TO JOAN!

I HOPE YOU ENJOY

1-13-15

Mark Aberdeen

2014, TWB Press

www.twbpress.com

Dex Territory
Copyright © 2014 by Mark Aberdeen

Edited by Terry Wright

Cover Art by Terry Wright

Pink Panther image by Paul Littlehale

ISBN: 978-1-936991-86-0

Acknowledgements

There are some important people I want to thank for their support: **Paul Littlehale** for his artistry, **Scott Goodspeed, Drew and Terri Cushman**, and **Henry and Jim Aberdeen** for the inspiration to write this story, my beta readers **John, Paul, Fiona, Gary** and **Mom**, and to **Jen Safrey** for her sage advice, and **Terry Wright** for his belief in me as a storyteller, and finally to my incredible wife, **Nadine**, for being my everything.

For Dad

Chapter One

I never liked morgues. There was never a happy reason to be in one, whether a body was standing upright or occupying a slab. This morgue, in particular, exhumed memories that I wished had stayed buried.

The medical examiner slid the body back into the cold storage vault. He slammed shut the door and it sealed with a tell-tale *whoosh-thunk*. The finality of that sound never failed to give me chills.

The spray from a water nozzle jarred me out of my contemplative moment. Blood, disinfectant, and tainted water spun down the drain as the M.E.'s assistant washed down the steel table.

The M.E. scribbled his signature on his autopsy report.

I stood patiently, choking back anger for the woman who now rested like a butchered animal behind a cold steel door. Images of her loved ones standing around a closed coffin swam in my head. I hoped to God that the family would never know that she lay in pieces. Evidence bags containing tissue samples were neatly stacked on the examiner's workbench.

He handed me the preliminary report. It read that the wounds appeared to have been made by a long inwardly curved blade, possibly a sword or sickle, but the angle of the cuts suggested something *unique.*

"Unique?" I pointed to the word on the report.

"I've seen this before." He spoke slowly with a hint of condescension in his voice then removed his glasses and wiped them thoroughly. "And like before, I couldn't find any trace particles. Maybe forensics will find something. They'll get back to you."

"Sounds familiar. In your opinion, do you think it's the same murder weapon that killed the others?"

"The lab should confirm it, but the marks look consistent." He pointed to an X-ray on the light board. "See the angle of the cut marks? And how the skin and muscle tissue looks smooth?"

He fell into forensic detail and threw in a

bunch of twenty-dollar words, and I nodded in understanding, but I couldn't tell one cut from another. He talked about how sharp the weapon had to be to cut through bone and the amount of force it must've taken, and he continued to explain until I got impatient and cut him off. "Could this be another Reaper killing?"

"Could be."

The Reaper. That's what the local paper called this serial killer. Overnight he became New London's Bigfoot. There were some blurry pictures of someone wearing a skull mask and robe and lurking in the shadows. This would have been easily dismissed as a hoax, but those pictures synced up in time and location to real crime scenes, all with the same gruesome MO. So far, six drug dealers had been butchered, and our little miss jigsaw puzzle now made number seven.

The M.E. took the report from me. "Got a handle on him yet, detective?"

"We're assuming the Reaper is a Dex."

The M.E. raised an eyebrow. "That's not good news."

Dex was short for spandex. The city had a community of people with superpowers who wore spandex costumes. Some called them superheroes. I called them a pain in my ass. They'd been lying low for some time, but lately their street presence had escalated. My job at the STF, Superhuman Task Force, was to keep them from getting out of control.

The M.E.'s concerned expression grew dark. "So what are you going to do about this person?"

"Doc, I don't know if I'd call who did this a person. Sort of fits snuggly into the *monster* category for me."

"He thinks he's the good guy. That makes him more dangerous."

I could tell he wanted to turn this into a debate, but luckily for me, my ear-bud radio squawked.

"O'Shea," I answered, tapping the receiver.

"Rick, seven-nineteen in progress. State Street, all units dispatched."

Seven-Nineteen: a riot? "Do you have an address?"

"Pick a corner, any corner, detective." The dispatcher's voice sounded haggard. "Just get there before somebody gets killed."

"Gotta go, doc."

"Keep your head down, O'Shea."

"Yeah, yeah." I was already out the door.

I'd been a cop for a long time, but every once in a while I'd get a call that would make my guts twist. Maybe it was the urgency in dispatcher's voice, I didn't know. I hated those kinds of calls, but as I allowed myself a quick glance in the direction of downtown, I couldn't help but feel this was *that* call.

The city looked as calm and peaceful as it ever did. The streetlights illuminated the night in an almost dreamy fashion. "Can't be that bad," I reassured myself and bolted for my car.

I couldn't have been more wrong.

I climbed in behind the wheel, flipped on the lights and siren, and raced toward downtown's famous State Street. Before my trip to the morgue, I'd been listening to an eighties station that I liked. The song playing now jangled my nerves, so I switched off the music in favor of the chatter over the STF police band.

It came in fast but didn't make much sense with everyone trying to talk at once. It sounded like every able-bodied officer at the station was preparing to deploy, along with the full brunt of the STF. If the STF was in full mobilization mode, the riot had to be a bad one, not that there was ever a good riot, and Dexes had to be involved.

I called dispatch to report my ETA. "I'm three minutes out."

"Detective Kapuscinski is on scene. He's in trouble."

"Roger, dispatch."

A voice blasted through my head. "O'Shea, where the hell are you?" The panicked words belonged to Detective Frank "Duke" Kapuscinski, my partner at STF. He had a voice so gritty it took paint off walls.

"I just turned off Jefferson. What the hell are we dealing with?"

"A nightmare. There are only three of us on scene. Me, myself, and that guy who looks like me in the mirror. Get here five minutes ago."

"I'm flying as low as I can." I gunned my car through a red light.

A high-pitched whine interrupted an extended silence and ended with Duke shouting, "Jesus. Fuck. Get down. Get the fuck down."

A loud noise followed, unbelievably loud, so overwhelming and distorted I couldn't figure out what made it. The blast felt like a blow to the head. I ripped the bud from ear, but not quick enough to stop the ringing. A million possible causes ran through my brain, from shotgun to nuclear. While this was indeed a brave new world with endless impossible dangers, I still had a job to do.

Anyone who tells you that they're not afraid going into the unknown is either a liar or insane.

A healthy dose of fear was not necessarily something to be avoided; it sharpened my senses and reflexes, gave me an edge to survive another day.

I jammed on the gas pedal. The engine responded immediately and growled as the tires chewed up the asphalt. I weaved in and out of traffic, crossed the median to get around slower cars, and careened up an embankment and down a sidewalk. I achieved a personal best in offensive driving.

I turned onto State Street with nearly four seconds to spare on my ETA. The scene before me killed any sense of accomplishment. "Shit!" I slammed on the brakes so hard the Charger came to a fish-tailing, wheel-screeching, tire-smoking halt.

For a breathless moment I sat there stunned. I'd traveled down State Street a thousand times or more, but where I expected a road, a collapsed building lay in rubble. Metal beams jutted from the pile of bricks and mortar like an oddly twisted skeleton. Bits of concrete and debris fell in a continuous shower from the exposed bones of the high-rise. Choking dust billowed from the remains, obscuring my view down the hill.

Where the hell is Duke?

Explosions rocked the earth. Intermittent multi-colored lights flashed across the walls of upright buildings, and deep, teeth-jarring rumbles reverberated off the cliffs of this manmade canyon. The most out of control rave had nothing on this mayhem.

A high-pitched helicopter whine came from overhead and was quickly lost in the noise beyond the rubble.

I jumped out of the car, grabbed my weapons and strapped them on. Then I mashed the ear-bud into my ear. "Duke! Where are you?"

Static.

I climbed on the car and stood on the roof. "Duke?"

"Glad you could make it," the familiar voice growled.

"I'm at the top of State Street."

"Then I must be at the bottom."

"There's a collapsed building. Road's

blocked. I'll get to you as fast as I can."

"Sooner would be better."

I searched for an alternative route around the rubble, but came up empty. I'd have to climb the pile. I started up. My footing gave way several times. Shards of broken bricks and glass threatened to tear into my flesh with every handhold. I grabbed at a girder, and it gave way, causing me to lose my uphill progress and a little skin. Nothing serious.

"Damn it." I scrambled back up and eventually reached the top. When I poked my head over the rubble pile, I got my first eyeful down State Street. There had to have been at least fifty Dexes and a hundred civilians involved in a full-out street fight. It raged from the debris pile all the way to the train station four blocks away. I'd never seen so many Dexes in one place.

Flames shot from the windows of the last tenement building left standing. A Dex I didn't recognize used some kind of telekinetic ability to keep the flames away from the doors while the residents fled, carrying whatever they could.

Another building lay partially crumbled. It didn't look like it would take much to bring it down completely. Debris littered the streets. Not only soda cans and newspapers, but broken and twisted cars and trucks strewn among building façades that had crumpled into boulder-sized chunks. Broken glass from hundreds of shattered windows covered everything in glitter. I hadn't seen this kind of destruction since Fallujah.

While the riot might have started as a single melee, it had spread into pockets of fighting that made no sense whatsoever. I saw Dexes slugging it out, friends fighting friends while those with bad blood between them ignored each other completely. Something fishy was going on.

"Duke, where's your position?"

"Pinned behind a car in front of Kendell's Furniture." He fired off a round from his weapon.

My eyes sought him out. He crouched behind a black Chevy Impala. I made out his dark jacket with the reflective word *POLICE* spelled across the back.

"I see you." And I saw a Dex I didn't know draw a bead on Duke. "Duck to your left!"

Duke didn't hesitate and rolled to a new position just before an energy beam ripped through his vacated spot, leaving a deep scar in the pavement.

"Thanks, Rick," he radioed back. "I think I

have a new part in my hair."

"You almost got it through your chest. Be right there."

Two pockets of fighting raged between us. When I saw who fought in the nearer pocket, my blood ran cold. Frost Warning and her partner, Zip, were often found on the wrong side of a bad situation. They liked figuring out ways to cash in on their abilities but did so with marginal success. I'd busted each on some small offenses, mostly minor drug charges, but the last time things got a little dicier. I had limped away with a pair of new scars, and the Dexes did a stretch in the Plum Island Correctional Facility.

This time it would be assault and battery. They fought a couple guys I didn't recognize. One stood a little over six feet and appeared dirty and unhealthy. He looked tired and strung out, probably homeless. His clothes were patched together, and I was close enough to know he smelled of old piss and smoke.

Zip rushed toward the old man, wielding an aluminum baseball bat. I opened my mouth to shout a warning to him, but he calmly held out his hand to Zip.

Oddly, Zip slowed, and the closer he got to

Mr. Homeless, the harder it became for Zip to move forward. He gritted his teeth as he struggled and clawed, fighting for every inch.

I could imagine the gears turning in his head as it dawned on him that something was very, very wrong. Bewilderment turned to panic on Zip's face as the homeless dude twisted his hand and let go of the unseen force. It flung Zip backward as if snapped back on a rubber band. He shrieked as he skipped across the street like a flat rock across a pond and impacted an SUV, caving in the fender, and he fell to the pavement, moaning. He didn't get up.

The other man faced Frost Warning. The man wore a business suit and looked like he'd stumbled out from a late night at the office. She flung an ice spear at him. He dodged it and charged Frost Warning head-on, but in a few steps, he vanished.

In panic, she swung her arm and sprayed some heavy projectiles at her invisible assailant. The ice just shattered harmlessly on the pavement. I heard a *woof* sound, and she doubled over gasping for breath. Her head whipped violently back as if her chin took a nasty uppercut. She wobbled, her arms spread out to get her bearings, but her knee buckled with a loud crack. She screamed in pain, and in fury she swung her arms in a last-ditch attempt to hit the invisible man, but each swipe came up empty. Her head snapped sideways, releasing a shower of snow from her mist-white hair.

She stagger-stepped back, and danger flashed in her pale eyes. She released a frustrated scream and a countless number of deadly ice shards shaped in a cone. The ice missile passed through her invisible assailant and into a crowd of civilians. Screams of fear and pain burst from the huddled group as the projectiles tore into them without mercy.

My feet skidded down the rubble pile, moving automatically while my pulse pistol fired burst after burst of searing energy at Frost. The pulse pistol was considered a non-lethal weapon because it affected the nervous system similar to a taser on steroids. If I set it to full power, the pulse could take down a Tyrannosaurus Rex and make it wish it had been dead for the last sixty-five million years.

Frost never saw me coming and a bolt hit home. Her body whirled as she twisted and jerked in spasmodic agony. She might have tried to scream, but it only came out as a pathetic yelp. She hit the ground, twitching.

"No!" Zip bellowed. His eyes filled with rage at seeing his partner pulsed. Somehow finding the energy, he jumped up from where he lay and came at me as fast as he could manage. If he wasn't hurt, I wouldn't have stood a chance. Still, I almost didn't get the next pulse off in time. He couldn't have been more than a yard or two away from me before his nervous system overloaded and he joined Frost in neuro-electric hell.

A flying Dex screamed from somewhere overhead. A clashing of steel came next, followed by a burst of gunshots. Battle reflexes flung me to the nearest cover. I rolled and came up with weapons hot. I fired off a wild shot, and it struck the stucco face of the O'Neill theatre. As the marquee exploded, the pulse dissipated in an electrical lightshow similar to Fourth of July fireworks.

A droplet of something warm landed on my cheek. I touched my finger to the drop, and it came away dabbed with blood. I looked up. Pitter-patters of blood droplets followed the fleeing flier. At the rate of blood loss, the poor bastard wouldn't make it far.

Bricks clattered behind me, and I turned to investigate. Something moved beneath the rubble.

"Hold on!" I ran over to help. Just as I was about to pull the loose concrete away, a figure sprang from the debris in a burst of choking dust. Standing in all his four-foot-four glory was Ruff 'N Tuff. I considered him the Dex equivalent to a cockroach, and that wasn't just a slight against his size. He was hard to hurt, harder to kill, and one couldn't get rid of him no matter how much bug-spray one used.

A story had circulated that one time he had been hit by a bus. The impact knocked him forty feet down the road. He got up no worse than being knocked over by a shopping cart. Then, when the driver ran over to check on him, he beat the man senseless. Several witnesses stated that Ruff 'N Tuff stepped in front of the bus on purpose.

Because his initials were RNT, I called him runt, not because he was a runt. "Runt, are you okay?"

"Fuck you, O'Shea!" He flipped me off.

"Hey! No need to get testy."

"Don't think I forgot last time!" The little jerk gave me an uppercut square in the gonads.

I dropped to my knees and could do nothing but wait as the sharp spike of pain wormed its way up to my brain. One time I was forced to suck the runt into an extremely large vacuum cleaner. For that he held a little resentment toward me, perhaps justifiably.

I reached out to grab him, fully prepared to commit murder, but he skipped out of reach and toddled off to make someone else's day unpleasant. I didn't know how it was possible to swagger and toddle at the same time, but he pulled it off.

A geological epoch later, the pain faded enough where I could crawl over to the wounded civilians. I did what I could for them, which wasn't much. Mostly, I reassured them that competent help was on the way.

A second pocket of brawlers fought between Duke and me. Fists, weapons, and colorful discharges of energy lit up the battlefield in flashes of whirling force. I didn't like my chances of getting through that mêlée intact. At least a dozen Dexes were involved in this fight, and the numbers kept changing as additional brawlers kept popping in and out. Trying to keep up with the tally made me dizzy.

It took a second to register, but some of the brawlers were dressed identically: green spandex, black boots, purple gloves, and a Yankee's ball cap. Upon closer inspection, I clearly saw they were, in fact, the same Dex called Multiplex. He continually added copies of himself as enraged combatants streamed in. He cloned himself to keep up, one for one, with the influx of all these unfamiliar Dexes.

The retrovirus responsible for Dexes had infected the population twenty years ago. By now, we knew most of the people with superpowers. They either revealed themselves over the years, or were *unmasked* by intrepid journalists, nosy neighbors, security cameras, or, if they were criminals, in law enforcement databases and courtrooms. Most Dexes designed and wore their own costumes and donned them for special events, charity functions, and whatever else a publicist booked for them. Tonight there were few costumes but lots of superpowers on display.

I grabbed one of Multiplex's doubles. "I need to get to Duke!"

"Come on." He created several more copies of himself. They surrounded me, ready to fight off any incoming threat.

I picked a clone and asked, "Do you have any idea where all these Dexes came from?"

"I just got here." They all spoke in unison.

"All right, you're deputized." I tapped one of them on both shoulders as if knighting him. Figured that would cover all of them. "Send a couple clones to help those civilians back there. Frost tore them up pretty bad. Just be careful, Plex. You're looking tapped out."

He gave me a nod.

Somehow above all the noise, I heard what sounded like mirthful laughter. I tried to block out the rest of the noise, which proved to be quite difficult and tracked the sound upward. A woman sat on the ledge of a building, swinging her legs as if in time to music. I could barely make out her features: light-colored hair and dragonfly wings on her back, which she fluttered at me seductively. Looked like she'd come out for the show, and as long as she just sat there, she could laugh her creepy little laugh until the riot ended for all I cared.

Multiplex got me clear of the fighting, and I rushed to the car where my partner was holed up. He wore a black ball cap and yellow-lens shooting glasses. Duke's grizzled face peered out from under the protective gear. He held a portable radio up to his mouth. "You heard me, shit-for-brains."

Everyone called him Duke, no one knew why. His demeanor reminded me of a wounded and highly rabid badger, but not nearly as friendly. He barked orders into the radio to the rest of the officers en route, the ones who should have been here already. He let them know he was pissed.

He slammed his fist into the car door and followed that with a string of very unkind words, then: "Just push the damn wreck out of the way!"

"Detective! Protect and serve, remember?" a woman's low voice fired back, a voice I recognized. Ramirez had a voice for radio: rich, deep, and smoky. "We're talking about civilians' property rights here. It's not their fault the wreck is blocking the road."

Duke growled through gritted teeth. "Then push it out of the way *protectively*!"

After a brief hesitation, the voice answered back to the affirmative.

Now I had his undivided attention. "Thanks for inviting me to your party." A sharp edge to my voice made me come off as stressed out.

"We'll have backup in ten."

"Ten seconds?" I asked hopefully.

He gave me a *don't-be-stupid* expression.

"What's got the Dexes all stirred up?"

He jerked a thumb over his shoulder. In the middle of the street, a wrecked armored car lay on its side. It was actually a steel-reinforced truck with bulletproof glass and tires, but it read *Brinker's Armored Car Service* on the side-panel, so that was reason enough to call it an armored car.

"Looks like a botched robbery."

Three Dexes protected the armored car: Thunderstorm, standing on top of the truck, Doublewide standing in front of the truck, and Talon, the lady of the bunch, standing on the cab door.

Thunderstorm was a giant of man, easily the most recognizable. He stood seven feet tall and had a long fierce beard. His face was cloudy gray, and his eyebrows resembled incoming storm fronts. He'd tied his lightning white hair back in a ponytail. In his biker leathers he looked like he belonged on an ancient battlefield, fighting off an attack on Valhalla.

Doublewide wasn't nearly as tall or as strong as Thunderstorm, but he could more than handle most situations. He wore his customary blue spandex overalls. The bulging muscles of his arms and chest made him look impressively broad. His shaved head gleamed under the street lights.

In stark contrast to the big men was Talon. She stood about five-foot-six and had a few too many curves to be a runway model, but that gave her a voluptuous beauty. Her golden hair rolled over her shoulders and flowed to an enormous pair of white wings on her back. Tonight she wore high heels and an elegant emerald green evening gown. Her having dressed to the nines meant she'd probably been on her way to a fundraiser for one of the many charities she supported. But now her eyes didn't suggest philanthropy, but burned with rage while her teeth were clenched in a fierce grimace. I quickly saw why.

A figure in black leather dived toward her from above. Nightflier was a bat-bastard who had no qualms against hitting a lady. He knocked her from the cab door of the armored car and smack into a solid brick wall. Talon twisted and rolled, and where I expected a bone-crushing impact, she planted her feet on the wall, bellowed a primal scream, and leapt into the sky, wings spread like an avenging angel. I tracked her path, and at the speed she could fly, Nightflier didn't stand a chance as he flew away, especially with murderous retribution radiating from her expression.

"Talon, stop!" I called after her, but she must not have heard me and disappeared into the night.

None of this made any sense. Talon made a living as a civil rights lawyer and defense attorney. She fought in the courtroom, not on the streets. What was she doing in the middle of an armored car heist?

Thunderstorm ripped the door from the armored car as easily as I'd pop the top on a can of beer, and with an almost casual flick of his arm, he sent the door whizzing like a Frisbee in an arc aimed at Hardball. He looked like a caveman, brutish and unkempt. His chest hairs protruded from a wife-beater shirt that stretched over a beer-barrel belly.

Teeth bared, Hardball braced for the impact, and the door crumpled like tinfoil against his thick skull. They didn't call him Hardball for nothing. "Was that supposed to hurt?"

Thunderstorm had only meant the door to be a distraction while he reached into the cab of the armored car and pulled the driver to safety.

While he did that, Doublewide faced an

attack from Metal Jim. Shards of metal formed all over the mercurial skin that sheathed the metal exoskeleton of his body, and I knew from some of my own nasty scars that he could launch those shards with deadly precision.

I had to warn Doublewide. "Take cover."

Metal shards zinged through the air.

Doublewide hit the ground behind the wrecked armored car.

Thump-thump-thump-thump. The shards stuck in the truck's side-panels like darts in a dartboard.

Duke poked his head over the hood of his car and frowned. "Do you have a plan?"

I let all the possible scenarios play out...got nothing. "Why do I always have to have a plan?"

"Just hoping. A plan would be really handy." He checked his weapon.

I eyed the battery level on my pulse pistol. The indicator bar registered in the green. "It's time to go to work."

We jumped up and shouted, "Police! Freeze!"

The response was immediate. Someone threw a freaking Honda at us. I dove to the side. A lucky bounce kept me from being crushed as the sedan hit Duke's car and tumbled down the road. The crumpled mass of metal eventually skidded to a halt against a pile of rubble.

I spun my head around to check on Duke.

"That was nasty," he grumbled. His face hardened, and he let a round loose from his Desert Eagle. The bullets were called HEAP rounds: High Explosive, Armor Piercing. Duke was old school and didn't believe in this non-lethal crap. If he shot a guy, Duke meant to shoot him, and the guy probably deserved it.

I chose my first target. It wasn't even a contest. I targeted Metal Jim. As a rule, I was not opposed to the use of deadly force when needed, but I'd seen bullets bounce off a few Dexes. While the pulse pistol I carried wasn't set to kill anyone, I'd never seen anyone get up after I shot them.

I fired a pulse at Metal Jim, and it rippled over the surface of his body without effect. I quickly revised my previous statement: I'd never seen anyone get up, and until now I'd never seen anyone not go down. I examined my weapon, shook it a little, and gave it a tap.

Shit. Metal Jim was going to be a problem.

"Down!" I shouted as he shot nasty bits of metal in my direction. I caught one in the chest, and while my vest offered great protection from bullets, knives and metal shards were a different matter. I felt the impact on my ribs. I gritted my teeth and tore the shard from my vest while shock kept me from feeling the pain. Blood smeared the shard-tip, but it hadn't gone in deep.

Screams echoed all around me. Metal Jim hadn't just shot steel projectiles in my direction. He went for maximum carnage as civilians, cops, and Dexes alike were felled indiscriminately.

I snarled as I cranked up the gain in my weapon to full Tyrannosaurus Rex. I knew this would drain the juice quicker, but I didn't care. Metal Jim had to be stopped.

By this time, he had reached the armored car. I chose my shot and fired. He turned in time to see the pulse streak toward him, and he thrust out his jaw defiantly. When the bolt hit him, sparks burst from various points on his body in showers of molten slag that sizzled as they hit the pavement.

"That was stupid, O'Shea! Now I have to kill you."

"Good luck with that." I smiled.

He didn't fully understand his situation until he tried to move and found that he couldn't. Panic flooded his liquid-metal face. Wherever he'd been touching the armored car, or the storm grate under him, or where'd he been touching himself, like his upper and lower lips and his arm to his side, all these contact points were welded together. The pointy barbs he'd loaded for his next round of projectiles were blackened and burnt. His skin no longer flowed like mercury, but instead, sloughed off him in clumps of slag, exposing chorded metal ropes, which were the equivalent of muscle tissue. Those too had been fused into a useless mockery of his biomechanical form.

He tried to shout *fuck*, but his mouth wouldn't work properly, so the word came out more like *ruck*.

"Stay put," I wise-assed to him and strode past.

After slapping a fresh battery into my weapon, I scanned for my next target. I felt the stirrings of situational awareness and started putting together a strategy to deal with this mayhem. I took a step, maybe two, when an incredibly loud explosion detonated near me and sent me sailing. I didn't know where it came from, but I took a couple hard bounces before landing on the other side of the street.

Stars whirled in drunken circles around me, and each breath brought with it a special level of agony. I ran my hand along my side and immediately found a couple bruised ribs. My hand came away bloody from a gash under my shredded vest. I'd caught some shrapnel from the blast.

I blinked a few times and tried to focus on a figure moving among the flames. He wore a fireproof Elvis costume, complete with high-back collar. The Dex let out a gleeful giggle and shot streams of fire from his wrists. Another car's gas tank exploded. I knew this Dex. He was the Arsonist.

"Boys make cheery fires." He giggled and scampered off, disappearing into thick smoke.

I bounced in and out of consciousness, not knowing which felt better. My decision leaned more toward unconscious. In a haze I gazed up and saw Talon flying overhead. She was back, and I wondered if Nightflier got away. I lay there mesmerized by her graceful wing strokes, the one fleeting echo of beauty in this nightmare. That ended when I saw a wicked looking sword in her fist. Her face twisted in rage. She hovered like a hawk above me, poised to attack someone on the ground.

And that someone looked like it was going to

be me.

I tried to shout *stop* but wasn't sure it came out loud enough.

I raised my hand, and my gun felt heavy in it, and my punch-drunk brain screamed in alarm to use it. But why was she out to kill me? What had I ever done to her? Again, her actions didn't make any sense. Talon turned an impossible arc, held the gleaming sword in front of her body, and dived toward me.

I pointed my pistol at her. The gain was still set to T-Rex, but I didn't have time to turn it down. I fired.

Without knowing if I hit her or not, I plummeted into unconsciousness.

Chapter Two

I felt a hand stroking my face. My head felt thick as mud, and I couldn't shake the grogginess. I'd had enough head injuries to recognize a concussion. I tried to make sense of my surroundings. Pulses of red and blue came from all directions at once, which didn't help orient me at all.

As my vision slowly cleared, a pink mask on a beautiful woman's face came into focus. She was crouched over me, protectively, caressing my cheek. The red and blue of emergency lights reflected in the whites of her concerned blue eyes.

"O'Shea? Can you hear me?"

"Panther?" I mumbled in disbelief.

Hope shined in her eyes. "Are you okay?"

"Am I standing?" My head pounded.

"Not exactly."

"Then I'm not okay." My words slurred out drunkenly.

"I'll be back in one second." She leapt straight up and delivered a roundhouse kick to a bad guy's head, a technique that would have made Chuck Norris jealous. She landed on all fours, again straddling me in her protective stance. Even in my condition I could appreciate the view of her curves. Apparently, my libido wasn't damaged in the explosion.

"O'Shea." Panther cupped my chin.

My eyes snapped back to hers. I blinked a couple of times. "I'll be all right."

She tapped my head with her knuckles. A wave of dizzying nausea hit me.

"You need a medic, right now."

"That can wait." I sat up and gave her a lopsided grin. "I've got a job to do."

She relaxed a little, but worry returned to her eyes. "Why do you have to be so stubborn?"

"Look, I've had worse knocks in the noggin."

She let out a resigned sigh. "It's a mistake getting back in the fight."

"Break-time is over."

"All right, O'Shea. I'll go first. You watch my backside." She gave me a wink.

"You mean *watch your back*?"

"I mean cover my ass." She sprang off me in a

flurry of pink spandex-clad limbs. I turned to see where she had gone. As usual, straight into danger, this time to confront Sunstroke. He shown so bright I couldn't look at him directly, and Minx was with him, the only other cat-themed Dex I knew about.

My fingers were still wrapped in a white knuckled death-grip around my pistol. I used my knees to steady my shaking hands and fired a pulse in Sunstroke's direction. His focus was affixed to Panther, but instead of getting a battery of fists and claws, which he expected from her, he received a face full of neuro-overload, T-Rex style. He jerked around on the ground until his daylight bright body turned dark as midnight. Surely, Pink Panther's claws and fists would have been kinder.

"Nice shot, O'Shea." Panther's full attention narrowed to a laser point on Minx. This catfight was a grudge match years in the making. I likened it to the unforgivable sin of them both showing up to the prom wearing the same dress.

While they scrapped, I reacquainted myself with breathing normally, and when the shakes subsided enough, I slowly stood up. My first attempt to take a step didn't work out so well; my knees buckled and I collapsed. Determined, I got up and tried again. This time I stayed upright, but with the surety of newborn calf.

I staggered back to Duke. "You all right," he asked.

"Do I look all right?"

Someone shouted, "Officer down."

The rioting stopped.

Chapter Three

Duke and I exchanged puzzled glances. Everyone stood around stunned. No one so much as twitched. The first signs of motion were tentative blinks. Dumbfounded expressions played over the combatants' faces. I imagined everyone thinking what I was thinking.

What the fuck?

Disoriented calm quickly morphed into blind panic, triggering a flight response. It seemed to me that most of the Dexes had no clue what was going on, like they'd been under the control of an outside force, which had suddenly let go. They awoke in a place they didn't remember coming to, fighting a battle they didn't know why they started. Now, running helter-skelter, it was all they could do to get back to familiar territory.

The next few moments did little to change my theory. Hardball, being the most experienced at criminal activity, bolted toward a debris-filled alley. Thunderstorm gave immediate chase.

Duke fired a HEAP round into the air. The explosion reminded me of the line in our national anthem: *bombs bursting in air*... That stopped the Dexes cold in their tracks.

"Nobody move!" Duke commanded.

The STF got to work and collared as many Dexes as they could take down. They bagged and tagged a bunch, but even their best efforts couldn't keep all the suspects from fleeing. We'd track them down later.

Ambulances and fire trucks stood by. Our emergency services weren't stupid enough to enter the scene until the area was secured. Instead, some of the Dexes and a few brave civilians helped carry the wounded to the emergency crews. One patient was Officer Stan Jebrowski. Someone said he wasn't going to make it.

Thunderstorm rushed up carrying Hardball and dropped him at our feet. He landed on the pavement with a satisfying *kerplunk.*

Duke shook Thunderstorm's hand. "Good work getting that armored car driver out."

Thunderstorm beamed. "If it wasn't for this asshole..." He reared his leg back as if to give Hardball a kick to the guts, but he stopped before acting. Good thing or we'd have had to pull Hardball down from orbit.

"How are they?" I gestured toward Doublewide and few other Dexes who fought on our side.

"We're okay...haven't seen Talon though. Ruff 'N Tuff tried to get into the fight." Thunderstorm jerked a thumb at a smoking crater about the size of an SUV. "You'll find him in the bottom of that hole."

"Is he dead?"

"Nothing can kill that cockroach." Thunderstorm peered down State Street, and his cloudy eyebrows furrowed. "Oh, shit! It's Zack."

He ran over to a body lying face-down on the pavement. The skinny guy wore fake leather spandex from head to toe. His patched and tattered blue cape lay over him like a funeral shroud. Zack could fly without wings, but not very well; his landings were especially frightening. Apparently, he'd come in on final approach and misjudged his altitude, significantly.

We gently rolled him over onto his back. The skin on his face was scoured away in the worst case of road rash I'd ever seen. His skin had already started to knit as his healing ability kicked into overdrive. Still, it would suck to be him for a while.

"Get him to an ambulance," I told Thunderstorm.

"You might think about finding one yourself. You don't look so good."

"I'll manage."

He gave me a *your-funeral* shrug and gently carried Zack toward medical help.

I stumbled over some debris, and a foreign hand kept me from falling. The hand wore a gray leather glove and belonged to a man dressed in a gray suit and overcoat. He wore a gray half-mask and a fedora cocked at an angle. He looked like he just walked off the set of *The Untouchables*. When dressed in this getup, he went by the name Phantasm. In his human persona, I knew him simply as Martin. He walked me toward a wall but, instead of stopping, we walked right through it.

Phantasm had the ability to alter his molecular density, lowering it to the point where he could pass through solid objects, or *phase*, as he called it. He had developed his power to the point where he could *phase* other objects or people with him, like me, unfortunately, and he could turn completely invisible.

The first time he'd *phased* me through a wall, I wanted to kill him afterwards. The fact that he had saved my life by doing so didn't enter my thoughts. I didn't appreciate feeling like I'd been strained through a chain-link fence.

This time I could *feel* the cinderblocks going through me. I also felt the tingle of electricity as a power cable passed through my abdomen. When we emerged on the other side of the wall and my body was solid again, I dropped to all fours and vomited. As I was being violently ill, Phantasm patted me on the back. "See? You're already doing better than last time."

When I could breathe again, I replied through dry heaves, "Don't. *Ever*. Do that. *Again!*"

We'd ended up in a little sporting goods store. I recognized it as the place my dad had brought me years ago to get my first Little League uniform. "What are we doing here?"

"Walk with me," he said, and we climbed a couple flights of stairs.

"What's up here?" I complained.

He *phased* me through a door, and right away I saw Talon lying on the roof. She looked hurt, bad. I knelt next to her. This was my fault. I'd shot her out of the sky.

"We have to get her down." Phantasm grabbed her feet. "I couldn't manage her by myself."

She had a nasty bump on the head and several cuts, and her white wing feathers were scorched black from the T-Rex knockout pulse my pistol had delivered, but nothing seemed to be broken.

I grabbed her under her arms. Phantasm extended his power and got us through the door, literally, and we wrestled her down to the first floor. Talon was lucky; she got to be unconscious for her first trip through a wall.

Once out in the street, it didn't take us long to get her to an EMS team. Word had been given, and they were now allowed into the area. Patches on their uniforms told me they had come in from surrounding towns to lend a hand.

Phantasm and I stepped into an alcove.

"It's going to be hell being one of us for a while," he said. "Tonight has given us Dexes a bad name."

"You might want to lie low as Phantasm." I scanned him up and down. "Take the time to put some color in your costume, at least until this blows over."

"Might take a long time." He indicated the crumbled buildings and devastation down State Street where emergency crews worked feverishly to clear debris and lend aid.

I turned him to face me. "What the hell's happened to everyone?"

"Seems Hardball and Metal Jim got a little too ambitious."

"Their plan wasn't very bright. Everyone witnessed the crime. They'd stick out in a line-up. Go to prison, and for what, a little money they'd never get to spend?"

"I don't think that armored car was carrying just money."

"Huh?" I mumbled, making full use of my genius.

"Rick, they transport money during the day when banks and businesses are open."

"Good point." I felt outsmarted by the Dex private-eye. "Late drop maybe?"

He shrugged. "I'd have a word with that driver, if I were you." He turned invisible.

"Martin?"

No answer. Now that was irritating.

I shuffle-walked up the street. Pink Panther

fell into step beside me. "How are you doing, O'Shea?"

"Got my ass kicked."

"That's what you get for fighting Dexes."

"You managed to get some ass-kicking in today."

"And I looked good doing it, too." She laughed and spun gracefully for me, showing me her latest battledress costume. It appeared to be a little sturdier than her usual costumes, and she had added some very sharp-looking claws at the tips of her fingers. Even with the added thickness of the material, there were plenty of curves to go around.

"Very nice," I said with sincerity.

"You could come over to my place and help me out of it." She had a playful twinkle in those big blue eyes, so I was sure she wasn't joking around.

"I can hardly walk much less try to peel you out of that outfit." I stopped. "Besides, my girlfriend frowns on me undressing other women."

She laid a hand on my face and regarded me. For a moment, the carefully crafted image of a super heroine dropped, and a touch of warmth from the woman beneath the mask radiated to the surface. Just as quickly, she dropped her hand, and the warmth went cold. "Duke was looking for you."

"Where is he?"

She pointed a clawed finger to a black police van with STF painted in white on the side.

"Thanks."

She gave me a forlorn smile. "I'm outta here." Then she flipped and tumbled her way down the street. She made a show of bounding up the side of a building and disappearing over the roof's edge with a signature Pink Panther flourish. I had to admit I enjoyed watching her body in motion.

Duke stood talking to a burly black man in a two-tone brown uniform. *Brinker's Security* was embroidered above the breast pocket. His nametag read: *Mason*. He was the armored car driver Thunderstorm had rescued. Two officers in riot gear stood with them. They greeted me when I approached. "Hi, detective"

"Ramirez, Jensen." I nodded to each officer.

Rachel Ramirez stood five-foot-five, and her body was all springy muscle. She also carried the largest weapon I'd ever seen a human handle without a tripod. I looked to her and then to the weapon.

She must have sensed my curiosity. "It's a rail gun," she informed me.

My *I'm-stupid* face must have remained because she continued, "Electric current runs along the rails of the weapon to create a magnetic field." She pointed to a battery pack. "It magnetically propels a conductive slug to seven times the speed of sound. There isn't much it can't stop." She wrinkled her nose. "Ask Ruff 'N Tuff."

"You shot him with that?"

"Buried him in his own little crater." She beamed.

I recalled Thunderstorm pointing it out to me, but I knew it would take more than a rail gun to put the runt down for good.

Jensen stood eye to eye with me. His sandy brown hair was neat, and a hint of stubble shadowed his face. He was new to the unit. We hadn't had time to bond yet. The fact that the rookie was standing with us hotshots spoke a lot about him. He had guts and smarts.

"You okay?" I asked him, keeping my tone neutral.

"Don't know yet, detective. I'm pretty shook up."

He was smart enough to be scared. "Kid, trust me, sometimes there isn't much that keeps me from crying like a little girl."

"Hey!" Ramirez barked. "Little girls are tougher than you think."

We all smiled.

Ramirez pulled me aside. "He tangled with a couple of Dexes back by the train station. One shot some kind of energy beam out of his eyes. It hit a pregnant woman before Jensen shot him. She never stood a chance."

I bowed my head. I knew the demons the rookie was going to sleep with. "Fuck." That mother and child were innocent bystanders caught up in the senseless violence. "Ramirez, take Jensen and check in with the medics. They probably need some help with civilian casualties."

She knew what I was asking: keep Jensen's mind occupied and focused on saving lives. It might give him a small measure of balance for the ones who didn't make it.

"Robinson!" Duke shouted at another officer. "Would you take Mr. Mason over to EMS and make sure he gets checked out?"

"Of course." He turned to the driver. "Sir, this way, please," he said with a polite-but-firm police voice. We watched them go until Duke turned back to me. "Rick, you had me worried."

"You and me both," I replied. "Are you doing okay? Pitched battles aren't good for your osteoporosis."

"The blast singed off your acne."

We each forced a smile.

I suddenly felt tired and achy as the chill from the night mixed with my injuries, making my neck stiffen. I put a hand to my side where shrapnel from the explosion had hit me. To my surprise, a bandage was taped across the wound. Panther must have put it on while I was out. "How long was I unconscious?"

"You were out for a while. Panther stayed with you and kept you safe." Duke snickered. "Yeah, that's some girlfriend you got there."

"She's not my girlfriend."

Duke knew full well that I was in a serious relationship with Dani. Pink Panther was anything *but* my girlfriend. I wondered if she was anyone's girlfriend.

I wanted to curse at Duke, but my heart wasn't in it, so I let it go with a surly grunt. We walked over to the Brinker armored car, ignoring Metal Jim's pleas for help.

Duke filled me in. "According to the driver, this was a special transport. He signed for three metal briefcases, and he'd been given an address." Duke handed me the shipping docket.

I frowned. The address wasn't a real place, at least not yet. It was a vacant lot slated for a huge construction project. "Maybe he was supposed to meet someone there."

"The instructions on his trip log told him to wait there for further directions."

"So somebody didn't want anyone to know where this delivery was going." I thumped the truck's flattened front tire. "But somebody did. How did the heist go down?"

"Hardball stood in the middle of State Street. The driver stopped, and that's when Metal Jim T-boned the armored car and knocked it over. The driver thinks there was a third Dex involved but can't be certain."

"Why does he think that?"

"By the time Metal Jim got the rear door open, one of the briefcases was gone."

"Let's have a look inside." We walked around the armored car. The entire area was strewn with blown up car parts, thanks to the Arsonist. In back of the truck, one door hung loosely on its hinges, no doubt the work of Metal Jim or the Jaws of Life. Duke pulled out a flashlight and we gazed inside. Two silver briefcases remained. I snapped on a pair of gloves, reached in, and took one of the cases. It wasn't locked, so I opened it. It contained money. "Small denominations."

Duke huffed. "That's weird."

I cocked my head. "But why leave two cases full of money, and what happened to the third?"

"I know who we can ask."

We walked around to the front of the armored car where Metal Jim was still attached to the hood like some kind of bizarre ornament. He cackled as we approached. Black stains dominated most of his metallic form. His outermost skin usually flowed like mercury. He could move very fast by using the flowing properties of his skin like rollerblades. As far as I could determine, his entire body, internal organs, muscles, and even his blood were made of different kinds of metal. He was one of the more extreme mutations caused by the retrovirus. The welding wouldn't do him any serious harm. His body would eventually absorb the metal hood, and he would be free to raise hell again.

A rescue crew with grinding wheels and

torches approached.

"Guys, give us a minute," Duke told the crew. "Let me borrow one of those welding torches."

Meanwhile, I moseyed up to our prisoner. "Hi, Jim. Havin' a bad day?"

"Screw you, O'Shea."

"Now. Now. Don't let this conversation get started off on the wrong foot."

Duke fired up the welding torch. With a hiss, a yellow and blue flame shot out the nozzle.

Metal Jim started clanking, a show of frazzled nerves. "What's he gonna do with that?"

"Jim, you have to focus on me," I told him. "What were you after in this armored car?"

"Nothin'! We didn't take nothin'!"

"Duke, what do you think? Is he telling the truth?"

"I don't believe him." He walked over, picked up a ragged license plate, and tack-welded it to the side of Jim's head. He squealed like a stuck pig. The ordeal gave a whole new meaning to the term *hot head*.

"Do you see anything here?" he pleaded. "We didn't take nothin'! It was just a job!"

"Who hired you?" I asked.

"I don't know."

"We could wait for Hardball to wake up, ask him, but Thunderstorm did a number on him, and his brain is going to be soft. He'll tell us. We'll make him a deal and you'll get the electric chair."

"I predict a total meltdown." Duke coughed. "This will go much better for you if you just tell us who hired you."

"I don't know, I tell ya!"

Duke grabbed a couple of hubcaps. He held them up appraisingly. "Jim, are you a Toyota man, or do you prefer a Kia?"

"Volkswagen. Ha! What are ya going to do now, tough guy? There ain't no stinkin' Volkswagen around here."

"Who hired you?" I made my tone sound bored.

"I don't know! Honest!"

"Kia it is." Duke tack-welded the Kia hubcap to Metal Jim's left ass-cheek. He shouted a string of profanities.

Yeah, that had to hurt. "Jim, one last time before Duke finds the other three to complete the set. You won't be able to sit down for a month."

"We got the contract through Geiger."

Duke and I exchanged *oh-shit* looks.

He signaled the work crew. "Okay, guys, cut him loose and lock him up."

We wandered off to confer over Jim's information. "Robbery might explain a part of this mess," I said. "But that couldn't have been what started the riot." I spread my arms to the ruined street.

"There was something else going on," Duke agreed. "Did you see all the Dexes?"

"I've never seen so many in one place before. A lot of new faces, too. Virus maybe—"

"Can't be." Duke shook his head. "There hasn't been a retrovirus outbreak since the first one. We'd be among the first alerted if there was a new outbreak."

"I don't know how else to explain it." I shrugged a painful shrug.

"At least we have a place to start."

"Yeah, Geiger." Why did it have to be Geiger?

We ambled away from the armored car and Metal Jim's girlish screams. Two things he couldn't handle: heat and electricity. He'd get more than his share of both before this was over.

I hadn't noticed before, but news choppers and lines of reporters had made their way here, and a small army of camera crews had set up shop. Reporters chattered with witnesses and those participants who hadn't been hospitalized or arrested, and I imagined the inane questions being asked.

Reporter: "So Nightflier dropped you when you were fifty feet in the air. How did you feel when you reached the ground?"

Nightflier's victim: "Unconscious, mostly."

That was the scene until Duke and I approached. Then, except for the reporters around Thunderstorm and couple of other celebrity Dexes, they all turned to us.

Duke and I were doused in floodlights and bombarded with questions. We grumbled, "No comment," until I heard my name called out by a voice I recognized.

I stood astonished as Ruff 'N Tuff ran toward me, and using a reporter as a springboard, he jumped up in a furious arc and came down on me. The last thing I remembered seeing was itty-bitty knuckles.

Chapter Four

I stumbled through the door to my house. Dani stood in the foyer. We had exchanged keys to each other's houses. She wore one of my UConn T-shirts; she wore them when she got upset. The shirt hung loosely on her graceful curves. Her short-cut brown hair was mussed, and tears had smudged her makeup. The olive skin of her Latina heritage made her look exotic, but her jaw was set, and equal parts anger and concern smoldered in her dark eyes. Both intensified when I turned to face her, and she regarded the full bloody mess I had become. "What the hell, Rick?"

"I didn't expect to see you here." I certainly didn't want her to see me like this. I had called her prior to my trip to the morgue, and we'd broken our date for tonight.

"I heard the news and came over."

The TV was on, and judging from the empty soda cans on the coffee table, it appeared she'd been waiting for me to get home for some time.

We'd talked about moving in together, getting married, but there were inherent risks in being the spouse of a cop, and I wanted to be sure she fully understood what this life was like before she committed to it. Tonight she got a practical lesson, and I could see a lot at play behind her eyes: fear, anger, guilt, and for the briefest moment, a touch of shame. I reached for her, but she pulled away and turned her back on me. Even the koi fish tattoo on the back of her neck seemed to scowl at me.

We'd been dating for quite a while and got to the point where unannounced visits happened more frequently. We even turned them into a little game to see who could find the other in the most awkward situation.

She hadn't yet come close to the time I found her dancing around in a bra and Superman boxers, trying to curl her eyelashes with one hand, shave her underarm with the other while simultaneously talking on a cell phone. The woman was a world-class multi-tasker. I had taken a picture and set it as my computer's wallpaper.

"Look. I'm sorry."

She spun on me. "What happened to you?" Now her voice was equal parts concern and anger.

"You should see the other guy." I couldn't resist saying that.

"Your job sucks." Her eyes, while normally warm and brown, looked like granite, hard and unforgiving.

I had to look away. The local TV news looped footage of *The Brawl*, as they were calling it. I could see why she was upset. It was big. The chopper footage ran the length of State Street and showed three buildings that had fully collapsed. Emergency crews still worked to control fires in two other high-rises.

An amazing shot from a handheld camera showed a violent explosion during the course of the fighting. It was the same explosion that had knocked me down. The camera joggled, but recovered enough to capture me tumbling to the spot where Pink Panther had found me. I stood slack-jawed as it dawned on me that I shouldn't have survived.

I saw several pillows on the couch. They told me that Dani had buried herself in the pile. She did that whenever I watched horror movies.

I pulled her in close, and after a little

resistance she eventually melted into me. Not a single word passed between us. She sobbed as I stroked her hair and kissed her neck. The fish tattoo stared at me. I had no idea how long I held her, but it got really hard to remain standing. I kissed her forehead. "I have to sit down."

Dani followed me to the Lazy Boy and stood behind me, gently massaging the back of my neck while I continued watching the news.

All told, the New London Police Department had made more than a dozen arrests, there were three confirmed dead, one being Officer Stan Jebrowski, and countless injured among all parties involved: Dexes, STF, and civilians. Jebrowski was NLPD, not a member of STF, and I didn't know him personally, but that didn't matter. He was a fellow cop, a brother in blue, just doing his job. I'd be at his funeral.

A statement by our captain, Timothy Grundle, came on the air. "This was a terrible tragedy. We have several of the participants in custody. Obviously there is a lot to sort out at this time. We are continuing to review the evidence and will work tirelessly to prosecute those responsible. Our hearts go out to the families of loved ones lost."

The news anchorman analyzed the events and provided a timeline of what had happened. Some of it was news to me. I only saw my little slice of the action, and that had my full attention. He did his best to identify the participants and powers they used. However, he seemed to have the same issue as I did; he had no clue who half the Dexes were.

One thing I did know was there'd never been a super battle-royale like this anywhere, ever. The news footage was picked up by every affiliate and had gone national on all the networks. New London became the biggest news story in the U.S., maybe in the world.

Nothing this big had happened since the accidental release of the Gentech retrovirus that created the Dexes twenty years ago. I sat through a reminder of that event more because of my body's refusal to move to the bedroom than any actual interest in hearing it. I'd heard it all before.

"It's just awful," Dani said.

I wanted to tell her that everything was okay and that it wasn't as bad as it appeared, but I didn't want to lie to her.

The anchorman got back to present-day news. "Even respected members of the superhero community were involved, including famed civil rights lawyer Talon, who was accidentally shot by police." The camera followed her down to where she crashed onto a rooftop. "She's currently in police custody at Lawrence Memorial Hospital."

I buried my head in my hands. "Shit. It was no accident."

"You shot her?"

"She attacked me."

"But she's your friend."

"I'm sure she didn't *want* to hurt me. She went crazy like all the Dexes."

Dani put a hand on my shoulder, but that did little to ease my guilt over shooting Talon. I would visit her tomorrow. I needed to get her side, ask her what she was thinking, but mostly I wanted to make sure she was all right.

There had to be a logical explanation for the craziness that went on tonight.

While watching the news coverage, something occurred to me. They had footage of our arrival on scene. How could news crews have been there before Duke and I arrived? They had footage of Hardball standing in the path of the armored truck. Then Metal Jim broadsided it, knocked it on its side, and went to work on the back doors. The camera flashed around to Thunderstorm barreling in.

As an added bonus I got to see footage I wished I hadn't. There we were: Duke, Thunderstorm, and I surrounded by the mob of reporters when Ruff 'N Tuff slammed into me. The pint-sized bastard smashed his diminutive fist into my face, leaving me sprawled on the ground, unconscious.

"I'm never going to hear the end of that."

Thunderstorm grabbed Ruff 'N Tuff and threw him. The camera followed the screaming form as the runt cleared the buildings and disappeared into the night, heading out for open water. I figured he'd splash-down sometime tomorrow.

"At least I got to see what happened after my lights went out." I turned off the TV.

Dani's eyes locked on me. I saw a glimpse of their usual sparkle. "You got taken out by a midget?" One corner of her mouth twitched in suppressed laughter.

"He's a dwarf with superpowers," I said in my own defense. "I don't want to talk about it."

Dani helped me stand and wrapped herself around me again. It would have been a beautiful and tender moment if I wasn't completely covered head to toe in bruises. I flinched and grimaced and let out a little yelp too. My reaction was enough for her to release me and step back.

She looked at her hand. "Oh my God, you're bleeding!"

"It must be the shrapnel wound." I tried for cavalier.

"You don't get to joke about this." Her eyes flashed dangerously. She pulled off my shirt and gasped at the sight of a blood-stained bandage.

"Somebody did a lousy job of patching you up."

Pink Panther had patched me up. I was sure she did the best she could under the battlefield conditions.

Dani grabbed a clean towel and put pressure on the wound until the bleeding stopped. "I can't believe they released you from the hospital."

"The hospital can wait, besides, all the doctors are going to be pretty busy tonight, treating people in worse shape than me."

"Doesn't matter. You need an x-ray, these ribs are broken." For emphasis she poked me gently.

I nearly dropped to my knees from the pain. "They're bruised..." I gasped, "...not broken. I know the difference."

"You don't know that for sure. Please, please get checked out tomorrow, promise me."

I mumbled an agreement I didn't mean. I had convinced myself that it was nothing a few hours of sleep and a bottle of scotch wouldn't cure.

She helped me undress and turned on the shower. A few minutes later, I stood under the hot water. Nothing ever felt so painfully good. The water rolled over me, and the grime, dried blood, and some of the stiffness swirled down the drain. I'd never been so happy to be anywhere in my life.

Once I emerged from the shower, Dani worked on me without saying a word. She massaged my damaged muscles, applied ice packs, patched up my wounds, and bandaged my ribs. As it turned out, she used up my entire supply of disinfectant and most of my gauze and tape.

By now, my left eye had completely swollen shut, courtesy of Ruff 'N Tuff, and each twist of my body sent a new spike of pain straight to my brain. I thought my brain was supposed to fight pain by releasing endorphins. My endorphins were probably on strike.

Dani went to the cupboard, portioned out

some ibuprofen for me, and put on some water for herbal tea, the two components of the Danielle Reyes' sure-fire cure-all.

She came back with another icepack for my eye. In the time it took her to return from the kitchen, her demeanor had changed. Her face appeared tranquil. She'd made up her mind about something, and it didn't take a brain surgeon to figure out what that was.

The teapot whistled.

I slipped into a robe and joined her at the kitchen table. She poured tea, and we just stared at each other for the longest time. Words didn't seem necessary.

I set the icepack on the table, lifted the tea cup, and drew first blood. "When are you leaving?"

"Tomorrow. I'll stay with you tonight. Someone needs to watch over you." She managed a sad smile. "This was a lot, Rick."

"Are you coming back?"

"I need to think harder about being a cop's wife. I hope you understand."

I sipped hot tea and wished it was scotch. I knew there was always the threat that I'd go to work one day and not come back. Dani had once told me that I'd be worth the risk. It was a nice thought, but the reality was brutal, as tonight had proven, hands down.

It appeared the house and kids and happy life just got replaced with cuts, bruises, pain, and heartache. No amount of ibuprofen and tea could cure those ills.

It was a dangerous world out there. I glanced at the drawer below the counter where I kept my dad's Colt. My first thought was to give it to her for protection, but she'd done all right without a gun all this time. Just because I needed one, didn't mean she would.

Live by the sword — die by the sword.

I got up from the table, and Dani helped me shuffle into the bedroom.

We kissed for what felt like the final time, and I fell into bed, dizzy with pain. She crawled in next to me and held me until I thankfully passed out.

Chapter Five

When I woke up in the morning, a note lay on the pillow next to me. She simply wrote, "Rick, I love you, goodbye, Dani." She had packed the few things she kept at my place. Tears welled up, but I choked them down. She'd escaped my world of cops and bad guys. Good for her.

My body had grown stiffer through the night. It took me the better part of an hour to go through my fifteen minute morning routine. I dragged myself to the car. Getting in took some doing, but I finally managed and drove to Y-Knots Diner, our usual breakfast haunt. I parked the car somewhere in the vicinity of the curb and shambled inside.

"Hey, Rick." Duke met me at the door. "You look like shit."

"You should see my insides." I was referring to my broken heart.

His face turned serious. "You better see the doc."

I shrugged.

Duke didn't look too bad. I guessed he'd learned how to keep his head down and avoid getting hit. We decided to sit at the counter so I wouldn't have to struggle getting in and out of our usual booth. While we ate breakfast, I told him about Dani leaving me.

He listened and nodded thoughtfully, then: "Rick, you did the right thing by letting her go. She wasn't ready for the glamour this job brings. Besides, now she doesn't have to sleep with someone so damn ugly anymore."

"Or as black and blue, I suppose." My bruises had become a rainbow. "Doesn't stop the hurt though."

"Don't write Dani off so quickly. Other than her lack of judgment in her choice of men, she's got a good head on her shoulders. She got scared last night is all. I see the way she looks at you. Give her some time. She might come around."

"You know, Duke, you're a romanticist."

"Fuck you, O'Shea."

"See? Crude but romantic."

"It's going to be a rough day."

"I can already visualize the captain's teeth chewing our asses." I polished off one last cup of the world's worst coffee. I was sure the beans were grown in a toxic waste dump.

On the way to my car, I was nearly run over by a kid on a skateboard, but decided it would be too much trouble to shoot the little bastard. I let him off with a warning.

Duke rode with me. Our normal route from Y-Knots took us down State Street, but in its current impassible condition, we took the long route to the station. Barricades and traffic cops kept non-official vehicles from getting downtown. Foot traffic was a different matter entirely as people did their best to get a glimpse of the smoking landscape that was once the heart of a city.

Outside the station, local and national news vans and crews had set up camp in the parking lot. Uniformed officers attempted to keep some semblance of order, but the intrepid reporters were hungry and jumped at anyone coming in or out. Our cleaning crew even got barraged for requests of overheard conversations and rumors.

One reporter decided to slip past the police barricade. Two officers immediately descended on her and hastily ushered her back to the others. A shout of police brutality echoed from a voice in the crowd. Cameras rolled and renewed protests fueled dissent to a fevered pitch.

I stopped at the barricade and got out my badge.

Duke shook his head in disgust. "Damn vultures."

"What did you expect?"

"I don't know, maybe some dignity."

"Not in this lifetime."

"We didn't start the fuckin' riot."

"But they blame us for not containing it."

I showed my badge to an officer. He let us through.

We rolled past the parking lot and entered the underground garage, avoiding the media circus. When I got out of the car, my legs didn't like the sudden change of position and nearly buckled. I grabbed the car door and used it to hold myself up until the ground felt solid again. I stood there and took a couple of deep breaths.

"Rick, you really need to get to the hospital."

"I'm okay!" I snapped at him harder than I meant to.

"Uh-huh." Duke didn't sound convinced.

I straightened up, and we walked in silence to the basement entrance.

The door to the station slid open, and when we stepped through, it felt like we just won the big game in overtime. Applause and cheers echoed through the squad room. There were pats on our backs, and everyone wanted to shake our hands. I had to admit it felt good to get such an ovation from our brothers in blue, even if only for a moment.

We shuffled over to the elevator, and Duke hit the button. "So we're heroes."

"I don't feel like a hero."

The door slid open. Ramirez was the sole occupant of the elevator. She had pulled her raven hair back into a ponytail and wore her uniform blues. We were normally a plain-clothes division.

"Ramirez," Duke greeted her.

"What's with the uniform?" I asked.

She cocked her head disparagingly. "Didn't you get the memo?"

"What memo?"

"We have VIPs coming in today."

"Imagine that," Duke growled. "I thought every day was VIP day."

We traded places with her on the elevator. I stopped the door from closing. "Hey, Ramirez. Good job with the rail gun yesterday."

"Thanks." Her face beamed. "But if I knew Ruff 'N Tuff would get up after I shot him with it, I'd have shot him twice."

"Might have saved me a black eye."

Her eyes softened. "O'Shea, shouldn't you be in the hospital?"

I groaned. "Not you too?"

"You should listen to us," Duke said.

"I'll get checked out later."

She gave us a crisp salute, spun on her heels, and walked away. I couldn't help but notice that Ramirez's uniform did amazing things for her backside. I let the elevator door close before my thoughts wandered to something unprofessional.

"That girl loves her weapons," Duke said.

"Everyone needs a hobby."

The world seemed to tilt on its axis as the elevator opened on the second floor. The sense of urgency hit me like a rogue tidal wave. Everyone looked frantic. The room contained a dozen suspects handcuffed to their chairs. If the detectives weren't on their phones, they were tapping away furiously at their computers as they interviewed witnesses and suspects. No one had slept much. There wasn't a clear eye in the bunch, and coffee was being slurped up like life itself depended on it.

Sprocketeer shouted at a haggard-looking Jensen. The Dex's voice was grating as metal-on-metal brakes as he repeated over and over, "I don't know how I got to State Street."

"That's what they all say," Jensen shot back. "You better start talking or no more lube jobs for you, sprocket head."

"Hey," Sprocketeer shouted to everyone in the room. "Did you hear that? He called me a sprocket head. That's police brutality."

"We must've been drugged," someone shouted.

Others chimed in, "It's the water, I tell ya. City water is poisoning us all." "I have to go to the bathroom." "When's my lawyer gettin' here? I'm innocent."

"Shut up," a cop shouted.

A defense lawyer from Talon's firm ushered past me. His tie was crooked and his hair was mussed. He appeared as stressed out as everyone else, probably more so with Talon incapacitated.

A fight broke out at one of the back desks, but shouts from gruff officers and a flurry of drawn weapons backed down the combatants, a couple of new Dexes I'd never seen before.

I drunkenly staggered toward my desk. On the way I took a peek in Captain Gundle's office window. Through chinks in the blinds I was able to make out Police Commissioner David Devlin and Mayor Nancy Klein. The mayor jabbed a pointed finger at the captain. The commissioner stood poised with his arms crossed over his barrel chest and didn't seem to be saying anything.

It did my heart good to see the mayor's face that shade of purple. A pleasant picture of her head popping like a zit came through my punch-drunk brain. I tapped Duke on the shoulder and pointed to the office. "Mayor's really laying into the captain."

"I hope you wore your shark-proof skivvies 'cause you can bet your butt we're next."

"Maybe we'll be lucky and they're having a really intense discussion about the best wine to serve with fish."

"We're cops." Duke continued on to his desk. "There's no such thing as lucky."

A female voice spoke over my shoulder. "Perhaps they're discussing the best wine to serve with fillet of O'Shea."

I turned to see Pink Panther.

"Just save a bite for me."

"What are you doing here?"

When she saw my face her flirty expression soured. "Let me take that back. You're not a fillet. You look more like ground chuck."

Pink Panther's pictures and even her Maxim Magazine photo-shoot spread didn't remotely do her justice. She had hit the genetic jackpot. Her body was the perfect balance of muscle tone and curves. Her face looked flawless with full, pouting lips and a playful sparkle in her blue eyes. Why she was doing this super-heroine gig and risking her life was beyond me.

She was dressed in a simple pink body suit with thigh-high pink leather boots and matching belt and gloves. Small fuzzy pink ears poked out of her blond ringlets. The effect made her look cute, lovable, and most importantly, nonthreatening.

She wrapped her arms around my chest and gave me a gentle squeeze. My ribs hurt, and her hug was worth the pain, but I had to play the sympathy card. "Ow!"

"Wuss," she responded but didn't smile. "Seriously, O'Shea, are you okay?"

"Check with me later." I tipped my head to the captain's office. "After my upcoming assendectomy."

"Hey, no matter what happens in there," she flipped the bird toward the office, "you did well out there last night." She pointed to the window with the view of downtown. "It was bad, but it could have been worse."

"Are you okay, Panther? Did you get hurt?"

"Me?" Her voice got a little quiet. "You don't have to worry about me." She donned a little pink mask that shaded those baby blues. Still, I saw a trace of vulnerability before it vanished behind her mask of bravado. She let out a musical laugh. "I got to kick butt last night, and unlike some detectives I know who shall remain nameless, I came away with my dignity intact."

"Don't say it!"

"Say what? That you were bitch-slapped by Ruff 'N Tuff?" She meowed. "Wouldn't even think of it."

"I'm never going to live that down, am I?"

"Not in this life." She stroked the side of my face. "Rickie, honestly, I'm saying this as your friend, you really need to see a doctor."

"Yeah, that seems to be the consensus. I was going for the *looking-really-terrible* look but decided that *near-death* was less effort." I tried to smile.

"Well, congratulations, you pulled it off. Let me take you to the hospital."

"I have to survive the next few hours. We'll talk about it then."

"Okay, but if you die, I'm going to have to find someone else to pester."

She still had her arms around me, and by now, most everyone in the squad room had stopped what they were doing to watch us. I suddenly felt uncomfortable. One day after Dani broke up with me and I was already in another woman's arms. I gently broke the embrace. That turned out to be a mistake. She'd been holding me steady. I staggered, almost fell over, would have if she hadn't grabbed my arm.

"What?" I snapped at everyone in the squad room. They immediately went back to what they were doing. I finally made it to my desk. Panther handed me a cup of water, which I drank greedily. That helped steady me a little.

"How long have they been in there?" I asked Jensen.

"Nearly two hours."

Panther purred. "And your names have come up a lot."

"You can hear what they're saying?"

She flicked her costume ears with clawed fingertips. "Parabolic microphones. I figured they'd come in handy today."

"Cool."

"Why does the mayor hate you so much?"

"I dated the mayor's daughter."

"Ah! That explains plenty."

"We were high school sweethearts."

"What happened to her?"

"I thought we were going to be a forever thing. She stuck with me through my stint in the Army and wrote me most every day during my two tours at war. It really kept me going. Her mom was running for mayor at that time, and having a future son-in-law fighting overseas didn't hurt her chances of winning. Her daughter loved me at that time, or at least the idea of me."

"What changed?"

"I came back with problems she didn't want to deal with, PTSD, night-sweats, bad dreams."

"But you're over all that now, right?"

"I'm over her."

Jensen cleared his throat and tipped his head toward the office.

The mayor, commissioner, and captain stood at the door and scanned the squad room until their gazes zeroed in on me.

"Good luck, and remember what I said." Panther blew me a little kiss and bounded off.

I turned to Duke's desk. His chair sat empty. My eyes darted around the room, and I spotted him casually making his way back from the water cooler.

The captain's voice boomed, "O'Shea! Kapuscinski! Gentlemen, would you please join us?"

Duke and I gave each other a helpless look and walked into the office. The trio of higher-ups looked pretty grim. It wasn't every day half their city got demolished, and it didn't take a powerfully deductive mind to figure out there weren't going to be any "at-a-boys" in our immediate future.

"Captain, commissioner, Your Honor," Duke addressed each.

I gave them a little wave.

Nobody offered us a chair, and I really needed to sit down.

The captain started off. "Detectives, this inquiry is informal at this time."

The mayor spoke next. "Half the downtown section of *my* city has been reduced to rubble.

News footage from the scene does not paint this department, or your team, or either of you SFT detectives in a favorable light."

"I don't know, Your Honor." I smirked. "I think they captured Duke's rugged manliness fairly well, but I looked fat in my bulletproof vest though. What do you think, sir?" I directed the question to the commissioner.

His mouth opened and closed a few times before he settled on a deep frown.

"Detective, this isn't a joke." The captain's tone took on a sharp edge.

I stabbed back. "Look, you can either believe the news crews and the piecemeal, sensationalized footage, in which case we've already lost our credibility, or we can do what we're supposed to do and gather facts, figure out what happened, and deal with those we find responsible appropriately." I thought I was going to keel over before I got all that off my chest.

A look of disdain passed over the mayor's face, directed at me. "The city council has asked for an investigation into the matter."

"Thank God for the city council. We're already on the case. I know these Dexes. They weren't acting normal. As for myself, I stand by my actions. Duke and I were just two cops in an impossible situation."

Duke backed me. "We did the best we could, Your Honor."

The Commissioner began with what I felt was a fairly standard opening address. "Gentlemen, I am not happy. The governor is due to arrive later today to survey the damage. He's expecting some answers on how these Dexes got out of control."

The captain chimed in using the same tone he'd use when talking over a jet engine. "How long before you can explain what happened?"

"Couldn't tell you, captain. As you can see..." I pointed to the mayhem outside the window. "We're working on it."

The mayor had daggers in her eyes. "How could you put me in this position?"

"I didn't. I voted for the other guy."

"Now isn't the time to be cute, O'Shea," the captain snapped.

Yup, I'd crossed the line. It was funny how I never knew where that line was until I'd stepped over it. "Sorry, mayor, but this isn't about you. The Dexes weren't acting like themselves."

"Explain it to her," Captain Grundle said.

"Their inhibitions were turned off. They

really let their powers loose out there. For some reason they were trying to kill each other and everyone who got in their way."

"They fight all the time, O'Shea." The captain stepped up to me. "We've arrested them for disorderly conduct and disturbing the peace."

"They're like plane crashes," Duke said.

The mayor turned on him with a frigid glare. "What is that supposed to mean?"

"Airplane crashes are actually pretty rare," Duke explained. "Statistically, it's the safest way to travel. But when one does crash, the ramifications are disastrous. The news media eats it up. It's the same thing here. There is less crime in the Dex population than in any other minority group. But when something bad happens, it gets noticed, exploited, argued, debated, making it the hotbed topic on every news channel."

"We saw a lot of new faces out there," I added. "New powers. New Dexes tend to show off. They use their powers because they can."

Duke jumped in. "It's something no one else can do, so they think it's cool."

"They rioted for no known reason," I put in.

"There've been no tensions building," Duke went on. "They've had no beef with the city. Why

~77~

they would destroy their city, their home, and try to kill each other—"

"And the STF," I interjected, though right at this moment, double vision made me think they'd succeeded in killing me.

"Their actions go way beyond anything that makes sense."

"Believe me, mayor, no one wanted this riot, including the Dexes."

"Well, obviously someone did."

The commissioner addressed us again. "Gentlemen, this is your one and only priority. Get to the bottom of it, find out who is responsible and why. Meanwhile, I'll deal with the governor and his shit-storm."

He continued to talk, but I couldn't focus my eyes. His words echoed down a long and darkening tunnel. My head pounded like it was beaten by Tyco Drummers.

"Are you okay?" the captain asked me.

"Why does...everyone keep...asking me that?"

Duke shouted to someone outside the room. "Call an ambulance. Now!"

My head hit the floor.

Chapter Six

"**R**ick? Rick. Wake up now. Rick?"

Consciousness returned to me, or so I thought. Felt more like clawing my way out of a body bag. I couldn't be sure if I was still alive.

"Rick? We need you to breathe for us."

She wanted me to breathe. The thought of not breathing alarmed me.

"Deep breaths."

I gasped.

"That's it."

I opened my eyes. Blinked a few times. A blurry bright light hung over me. *Don't go into the light.*

Masked figures were sticking various needles and tubes into me, and in some places attaching wires with cold, sticky pads. I was either in a hospital emergency room, or I'd been abducted by aliens.

They had fitted a breather cup over my

mouth and nose.

"Do you know what day it is?" she asked.

I didn't have a clue.

"Who is President of the United States?"

"George Washington," I muttered.

"Concussion," she told someone next to her.

I drifted in and out, dreamed of Duke standing over me, Pink Panther, and Dani. Everyone looked grief stricken and sad. I was lying in an open coffin, and there was a burly guy standing by with a shovel. A nurse kept leaning in to see if I was still dead.

I awoke in a hospital room, accompanied by monitors and beeping instruments. Panic-fueled adrenaline shot through me. I didn't remember how I got there. What the hell happened? I looked at my hands, wiggled my toes, felt my face, two-day stubble, and discovered a bandage wrapped around my head. Brain surgery was the first thing that came to mind. Fuck! I groped the sheet, found the call button. This wasn't my first rodeo.

A nurse rushed in, young and eye-pleasing, pressed a button on the wall, then came to my bedside. "Detective O'Shea, it's nice to have you back."

"What happened?"

The look in her eyes said, *I've waded through my share of hell, and I have the scrubs to prove it.*

"You were in pretty rough shape when they brought you in, but they got you into surgery right away. The operation went fine, and *voila,* here you are!"

"What was wrong with me?"

"The doctor will tell you the details. He should be here shortly. Are you hungry? Can I bring you some breakfast?"

"I'd love breakfast in bed."

"The service here is impeccable." Her eyes sparkled.

"I have no doubt." I rubbed the stubble on my chin. "How's the food?"

"Can you settle for two stars?"

"I lived on bugs for three days when I was in the Army."

"I promise it won't be that bad."

She adjusted my pillows, checked the bandage around my head, and fiddled with the assorted gadgets around me.

I noticed a large collection of balloons, chocolates, and flowers on the nightstand. One flower arrangement stood out. It contained one of every color of rose. It reminded me of one bouquet

I'd given Dani on her birthday last year. Yellow was for friendship, white for honor, orange for passion, red for love. I felt my heart pang and I suddenly felt lonely.

Pink Panther left a card with pink lip prints on the cover. It read: "O'Shea, I couldn't think of anything inappropriate to say." I opened the card and there was a picture of Pink Panther wearing nothing but her mask and strategically placed ribbons.

"Wow. That could bring back a dead man," I said aloud.

Duke had brought me an assortment of baseball magazines. I hoped that didn't mean he expected me to be here a long time.

I turned on the TV and it came on during an interview with Jonathan Ford, CEO of UltraGen.

He smiled a shark's smile. My guess was he'd earned it after he'd made his first billion.

The interviewer said, "You single handedly created UltraGen from the ashes of Gentech. That certainly was a bold move considering the dubious nature of Gentech's past."

That was an understatement. The retrovirus was their fault.

"No doubt Gentech caused a lot of harm,"

Ford responded with the sincerity of a judge. "But we at UltraGen believe we owe a cure to those affected by this terrible virus."

"What progress have you made?"

"Let me assure you, we refer to the project as P-1 for priority-one."

"Do we need to be concerned about another outbreak?"

Jonathan's expression remained serious. "The influx of new Dexes is being researched as we speak, and we have high hopes for an inoculation soon."

He'd said the same thing ten years ago. I wanted to punch him.

"So Jonathan, what's new for UltraGen?"

"I am glad you asked. We are expanding our Thames River waterfront facility in Groton, Connecticut, and building a new complex across the river in New London. That facility alone will create jobs and those workers will pump dollars into the community. The benefits will be immeasurable."

"And what's the main purpose of the new facility?"

"The new center will be dedicated to finding a cure for the retrovirus." Jonathan raised both arms like Jesus on the mount. "Rest assured, what happened downtown will never happen again. The Dexes will be cured."

Sure, a cure would be beneficial for many, but I couldn't imagine a world without Pink Panther and Talon and Thunderstorm. The STF would be out of business. I'd be out of a job, along with Duke and all my friends. Every good thing had its downside.

A doctor entered my room. I turned off the TV, happy to put an end to Jonathan's grandstanding.

"Detective Rick O'Shea. Welcome back." He checked my wristband as if to be sure I was who he thought I was.

"What happened to me?"

He studied my chart and scribbled something.

"Doc?"

"It's Dr. Brooks, if you please."

"No disrespect intended, doc."

His jaw clenched as he set down the chart. "Internal bleeding in your skull put pressure on your brain. That's why you passed out. Why you didn't come in right after you got that concussion, I can't comprehend."

"I was busy."

"You were almost dead."

"When can I get out of here?"

"In a few days. I'm holding you for observation. I saw your medical file. Don't recall seeing one that thick before."

"I'm accident prone."

"You're no stranger to head injuries. I'll prescribe something for the pain. Any questions?"

"I don't feel so bad now, so I can go home, right?"

"I've got you hooked up to a morphine drip." He checked the IV tube. "I'll take you off in a day or so. Then you'll beg me not to let you go home. Anything else?"

"When's my breakfast getting here?"

"Not my department." He left the room.

A sensitive guy would have been hurt by his abrupt bedside manner. Lucky for me, I had the sensitivity of a rock.

Duke came by that afternoon. "You're not dead?"

"Wasn't for a lack of trying," I had to admit.

"If you ever fail to listen to me again, I'm going to let your stupid-ass die."

"Good to know."

Duke perused the table-o-cheer, took an apple out of a fruit basket, and started munching.

"That came from the mayor," I warned. "The wicked witch."

"Well, I ain't Snow White, so no problem." He continued eating.

"What's the scuttlebutt?"

"Hardball and Metal Jim are cooling their heels on Plum Island, awaiting arraignment, and we're rounding up the stragglers."

"Just as long as Ruff 'N Tuff gets dropped in the deepest hole they can find."

"That's the bad news. Coast Guard searched for him but came up empty. Maybe he's washed out to sea, never to be heard from again."

I shook my head. "He'll turn up. He always does."

"We'll find him. Assault and battery on a police officer. Got it all on video."

"He sucker punched me."

"And you went down like a dropped sack of mail." Duke laughed.

"Et tu, Brutus."

He shrugged.

"What's going on at the station?"

Duke swallowed. "Dignitaries, politicians,

and publicists all trying to spin the riot in every conceivable direction. I don't see us coming away from this without some kind of oversight, probably federal."

I sighed.

"It could be worse, Rick. We could both be suspended."

"Yeah, that's fortunate."

"By the way, you're suspended."

I groaned. "What for?"

"Officially? Insubordination...with pay. You're ambulatory now, but when you're on your feet again, the captain needs you to work under the radar...to nose around."

"Where?"

"UltraGen."

I nodded.

"Until then you're just going to have to do nothing."

Looked like I had a forced vacation on my hands. "Yay," I said without enthusiasm.

After he left, I lay in the bed with my thoughts. I replayed the events in my head and remembered Dani's reaction to the violent lifestyle I lived. She'd left me. That pain felt worse than my injuries. The roses she'd brought gave me hope.

Lucky for me I had morphine.

I slept a lot over the next couple days. Doctor Brooks removed the morphine as promised. I was sorry to see that go. A nurse removed my IV. I wasn't sorry to see that go.

The duty nurse, Paige Greene, stopped by often and kept me company. I didn't know if she paid this much attention to everyone, but I liked to think that we shared a bond. We chatted about work and gave each other little details of our lives, swapped war stories and the like. We spent equal amounts of time laughing and crying.

"Paige, I don't know how you can remain so calm after wading in guts and blood all day."

"It's not like that every day, but this new drug that's out there, it's creating a lot of problems for us."

"What drug?"

"I'm trying to figure that out, doing some research, taking notes. Most everything is hearsay and rumor. If I can find its source, maybe McDonalds won't be so busy."

"McDonalds?"

"That's what we call this floor. We serve hamburger."

"Colorful."

She sucked a breath through her teeth. "We get most of the injured and sick Dexes on this floor. The ICU is up here too."

"You guys that good?"

"We're experienced with the severest trauma. Most of us are ex-military."

"I'd say you were Navy?"

She gave me a half-cocked smile and pushed a stray blonde lock of hair behind her ear. "Marine."

"*Semper Fi.*" I bowed my head in respect.

"You?"

"Army Ranger."

"Where?"

"Vacation spots mostly." I scratched at the stubble on my face. "Surf, sand, snipers, you get the point." I left out the specifics, though her arched eyebrows told me she expected more, but I allowed an awkward silence.

She tilted her head. "Can't talk about it?"

"Not can't, more like won't."

She didn't press the issue. That earned her extra points in my book. Before we reached another awkward moment, I changed the subject. "What's the deal with Dr. Brooks?"

"What do you mean?"

"His bedside manner sucks."

"He's a cold one, I know, but he's good at what he does. Saved your life, anyway."

"Maybe he just has a bad day every day." I scratched at my stubble. "Could you rustle up a razor for me?"

She scrutinized my face while tapping her chin playfully. "I don't know. I think stubble adds a certain manly charm, on the right face."

"Are you saying I have one of *those* faces?"

"Hardly." She smirked. "I'll get you a razor and give you a shave right after your sponge bath."

Sponge bath: the best part of my day. Paige and I became fast friends.

My strength returned enough for me to take short walks. The first walk I took led me directly to Talon's room. An officer stood guard outside her door. Duke told me that she was still considered a person of interest in the investigation. After all, she did attack me for no reason. They had the evidence on camera.

"Detective, I can't let you go in there," the officer said. The name on his badge read *Kilmer*. He couldn't have been older than twenty-five. He still had that new cop stature: squared shoulders, straight back, but from the bruises and nicks on him, I knew he'd seen some action during The Brawl. More action like that would kick the *rookie* out of him in a hurry.

"Kilmer, I just want to visit my friend. Off the record."

"Sorry, detective. You know the rules."

I moved in closer. "Look, I'm the one who shot her down. I owe her an apology."

"Send her a card that says I'm sorry."

"Okay, how about I do that right after I send you a get well card."

He looked at me funny. "I'm not sick."

I showed him my fist. "You will be."

He nodded. "I think I'll go to the rest room now. You have until I get back."

"Take your time. Grab a magazine."

When he was out of sight down the hall I knocked gently on Talon's door but didn't wait for an answer before I slipped inside.

Relief washed over her face at seeing me. "I was hoping you'd stop by."

It hurt to see her wings bound with rope. There were several fliers in the city, but none quite like Talon. She had genuine feathered wings. Some fliers used mechanical methods to fly like jet packs or spring-loaded boots, but with Talon it was all about the grace and beauty of her wings. Now she looked like a hobbled angel. And that was my fault.

"I just want to see how you're doing."

She gestured to a chair by the bed. I took the seat and regarded her for a moment.

Her face paled as she scanned me up and down. "I heard you were hurt, Rick, but I had no idea it was this bad."

"Internal bleeding, a concussion, a few bruised ribs, all in a day's work."

"How many did we lose?"

"Dexes, four dead. Cops, we lost one." I forced a smile. "Almost two."

"Oh my God, I'm so sorry this happened." Tears flooded her eyes.

"Me too, Talon." I put her hand between mine. "I'm sorry I had to shoot you."

"You? You shot me." She looked at her hand, the one I was holding, as if struggling with the notion to pull away, but she didn't. "That explains a lot."

"What happened out there? Can you tell me anything?"

Her lower lip quivered, and tears trickled

down her cheeks.

I wanted to hug her. I couldn't stand seeing a woman cry. The last time I ever saw my mother, she was crying. I was too young to know what words like lymphoma meant, but I knew what tears meant. She kissed me and told me to be brave. When she died, I wiped her last tear away with my thumb. I always flashed back to that moment whenever I saw a woman crying.

I let go of her hand so she could reach for a tissue. This wasn't the same woman I'd witnessed in court, arguing with opposition lawyers, activist groups, and judges. Here she lay helpless and vulnerable, and not just because of the bindings on her wings.

"What do you remember?" I pressed.

"Rick, you know I can't talk to the cops."

"I'm not here as a cop, Talon. I'm here as your friend, and if you want to be technical, I'm suspended from the STF. I have no official authority here anyway."

"Suspended?" Outrage flashed in her eyes.

"I had a run-in with the mayor," I lied. "It didn't go well."

Talon drank some water and set down the glass, as if taking her time to decide to talk to me or not. "Okay, Rick, this is strictly between us and off the record."

I nodded.

"I don't recall a lot of what happened. It seemed like I was having a bad dream. It's like I was outside of myself, almost like someone was operating me by remote control. I knew what was happening and I wanted it to stop, but I couldn't."

"What made you attack me?" The million-dollar question.

"I remember getting angry, really, really angry and needing to lash out. I don't know why. I saw you on the ground, and I knew I had to...I had to kill you. And I didn't care if I died doing it." She swallowed hard. "I folded my wings and dived, and the next thing I knew, I was plummeting toward a rooftop."

She took another drink and her words slowed down. "It felt like I was struck by lightning. Everything was out of control. I believed I was going to die and didn't know why." She rubbed her neck. "But now I know why. You shot me down like a duck over a pond."

"Talon, you were going to kill me with a sword."

"Oh God! What sword?"

She didn't know. I was convinced. "It wasn't your fault, Talon."

She gave me a tearful nod, leaned over, and we touched foreheads.

"I'm going to figure out why this happened. I promise."

"I know, Rick, I know. And I know a pretty good lawyer just in case you need one. Suspended. I'll sue their asses."

I kissed her on the forehead as we clasped hands. "I'm glad you're going to be all right."

"Likewise."

A knock at the door told me that my time was up.

"We'll talk soon."

I purloined a pudding cup from the duty nurse and got back to my room.

Dr. Brooks stood at the foot of my bed. His expression was pissed off. "Detective, why are you up?"

"Just stretching my legs." I set the pudding cup on my nightstand. "Is that a problem?"

"It is when you're disturbing the other patients." There was a gruff edge to his voice.

He must've known I'd been to see Talon. "Who says I'm disturbing them? I'll happily apologize."

He bared his teeth. "Always the wise guy, O'Shea. You're a loose cannon, a rogue cop. You shouldn't even be a cop. You should be—"

"Whoa, doc, what's eating you?"

"I've got a ward full of injured Dexes, all because you're not fit to be on the Dex squad. It's your fault the Dexes got out of control, and it's your fault Jebrowski got killed. If you'd done your job, none of this would have happened."

"I was on the Reaper case when all hell broke loose. You can't blame that on me."

"You're not smart enough to catch the Reaper. You should be selling shoes."

"I'm no good in sales, too abrasive. Go back to your patients and leave the Reaper to me."

"Just stay in your room."

The doc was being a prick. I decided to push the issue. "I need to stretch my legs once in a while."

"I can have you restrained." His expression turned menacing.

I smiled at him. "I've got a gun. Care to threaten me again?"

"You wouldn't dare."

I should've killed him on general principles,

for being an asshole, but: "Doc, clearly we're on opposite sides of the fence. I break them, you put them back together. I get that. But we're actually on the same team. Let's just agree to disagree."

"I've got a better idea. I'll release you tomorrow, and we can both go our merry ways."

"Fair enough."

"Until then, stay in your room!"

He brushed past me. I got the distinct impression that he wanted to shoulder-check me out of spite. He stormed from the room and down the hall, and I no longer thought he was *just* having a bad day.

I turned back to my bed to find Phantasm stretched out on it, eating my pudding cup. He must've walked in under his cloak of invisibility. "Crap, Martin, you scared the shit out of me."

"I've been keeping an eye on you."

"How much of that conversation did you catch?"

"That man has issues." He moved off the bed. "Thanks for the pudding."

He checked out my table of well wishes, held up Pink Panther's card, opened it, and whistled. "Nice." A box of chocolates got his attention. He tore into it. "Rick..." He slumped in the chair.

"Like I told you, I think there's something not right going on here."

"You're in good company thinking that."

He offered me a chocolate.

I declined. "Let's assume no one wanted this to happen. Hardball and Metal Jim were just pulling a job, opportunists looking to score some quick scratch, and got stupid."

Martin rolled that around while making a face at a chocolate that didn't agree with him. He placed it back in the box and selected another one. "They're not the sharpest tools in the shed." He popped the chocolate into his mouth and talked while chewing. "But even they had to know their caper would go south. Instead, they were nothing short of reckless."

"The armored car driver thought there might have been a third culprit."

Martin bit into a bonbon. "Might explain where that missing briefcase went." He chewed some gooey caramel filling. "Maybe, if I could see surveillance footage of the area. Maybe, if I had a friend in the police department with access."

I shook my head. "I'm suspended right now. You'll have to ask Duke. However, I learned something interesting from one of the suspects." I told him about Talon's experience of induced rage and how Sprocketeer didn't know how he got on State Street and landed in the middle of a riot. "I'll bet you a steak dinner at Hughie's that the other Dexes' statements are similar."

"No bet. I've already talked to several Dexes who were involved. None of them had any business downtown, and none of them knew how they got there. Compelled was a word they used a lot. They felt compelled to be there."

"How about you, Martin? What made you go down there?"

He tossed the empty box into the trash. "I was there to kill someone."

"Who?"

"You, Rick."

I suddenly felt cold. "You have my undivided attention."

"Or any cop would have sufficed." He picked a fingernail at caramel stuck in his teeth. "Don't know why, but I have a theory."

"I suspected you might."

"There's nothing more attention-grabbing than a cop getting killed in a fight with Dexes."

"You're referring to Jebrowski."

"Exactly. He gets a hero's funeral, and the

Dexes are the bad guys in all of this. Goal accomplished."

"Who benefits?"

Martin laughed. "Everyone that isn't us."

I scowled. "That certainly narrows it down."

"The feds bring in resources, suddenly there are contracts for new construction. New London gets a makeover and UltraGen gets money for their supposed cure research, because the government is going to throw money at the problem. Expect new legislation, federal oversight, our rights to use our powers taken away, hell, maybe we'll all be rounded up and exterminated, and all it cost to get the ball rolling was the life of a good cop, a few burned down buildings, and our freedom."

"Sounds like someone got a bargain."

"How did you not figure it out?"

"My brain is a little addled."

"What about your doctor buddy? The hospital needs funding."

"You think Brooks has something to do with this? He's an asshole, sure, but hardly a criminal mastermind. Besides, your theory doesn't play. He's stuck with fixing Dexes and upset about the number of casualties he has to deal with. You're grasping at straws."

"He definitely doesn't want you on the case nosing around, that's for sure." Martin got up. "Sleep on it. You still look like shit." He snagged one of my apples on the way out.

I tried to get some sleep, but it didn't come. So I just lay there alone with my thoughts, trying to figure out why Dr. Brooks would have a dog in this fight.

Chapter Seven

"Discharging you?" Duke growled into the phone. "I'm no doctor, but you need more convalescent time in there."

"I can rest at home."

"I'll be there to get you. Meanwhile, don't do anything stupid."

I got dressed and signed the last of my discharge papers. The nurse handed me a fistful of prescriptions and told me to follow up with my doctor. I couldn't have been happier.

"Detective, I hope we never see you like that again, but given your track record...never mind." She smiled. "Just make sure your health insurance is paid and up to date."

"I was hoping to catch Paige on the way out and thank her."

"I'm pulling a double because she had something to do today."

"Is that like her...to take time off?"

"No, but it sounded like something she needed to do."

After writing my cell number on the back of my card, I handed it to the nurse. "Would you be sure she gets this?"

"Sure, sweetie." Her cell phone rang. She examined the screen. "Ah, speak of the devil, that's her now."

I had started to walk off, but she stopped me. "Detective O'Shea. Paige wants to say goodbye."

I took the phone and told her I was discharged.

"This soon?" She didn't sound happy about that.

"I left my number with the nurse here. Call me anytime you want to swap war stories."

"Don't be surprised if I check up on you."

"I'd like that. Gotta go. A guy's waiting with a wheelchair."

A volunteer wheeled me into the elevator.

The door was about to close when an arm stopped it. The arm belonged to Dr. Brooks. He entered the elevator smiling, until he saw me. His expression turned stone cold. "Go ahead. I'll take the next one."

"Don't be silly, doc," I told him. "There's

plenty of room in here."

Wordlessly, Dr. Brooks stood with his back to us as the door closed. I had time to observe him. Detectives used body language when interviewing suspects and witnesses. It wasn't hard to tell when someone was lying or hiding something.

In this case, it didn't take an expert to know there was more going on with the good doctor than met the eye. Eye contact, for one, was non-existent, and he stood stiff as a board while faced away from me, as if every muscle in his body was made of granite. The hem of his trousers shuddered. Every nerve in his body was on high alert. After what seemed like an eternity, the door opened and Brooks fled the elevator like a rat fleeing a fire. Yeah, I had his number pegged; he was guilty of something.

My volunteer wheeled me to the curb where Duke waited with his butt leaned against the squad car's fender.

It felt good to have the sun on my face instead of florescent lighting. I took in a deep breath. I didn't even mind the tinge of pain that accompanied it. The air didn't smell of antiseptic, and that made it worth the discomfort.

"Come on. I ain't got all day." Duke slid in

behind the wheel. He waited until I was fully in the seat and strapped in before speeding off.

After a few moments of silence he asked, "How did you bamboozle your way out of there, Rick?"

"Pissed off my doctor."

"Why do I believe that?" He turned the car down Roosevelt, heading toward my place.

I peeled the bandage off from around my head and hoped I wouldn't start bleeding all over the front seat. "How goes the investigation?"

He sighed. "Since your swan dive in Grundle's office, things got real bad. The department's being bent over and violated without lubricant. A senate subcommittee is looking at disciplinary action against the department. The only reason we haven't all been reassigned to sewage treatment is because..." Duke glanced at me with a *fuck-if-know* tilt on his brow. "Honestly, I don't know why we aren't shoveling shit right now."

"I'll have a word with the motherfuckers."

"Whoa, Silver. Last thing we need is you pissing these guys off."

"But—"

"Shut up."

I shut up.

"Everybody thinks we could have done more to stop that riot. We should've seen it coming."

"No one's going to be satisfied until we find out why it happened. There'll be plenty of time to take heads off later. I figure that's why they're leaving me on the case."

"You've earned a lot of goodwill with the Dex population. They'll talk to you."

"They haven't helped me find the Reaper."

"Maybe he's not a Dex."

"He's got to be a Dex. Otherwise we'd have caught him by now."

"Nothing brings the community together like a psychopath." He braked for a red light. "There might also be some merit to the theory that something had messed with the Dexes' heads. We have too many stories pointing us in that direction, too many to ignore. The problem is we have a serious lack of hard evidence."

"Who would have a motive?"

"It's your job to find out."

My brain started working. "While I'm clandestinely convalescing, who do I report to?"

Duke grinned. "Yours truly, of course."

"That works for me. And since I'm reporting

to you, here's a little something to get you started."

I highlighted my conversations with Talon and Phantasm.

Duke listened intently. When I finished, he whistled a low whistle and shook his head. "That fits with what we're getting."

"I understand a couple supers playing the Good Samaritan and trying to stop the robbery and helping others, Panther and Thunderstorm in particular, but the others had gone completely mad."

Duke banged the heel of his palm on the steering wheel. "It's like they were hopped up on something."

"Exactly!"

"Where do you want to start?"

"Money, power, sex," I ticked off. "The three great motivators, and I know someone who has his fingers in two of them."

Duke gave me a *what-the-fuck-are-you-talking-about* glance.

"Jonathan Ford. UltraGen."

"Why him? He's going to find a cure for the retrovirus."

"You don't really believe that shit."

"Doesn't matter what I believe. We have two days before American Eagle and his federal task force, or I should say farce, get here and take over the investigation."

I groaned. The last time we had a FBI federal task force come in to deal with a Dex related issue, it led to a national day of mourning, a shiny new maximum security prison, and the creation of our friendly neighborhood STF. Our lives hadn't been the same since.

Each major city had an STF, which suited everyone just fine. It kept jurisdiction local. The last thing anyone here needed was the federal government to *fix* things. The FBI could act as a safety net if our asses were truly in a creek, but that seldom turned out well.

"We've got to crack this case before they fuck it up."

"Okay, Rick. You've got two days."

"I've got to find that third briefcase."

"Is that all?" Duke gave me his best *don't-be-stupid* look.

Then it dawned on me. "The money was a cover. It was never about cash. Maybe that third case held something else." A list of possibilities ran through my head. "Corporate documents, research or cooked books. Who knows? It was a hell of a lot of security for relatively little money."

"Find out what was in the third briefcase, you'll solve the mystery. Oh...and did I mention...*do it quietly*?"

"I'll make a church mouse sound like a heavy metal concert. Does anyone else know?"

"The captain."

"Any backup?"

"You're resourceful. You didn't hear this from me, but it's rumored that Pink Panther is suffering a little PTSD after The Brawl and took a leave of absence to get her head straight, a shampoo and manicure, maybe."

We traded grins. I got the message loud and clear. My new partner. Meow.

Duke dropped me off at my place. After checking my mail, bills, bills, and more bills, I stood at my door, hoping for a spit second, to find Dani waiting for me inside. As expected, the house was just the way I'd left it. Empty.

Damn.

After hanging up my coat and gun belt, I steeled my bleeding heart and opened the fridge to pull out a beer. My answering machine had thirty-four new messages, and my cell phone batteries were long dead. I stabbed the cell in the charger and sat back in the easy chair to wade through my messages. About half were people wanting to borrow money and the other half were people wanting to loan me money. Someday I would figure out how to get them to talk to each other and me leave out of it.

There was no word from Dani, not a *Get well, baby* or a *Go to hell, asshole.* A message that interested me most came from Mighty T. *"Hey, O'Shea, it's T. Got something for ya,"* was all it said. T ranked near the top of my *watch-out* list. He could turn on his best friend like a pet tiger cooped up in a Bronx apartment. An invitation always made it easier to see him. I erased the other the messages and went toward my bedroom. As much fun as the sponge baths were, I really wanted a proper shower.

I turned on the bedroom light and nearly jumped out of my skin when I saw that my bed was occupied. I reached for my holstered weapon, but fumbled when my hand came up empty. My pulse pistol hung in the holster on my coat rack.

The woman in pink spandex giggled. "Love those cat-like reflexes, O'Shea."

"I could have shot you."

"You have a very comfy bed."

"I'll be sure to send your endorsement to the mattress company, Panther."

She was stretched out on the bed covers, and to say she wasn't alluring would have been a lie. "Care to join me?"

"Get out of my bed."

She rolled off the bed and did a little handstand then lazily stood upright in front of me. The way her body moved...well, it just...

I decided to make my shower a cold one.

"Did Duke tell you?" she breathed.

"You have post-traumatic stress disorder," I said gravely. "Sounds serious."

"The battle just got to me, all that fighting and punching and kicking, too much for semi-sweet, semi-innocent little ol' me." She threw in a passable Southern drawl for effect.

"Okay, if we're going to be partners, no costumes and we keep a low profile. A pink leather dominatrix outfit does a lot of things, but it doesn't scream discretion."

"Can I wear pink underwear?" Her lips were just a breath away from mine.

"Any color you like." My lips were almost touching hers, in fact, a lot of me was almost touching her. "As long as I don't have to see them."

Her eyes hardened, "Your loss," but never lost contact with mine.

"I know," I answered with regret in my tone. "But that's how it has to be. Right now I'm going to shower and get some real food. You can join me."

"Sure. I'd love a shower." She bubbled.

"I meant join me for dinner."

"I'll take a rain check. I have a saucer of milk waiting for me at home." She grabbed a pen and pad from the top of my dresser and wrote down her address. Before she handed it to me, the playfulness exited her expression. "No one knows where I live."

I matched her serious manner. "Your secret is safe with me."

"I know."

"I'll pick you up tomorrow."

Panther left through the window she'd jimmied to get in. I thought about locking it, but there wasn't much point with the friends I kept. I'd just end up replacing a broken window.

I swallowed a pain pill and examined my head wound in the bathroom mirror. Asshole Dr.

Brooks had shaved off a spot of hair and left a scabbed-over hole in the center of the bare patch. Ugly, but the drain tube that had been in it had saved my life.

After a long scalding shower, a shave, and a change of clothes, I felt half-human. In fact, I felt good enough to venture out in search of something good to eat. Duke had my car delivered while I was luxuriating in the hospital. I grabbed the keys and put a ball cap over my patch. Out on the highway, I motored to the coast and a little spot I knew.

The Gull Grill's claim to fame was its whole-belly clams. I particularly loved their clam fritters. Barely a dozen people were in the place. The summer tourists were a distant memory, and the autumn foliage had peaked. The last surge of tourism would come for Halloween. It had become New London's answer to Mardi Gras. Folks traveled from all over the world to let their freak flag fly in our little berg.

My mouth watered when I smelled the aroma of fresh seafood cooking. I seated myself, and a waiter ambled up. I ordered a bowl of clear broth clam chowder and a half-a-dozen fritters then watched the sun set on Long Island Sound. The silhouettes of gulls dotted the last rays of the sun before it dropped below the horizon.

I felt my heart pang. The last time I sat with my dad, we were on the dock outside, and the evening was much like this one. We watched the sun set over a darkening blue sky. Reds and oranges reflected in the still waters of the Sound. We had a couple of fishing lines in the water but didn't even bother to bait the hooks. A day later I shipped out to Iraq. Eight months later I got the letter.

I sat alone with my thoughts until my food arrived. I dug in and showed my dinner no mercy. The hospital could keep its two stars. This was bliss. I washed my meal down with some fresh-squeezed lemonade then sat back after my feast.

The waiter came by to pick up my plate. "I recognize you," the teenage boy exclaimed.

"Do I know you?"

"I'm Jeremy and you're that dude on TV, doing battle with super-villains. Man, you rock!"

I didn't know what to say.

He went on and on about what he saw and how I took out this guy and beat up that guy, 'til I got punched out by the little guy. He asked me for an autograph.

I politely declined. "Jeremy, they weren't super-villains. They're people who got mixed up, and some got hurt."

"Yeah, I was talking to Brad, my best friend, and we thought there was something fucked up going on there. We'd met Talon once. She is way hot. Anyway, she was totally not cool and Brad said, 'I wonder if she was being mind-controlled.' And I said, 'Yeah, that'd be it.' Then he said, 'Totally, probably the Chess Dude.'" Jeremy was talking a mile a minute. Stopping him was like roping a speeding Mack truck.

"What Chess Dude?"

"He can totally mind-control you and make you his pawn." Jeremy folded his arms and gave me a proud smile. "You'll do anything he says."

"Where did you hear about him?"

"The Internet." He looked at me like I was an idiot. "Almost every super-hero and villain has a webpage, or they're on Facebook, but..." he leaned in close, "there's this one site where it's like fantasy football league. You can pick a Dex, and when they fight another Dex, you earn points."

"What do you do with these points?"

"It's just for fun, man."

"What about the Chess guy?"

"He just appeared on the website. He's like some kind of boogieman, probably played by the site admin. As far as I know, he just fucks shit up. No one can play him."

I figured it was probably no more than an urban legend or Internet prank, but given my lack of clues, it seemed like a decent straw to grasp. I'd get Martin to follow up on the Chess Dude. He lived for that sort of thing. Hell, he'd probably link it to a CIA conspiracy or UFO crash cover-up. Me? I thought computer games reached their pinnacle with Pong.

Jeremy wrote down the website name for me: *Dex Territory,* and I left him a good tip. He earned it.

Chapter Eight

I returned home and fell into my chair. Every muscle in my body was punishing me for not going straight to bed. I grabbed the phone and called Martin, got his machine, and left him a message, giving him the lowdown on the website lead I'd gotten from Jeremy. My eyes shifted to my computer on the table across the room. I could have looked up Dex Territory myself, but I wouldn't know what I was looking at. Martin would figure it out.

I flipped on the TV. I don't know when I fell asleep, but I woke to a phone call. I mumbled something unkind and the answering machine picked up. I heard a familiar voice and snapped up the phone, "Hello?"

"Rick, it's Paige," she whispered. "I need help, he's in the house. I haven't been able to—"

Clunk!

The phone clattered on the floor.

A scream.

"Paige?"

My heartbeat went through the roof.

I heard scuffling and her pleading voice. "No, please, no." Dragging sounds, kicking feet, muffled gagging.

"Oh my God!"

Thump!

Footsteps on hardwood.

Click!

The phone went dead.

"Son-of-a-bitch!"

I dialed 911.

"911. What's the address of your emergency?"

Shit! I didn't have her address. But I had her phone number. "I need a welfare check right away, to the address listed for this phone number." I read it off my cell phone screen. "I was on the phone with Paige Greene when an intruder attacked her. She's in immediate danger."

"Who's calling, please?"

"Detective Rick O'Shea, STF. Call it in, now!"

"You're suspended, detective, I can't—"

"This isn't about me. It's about saving her life."

"But—"

"Just do your job or you'll find Thunderstorm playing bongos on your doorstep."

"All right, chill, O'Shea."

I heard him call it in. "Calling all cars in the vicinity of 778 Beach. 10-42. Possible intruder. Proceed with caution."

Seventh and Beach? I couldn't believe her address was only two blocks away. I hung up the phone, grabbed my pulse gun from the holster on the coat rack, and ran out the door. I thought about the car briefly, but I'd left the keys in the house, so I ran past it and headed down the block. Running was a mistake, and my body let me know it. By the time I reached Paige's house, two black-and-whites had pulled up in front. A pair of officers got out.

I flashed my gold shield at them, and they fell in step behind me. I motioned one to go around back. The other officer and I rushed up the front stairs to the door.

"Ms. Greene!" I banged on the door.

No answer.

"Paige! It's Detective O'Shea! Are you okay?"

No answer.

I tried the doorknob, locked. I gestured to the

door and stepped back. The officer kicked it in.

We stalked inside, gun barrels leading the way.

"Paige?" I called again.

The second officer came in through the back. "Clear."

We systematically cleared the lower level. I was so pumped with adrenaline my pains had evaporated.

I grabbed a flashlight off the cop behind me and steadied my shooting hand with a tactical stance, keeping the weapon and light pointed directly in front of me as I led them up the stairs. We alternately checked the rooms down a short hall until we came to a back bedroom.

My stomach twisted as I reached for the doorknob. The two officers behind me breathed heavily. I gritted my teeth and swung open the door.

"Shit!"

I didn't know who said it. Could have been me. The officer standing directly behind said, "Dear God."

Steeling my nerves, I shuffled to the body, gun on a swivel in case the intruder jumped out from the shadows.

Paige lay naked on the floor. Her body had been carefully posed in a spread-eagle position just like Leonardo da Vinci's Vitruvian Man. At each of her joints a thin line of crimson oozed from the cuts. Additional cuts ran across her neck, under her breasts, through her ribcage and her abdomen. Blood pooled on the carpet, slowly soaking into the fibers.

She couldn't have been dead more than a minute.

The stillness made the room seem peaceful, which lasted until I saw the twisted expression of horror on Paige's face. Her mouth gaped open in a silent scream, and her unblinking eyes were forever fixed in a blank stare.

As long as I lived, I would never forget seeing her that way.

The officers got to work, one on the crime scene tape, the other on the radio to call Emergency Service and the M.E. I stayed with Paige. I had no idea how long it took for the forensic team to arrive, but sufficient time had passed for me to lose feeling in my legs as I crouched over her.

Crime scene investigators catalogued and photographed the scene. As some point Duke arrived and took over the investigation. "Rick, what the hell are you doing here?"

"She called me...scared to death. Someone was in her house."

"Outside. Now. That isn't a request."

"I didn't touch anything," I assured him as he led me outside.

The M.E. arrived. He looked at me with disdain and stomped up the front steps to disappear inside.

"Why didn't she call 911?"

I shook my head.

Duke had his hands full and didn't need me getting in the way. I hated to admit it, but he wasn't wrong. I ducked under the yellow and black crime scene tape stretched along the sidewalk and waded into the growing crowd of neighbors eager to see what the commotion was about. I asked if anyone had seen anything. No one had. That didn't surprise me, especially in the early hours.

The body came out on a gurney. The M.E. accompanied it but veered over to talk to Duke and me. He droned on about angles of the slashes, they were awkward and random, and that to cut through bone the weapon had to be very sharp, but this one only scraped bone, and there had to have been a lot of hacking force used. But this perpetrator wasn't very skilled with his blade.

I'd had a similar conversation with him before. Dead girl number seven. "Like the Reaper?"

"Was she a drug dealer?" He indicated the gurney.

"No, she was a nurse. A damn good one."

"Think about it, O'Shea. She doesn't fit the Reaper's MO." He hopped in the coroner's van with the body. "But the killer wants us to think it was the Reaper." The door closed and they left without sirens.

My throat turned to sand. So it wasn't the Reaper...but a damn poor copycat? Dr. Brooks...he could have done this. Motive and opportunity. He knew the victim, he knew I liked her, and he knew killing her would piss me off. If so, he'd succeeded.

Or maybe Brooks was the Reaper, maybe he'd butchered Paige differently to throw me off, maybe I was getting too close, and this was just a warning. Or maybe he had nothing to gain by killing Paige, just killed her for fun. Still, who else? It was enough to make my head hurt.

Duke shook my arm. "Rick, go home. That's an order. I got this. I'll keep you in the loop."

"You'd better."

"Get some sleep."

Fat chance.

Chapter Nine

I walked back to my place. By the time I got there the first rays of the sun were poking over the trees. I took a moment to watch the light dance on the dewy red and yellow autumn leaves, creating a thousand little rainbows. The beauty of those leaves seemed foreign to me after the horror I'd just witnessed. I let my eyes linger over the gift of that moment before facing my empty house. The thought of going inside made my heart ache.

I got in the car and drove to a local coffee shop where I ordered the largest coffee they had and a second cup with heavy cream and a teaspoon of honey, and then I drove to the address Panther had given me.

It turned out that this big-time celebrity superhero lived in a very modest brownstone in a blue-collar neighborhood.

I shuffled up the stairs and rang the bell.

"Come in," I heard Panther shout from

behind the door.

I let myself in. The place was not what I expected given the nature of her over-the-top costumes. I had money bet on a dungeon filled with pink restraints and a host of criminals' pictures adorning the walls like trophies.

Instead, the place might have belonged to her grandmother. The floors were hardwood. The window coverings were rich and elegant. The furniture looked comfortable and sturdy. Antiques dotted the place making it a residence of a Home and Garden enthusiast rather than a rock star.

Mail lay scattered on the coffee table. I got nosy. There were fan letters to Pink Panther addressed to a P.O. Box. Other mail had been addressed to Monica Voight, bills and such.

A spot on the pillow-laden couch had been cleared. In front of it, on the coffee table, sat a half-finished glass of fruit juice and the remnants of a very substantial breakfast: two empty boxes of cereal, two plates of toast crumbs, a giant bowl of mixed fruit salad nearly empty, another plate smeared with pancake syrup, and an empty bag from a bagel shop up the road.

"Hungry this morning?" I shouted.

"That should keep me for a couple of hours."

Panther's voice came from upstairs. "Be there in a second."

I noticed she had no television in living room, but a shelving unit held an impressive stereo and a music collection brimming with vintage vinyl records. I picked up a Frank Sinatra album and whispered, "Not bad, Monica Voight."

"Glad you like it."

I spun around and saw the smiling face of someone I'd never seen before. The woman before me bore only the slightest resemblance to Pink Panther. She had the same size and build, but I would have walked by this woman on the street and not given her a second look.

Chestnut hair hung to her shoulders in a conservative, bland cut. She wore a little eyeliner that made her skin appear pale. I'd seen Panther in skin-tight outfits and even a bikini, but little trace of that body showed in the loose-fitting jeans and brown leather jacket Monica wore. Her mundane makeover was punctuated with a very common pair of black and white sneakers.

"How do I look?" She spun without the famous Pink Panther grace.

"Ordinary."

She beamed as though I'd given her the

greatest compliment in the world.

I put away the record. She ate some more fruit salad and finished her glass of juice. I helped her carry the dishes into the kitchen. She grabbed an apple and offered me one.

"No thanks. Something that good for me this early might wreak havoc with my system."

She led me outside and got into the car. When seated, I handed her the coffee I had brought for her. She took a sip and smiled, showing a bumper crop of dimples. "I could get used to this."

"O'Shea's first rule: always take care of your partner."

"Are you one of those guys who has a hundred and thirteen rules to live by, for doing the job, or taking a dump?"

"Nah."

"Thank god."

"Only a hundred and eight."

She shook her head and drank her coffee. We drove out of the neighborhood and headed toward the highway.

"Where are we off to first?" Monica asked between sips.

"You up for a drive in the country?"

"Let's go, cowboy."

I turned north on I-95 and drove to a small town way out in the suburbs. At the bottom of the off ramp I took a few secondary roads. After running through the center of town, the subdivision started giving way to small farms, mostly dairy.

Driving out here, I could breathe. The death scene I'd witnessed just a few hours ago felt like a distant memory. Lakes and trickling brooks adorned the roadside views.

After passing a large lake, I turned down a gravel driveway. Massive cherry trees acted like sentinels along the way to a farmhouse.

The farm was like many small New England farms: planted fields, a lovingly tended barn, and dairy cows lazily moving around fenced-in pastures.

I parked the car in front of the barn, and we got out. I closed my eyes and took the pleasure of a long inhale. The fragrances of the grasses, the sweetness of the fallen leaves, autumn flowers and dust, all greeted me lovingly.

Thunderstorm met us at the gate. He eyed me suspiciously. "You here for a reason, bro?"

Monica extended her hand and smiled at him warmly. "I'm Monica."

"My new partner," I put in.

He hesitated to take her hand. "You look familiar."

"You too."

"Henry, my name's Henry." He shook her hand.

"Pleased to meet you, Henry. I've heard a lot about you."

"Good, I hope."

He leaned against the metal fence of a corral.

"So what brings you to my humble abode?"

"Questions."

"I told Duke everything I remembered."

"Henry, I need you to think really hard. You and Talon were the first to see Metal Jim and Hardball take out the armored car."

He nodded.

"Who else did you see?"

"I walked out of Graffiti's and saw Metal Jim and Hardball standing in front of the armored car."

"Graffiti's is a mile and half away from State Street. How could you have seen them?"

"I don't know. I just saw them."

Monica and I exchanged skeptical looks.

"I knew she and Metal Jim were up to

something."

"She?"

"What?" Henry eyed me warily.

"You said she."

"Did I? I meant Hardball."

"No, you meant *she*. It's called a Freudian slip. Your subconscious saw her. Who is she?"

"I don't know who you're talking about, bro."

"With Metal Jim and Hardball, she was there."

Henry's face reddened as he balled his fists. "Who?"

"I don't know. You saw her. You were there and you saw her. Maybe right next to Metal Jim and Hardball. Who was she, Henry?" I made sure my voice sounded demanding.

Henry put up his hands and grabbed the sides of his head. "I don't know."

Monica looked at me with alarm in her eyes.

I gave her a single nod: *everything is all right.* "Come on, Henry. She was there, you saw her. You did. She played you, Henry. You know her face. Tell me. Tell me now."

He let out a frustrated cry and flung a lightning bolt at a nearby tree. It exploded to splinters. Henry's eyes looked stormy and lethal.

I held up my hands and backed away a step. He gritted his teeth, took an angry step toward me. I felt some unease at this, actually a lot of unease.

As he took another step closer, Monica came to full alert, and Pink Panther's protective nature crept in. She stepped in front of me, her hands outstretched to Henry, her fingers poised like claws. He stopped and cocked his head. The threat of bodily harm suddenly dissipated.

"What?" I asked.

He unclenched his fists struck a thoughtful pose. "You're right, Rick. There *was* a girl."

"Who?"

"I can't remember."

Chapter Ten

I'd have to hypnotize Thunderstorm. That would be like controlling the weather, but I had to try. The identity of the girl involved in the armored car heist was crucial. She could have taken the third briefcase.

"Monica, I need your help."

"With what?"

"We've got to hypnotize Henry."

"You know how to do that?"

"I've had therapy, and believe me, I've got a good idea how it works."

"If I were you I wouldn't brag about that."

We grabbed a couple hay bales and positioned them about two feet apart facing each other.

"Take a seat, Henry. I need you relaxed for this."

He sat on one hay bale, and I instructed Monica to sit facing him on the other.

I stood behind him. "Henry, I want you to look into Monica's eyes and listen to me very carefully. Breathe slow and deep."

He breathed in and out a few times. "This is stupid."

"Henry, try again. Concentrate."

Monica stared into Henry's eyes and demonstrated how to breathe slow and deep. If she were wearing her pink spandex costume, it would have been quite an erotic show.

He relaxed a little. His eyes remained fixed on Monica's baby blues. He mimicked her breathing to the letter this time.

"Henry?" I kept my voice soft. "Can you hear me?"

"Yes."

"Think back to the night of The Brawl. You're at Graffiti's. Who's there you with?"

"Zack."

"What is he doing?"

"Dancing with a girl."

"Who is the girl?"

"A regular, Julia."

Monica and I exchanged shrugs. She shook her head. *Not the one.*

I moved to a position to where I could see his

face. His eyes were staring at a point beyond Monica. "Is she leaving the bar with you?"

"No." His eyebrows narrowed.

"What do you see?"

"Metal Jim and Hardball."

"Henry, are you're standing in front of Graffiti's?"

"Yes."

"Can you see State Street?"

"I can't."

That stumped me. He could see the Dexes but not the street. So he must've had a vision. I'd have to be very careful with my next line of questioning. "What do you hear?"

"Voice in my head."

"A familiar voice?"

"No."

"What is he saying?"

"Go to State Street."

"What are you doing now?"

"Running...trouble...running...trouble."

"What do you see?"

"Metal Jim. Hardball. Armored car. It's on its side. Driver trapped."

"What are you doing?"

"I'm standing on the truck."

"Why?"

"I must protect the driver."

"Do you see the girl?"

"Yes."

"What does she look like?"

"Cat burglar, black and purple spandex."

"What color is her hair?"

"I can't see her hair."

"Why?"

"Skull cap."

"What is she doing?"

"Moving very fast. A blur. Running away."

"Does she have anything in her hand?"

"Briefcase."

Bingo. "Do you see anything else about her?"

"Tattoo."

Sleeveless spandex? "On her arm?"

"Neck. In the back."

Her hair was tucked up under a skull cap, sure, Henry could have seen the back of her neck. "Can you see the tattoo now?"

"Yes."

"What does it look like?"

"A fish."

My blood ran cold. *A fish?*

Monica gave me a sideways glance. "What?"

"Dani has a koi fish tattooed on the back of her neck. I hate the damn thing."

"Do you think it could be her?"

"There are a lot of people with those tattoos, besides, she was at my place all night." I recalled the pop cans and pillows. "Couldn't be her."

"Are you sure?"

Recalling the conversation I had with her on the phone before I went to the morgue, she'd said something about a parent-teacher conference. That was why we'd broken our date. Technically she wasn't at my place *all* night. But Dani involved in an armored car heist? Dani a Dex with super-speed powers? That didn't make any sense.

"How well do you know her?" Monica pried.

"She's a kindergarten teacher, for Christ sake. All the kids love Miss Reyes."

"Reyes?" Monica's eyebrows shot up. "Any relation to Fernando Reyes?"

"She's never talked about her family."

"So you *don't* know her very well. No background check?"

"Hell no! Why would I? There's this thing called trust. I love her. I know her. I'm a detective and fairly good at it most days. I can tell when someone's lying to me. I notice things."

"Except this time, you didn't."

I replayed recent events in my mind. Things that seemed innocuous at the time, but put in another light, were very noticeable, had I looked. Dani's workouts went way beyond a health routine. I didn't train that hard in the Rangers. A couple times she visited her college roommate in Miami. Dani came back with pictures of them on the beach and she brought me a lemon tree. Was that all a lie? If so, where did she go?

Then there was an incident when an elderly Latino couple recognized her in a restaurant. They were genuinely delighted to see her. She'd claimed it was a case of mistaken identity.

My brain kick-started. Dani was a kindergarten teacher, which gave her a lot of free time: summers off, holidays. Her job carried an air of respectability. Who wouldn't think well of a kindergarten teacher? But the job might rank in the top ten of undercover identities. Everything about her could have been a lie.

But she was at my place waiting for me that night. I'd vouch for her alibi anytime.

Monica had talked Henry out of the trance. I studied her *Monica* disguise, very convincing, and then reminded myself that she was Pink Panther.

Worse yet, I knew she was Pink Panther, but after only a few hours, she became Monica Voight to me. In reality, she was both personas. While I didn't buy the speedy mystery woman was Dani, I had to admit it was possible.

I wanted to be sick.

Chapter Eleven

*T*he only way to describe *The Loon* was to compare it to a natural disaster in the middle of a war zone ravaged by an apocalypse. The place had the charm of a fungal infection. Its owner was a man of diminutive stature, a little like Ruff 'N Tuff. He went by the name Mighty T. Everyone called him T for short, but intended no pun.

T was a victim of the same retrovirus responsible for the Dexes. Some of the more unfortunate victims were altered radically. Before the outbreak, T was six-foot-four, and he used to do some modeling work, underwear mostly.

During his illness, his body deteriorated and disfigured, and when he emerged transformed, he stood only four feet and an inch. His facial features changed. One eye grew disturbingly large, and his nose became bulbous. One of his legs was slightly longer than the other, and he lost most of his hair, which sprouted in sad little tufts unevenly on his head.

I found him behind the bar, a stained white towel draped over his shoulder. He wore a green Leprechaun hat and a red kilt skirt with gold tassels.

"Hey, T."

"Well if it ain't O'Shea. I heard you got your lily-white ass wasted by the midget." He used a fake Irish accent in an attempt at branding, but he was as Irish as Napoleon Bonaparte.

"Ruff 'N Tuff is a dwarf, T," I corrected him as Monica and I claimed stools at the bar. "He sucker-punched me."

"Asshole!" T jerked a thumb at himself. "I'm a dwarf. We're hearty. Ruff-n-Tuff's a midget."

"In case you hadn't noticed, he's invulnerable to most causes of death."

"I hope he can tread water a long time."

The Coast Guard still hadn't found him. There was a long-standing feud between the two little people. They were more similar than either man realized.

"Get to the point, T. You called me, remember?"

"About damn time you got back to me. Who's the bitch?" He motioned his chin toward Monica.

"Doesn't look like much, does she?"

"Leave the lady alone, or I might just let her whoop your ass."

"Ha! Like that'd happen." He leaned over the bar and looked her up and down, giving her a full appraisal. "Some nice lines, a wee frumpy. O'Shea..." he looked at me, "if you're that hard up, you should have talked to me. I have this new girl. She'd knock your dick in the dirt."

At that, Monica jumped in. "Fuck you, short stack. One more word out of you and I'll remove your tonsils rectally and use your funny little hat for a butt plug."

"Feisty." T gave her an exaggerated wink. "O'Shea. You have my approval."

"That makes me so happy, T." My voice dripped with sarcasm. "You said you had something for me?"

T scanned the barroom and must've decided it was safe to talk. "There's a new player in town. No one's seen her before. She was at the ruckus on State Street. Only a couple of the guys actually caught a glimpse of her. She made off with somethin' from Hardball and Metal Jim's armored car heist while you STF guys were lickin' your pussies."

"Tell me something I don't already know."

"Rumor has it, she's fast and agile. She could give the pink lass a run for her money."

Monica snorted.

He squinted at her. "I'd actually like to see that, a cat fight in a big ol' tub of puddin'."

I think Monica bit her tongue a little. "Focus everybody."

T handed me two large envelopes.

"What's this?"

"O'Shea, you could sit there and ask stupid questions, or you could open them and find out for yourself."

I opened the first envelope. There were pictures of the Arsonist in his fireproof costume tailored after Elvis's famous stage getup. On the back of the photo an address was written.

"That's his last known location."

"He's wanted for blowing up shit during The Brawl." Monica snatched the picture from me. "I'll take care of him."

I opened the second envelope. Two pictures. The first was dark with a lot of shadows. A figure in black was silhouetted against the background. The second picture was better: a skull mask clearly popped out of the figure's inky blackness. Light glinted off a scythe blade. The weapon looked deadly, and there was no mistaking it for a Halloween prop. The picture was date and time stamped the night Paige was murdered.

"Where did you get these?"

"I got my connections."

"Where were they taken?"

"Mill Creek Road."

"That's my neighborhood."

The picture was taken minutes before I received the call from Paige. That put the Reaper at the scene of the crime. Brooks had motive and opportunity, and now I could prove he was there. I felt like I'd been gut punched. I pounded my fist on the bar. "I should have killed Brooks when I found out he was an asshole"

"Brooks is the Reaper?" Monica asked.

"It's a theory I've been working on."

"Let's go find him."

"I know where he is. I'll need to connect him to the Reaper first. Meanwhile, I'm declaring war on anyone with a skull mask."

Monica grabbed me and spun me around to face her. "Easy, O'Shea! Losing your cool won't do anyone any good."

"The bastard is fucking with me!"

"I understand your frustration. You've been chasing him a long time." She thumped me on the forehead with her index finger. "You're going to catch him with this, your street smarts." She held up my clenched fist. "This is just going to get you in trouble."

"Your dumpy broad's right, O'Shea. None of us want this asshole on the street. The Reaper's givin' us Dexes a bad rap. Everyone's looking for him. I don't know how you take out these fuckers like you do, but there's a reason you're good at it."

I'd never heard T compliment anyone before. That pulled me out of my rage.

I'd gotten lucky a few times in the past, took out some really bad bad-guys. That part was true. There were more than a few Dex criminals locked tightly away on Plum Island.

I looked at the picture of the Reaper and his weapon of death. "You're next," I muttered.

Chapter Twelve

We left *The Loon* and just walked. After a few blocks it began to rain and we stepped under an awning to wait out the passing shower.

Too many things swam around in my head. Dani's leaving stung but not nearly as bad as the suspicions I had about her being a Dex criminal. I couldn't wrap my head around her secrets and false identity. Paige's death weighed heavily, and I couldn't even throw myself into the investigation, because technically I was out in the cold, like a burned spy. I was bone-weary tired and hurt.

Monica broke the silence. "Rick, no one knows for certain Dani is the new player in town."

"We don't have any facts, just secondhand information and circumstantial evidence. Even entertaining this scenario probably says something negative about my character."

"Hey, character flaws make interesting characters."

"I feel guilty for doubting her, yet I curse her at the same time for lying to me."

"You're mad at her for leaving. Keep an open mind and follow the facts."

Monica put her arm in mine, and her touch felt reassuring. We stepped out from under the awning and walked in the light rain. "Why does T hate you so much?"

"He respects me."

"To listen to him, it sounds like you killed his mother."

"He hates calling on me for help. The Reaper's got them all on edge."

"Why don't they like dealing with you?"

"Would you come to me if there was something you couldn't handle as Pink Panther?"

"If it was something I couldn't handle, it would break you in half."

"But it's still my job to take on dangerous cases, and T knows it. I've done him a solid a time or two. Wouldn't it be hard for Pink Panther, who is a superhero with action figures and a breakfast cereal, to ask anyone for help?"

"The cereal was originally called Pink-Os." She shuddered. "Thankfully, someone got wise before that name hit the market."

"Pink Panther is iconic. There's nothing she can't handle, but you don't have the authority. I mean this with the highest possible respect, even though you consult and work with STF and give back to the community in a thousand different ways, you don't have the power that I do."

I could tell that stung her by the way she bit her lower lip.

"I'm sorry, that's the legality of our situation. But reality is much simpler. Those with the power are the ones who can affect the most change. I'm all for those who use their power to change society for the better. I get a little cranky when they use their power to hurt people."

"You just hate competition."

"Maybe." I laughed. "But why do it? As Pink Panther, you're famous. You have fans and magazine spreads. I bet you've even had some movie deal in the works. Why slum with us lowly civil servants of STF?"

She pulled me to a stop and put her hand on my chest. "Short answer, there are people I care about and want to help. Never once has my celebrity status really helped anyone other than ad execs, lawyers, and agents. I want to make a difference in New London. It's my home. It's as simple as that."

I looked into her eyes. It was the first time I saw the woman behind Pink Panther. There were all kinds of masks. I never thought hers extended beyond the one she wore as part of her costume. I saw a deep hurt in her eyes. "What happened to you?"

"I was a little girl when I got sick with the retrovirus. My parents were afraid I was going to be deformed like T, or turn into some freak like Metal Jim, or die like the lucky ones had. They were scared. I was scared too."

"I can't imagine." The statement sounded hollow.

"Everyone was so happy when I got better, and there didn't seem to be anything wrong with me."

"When did you learn about your powers?"

"Olympic gymnastics."

We started walking again. She moved in closer to me, almost threw me a little off balance, but she looped an arm around me and steadied us both.

"I was watching Jesse Kreegan perform. Her routine was amazing. I remember being in awe of her back flips and twists. I thought I would like to do that. In my living room I tried and discovered I could not only do them but do them better than her. Talk about being excited. I ran out to the backyard and did more tricks. Soon, I was bouncing off the swing set and jungle gym, flipping and tumbling and doing stunts that Jesse Kreegan couldn't even imagine."

"And she was a world champion," I added.

"I called my mom outside so she could see. I remember the horror on her face. 'My little girl is a freak.'"

"She didn't understand."

"She thought I was going to become some kind of monster. All she'd heard were news reports how everyone who'd been affected by the retrovirus was dangerous."

"I remember a lot of wild speculation during the outbreak."

"It took time for reason to beat back the panic. I dreaded what would happen when my dad got home from work. Mom had locked me in my room. Dad walked into the house, and I heard Mom's voice, shrill and terrible. They fought and cried then shipped me off to my grandma's house. Their bodies were found two days later. Murder suicide they called it. The thought of having a Dex child was too much for them to handle."

I held her there in the rain until she started shivering. Losing her parents was a traumatic event made worse because she thought their deaths were her fault. That was enough to change a person. She grew up trying to show the world that all Dexes weren't dangerous.

By the time we got to the car, we were both cold and wet. I pulled up in front of Monica's place, but before getting out, she took the envelope she'd snatched from me out of her pocket. "I'll track down the little firebug. Something physical will do me good."

"I don't want you detaining him without backup."

She gave me a girlish smile. "I can handle him."

"Yeah, that's what worries me." I smiled back at her. "I need to see Martin tonight."

She got out and stepped to the curb. "O'Shea." She bent to the open window. "I've never told anyone about my parents, so don't tell anyone else or I'll cripple you, and not in a good way."

"There's a good way to be crippled?"

"Do you want to pee with or without the aid

of a catheter?"

"I get your point."

She curtsied, spun on her tiptoes, and sauntered to her front door.

I didn't know what I'd done to earn her trust, but it was very important I kept it.

Chapter Thirteen

I stopped at my house and took a hot shower. It did a lot to pull the chill out of my body. I eyed the bottle of pain pills, but my injuries didn't hurt as bad after the shower had done its work. Now to deal with Dani. I picked up the phone and dialed her number but got the answering machine.

"I miss you and want to see you. Call me." Actually I wanted to interrogate her about her whereabouts during *The Brawl.*

I called Duke next.

He picked up. "Hey, Rick, how ya' feeling?"

"What's the chance of me getting in to see Hardball and Metal Jim?"

"What do you want with them?"

I told him about my chat with Thunderstorm and gave him the description of the mystery woman verbatim, but I kept my suspicions about Dani to myself.

Then he gave me the bad news. "Martin and I checked the State Street security cameras. If she was there, she knew where the cameras were located and the areas they didn't cover. We only saw Hardball and Jim."

"Check them again. Meanwhile I want to grill those idiots about an accomplice. Maybe they'll sing if I offer them a deal."

"The Feds won't agree to a deal. Those boys are up for some hard time."

"The Feds?"

"They've got our perps locked down tight, maximum security."

A knot tightened in my stomach. "The Feds weren't supposed to be here for two more days."

"Someone got ambitious," Duke growled out. "Homeland Security sent in an advance unit. The STF is officially off the case."

"And me?"

"They don't know you're out there nosing around. You're the only hope we've got to beat them to the punch."

"If STF is off the case, who do I report to?"

"It gets worse. Since I was lead detective on the scene, I'm flying a desk now. We aren't partners anymore."

"This isn't happening." I felt gut-punched. "I'm sorry, Duke. I'll do everything I can to get your job back. Who's filling your shoes now?"

"Hold on to your panties, Rick. It's American Eagle."

I set a new world's record for the most amount of swear words strung together. "The Dex is a fucking Fed? How does he get local control?"

"Homeland Security is calling it a lateral transfer. They want a Dex in charge of the investigation so it doesn't look like it's us against them. Might stem another riot."

I squeezed the phone as if this turn of events was the phone's fault. "Only an idiot would think that."

"Don't underestimate the power of idiots. Half the population has lower than average intelligence. Blame the Internet and video games."

"You're starting to sound like Martin."

"I'm keeping him in the loop so he can keep you informed."

"Speaking of which..." I thought about the Reaper. "I have a picture I want forensics to take a look at, make sure it wasn't doctored. If it's legit, I have proof the Reaper was in the area when Paige was murdered."

"You can't come anywhere near the station. You've gotta lay low. I'll meet you at Y-Knots."

"Seven A.M. okay?"

"We'll have breakfast," he chirped.

"Do we have to?"

He hung up.

Outside, it was pouring rain. I went to the coat rack and grabbed my tan trench coat, slipped it on, and got it cinched up. When I stuck my cell phone in the pocket, I felt a folded piece of paper.

The surreptitious note contained an unfamiliar phone number. I'd recognize the handwriting anywhere. It was Dani's. My neck hairs prickled. When did she slip this into my pocket...and why?

I reached for my phone but stopped. The Feds could have bugged it. But who would be interested in my activities? Everyone thought I was the black sheep of STF. Still, to be on the safe side, I needed a burner phone.

It was time to visit Martin.

Chapter Fourteen

*M*artin's office was located in the part of town where it was a good idea to lock the doors. The neighborhood had seen better days. Once-proud storefronts were now covered with iron gates, and graffiti dotted the walls like colorful scabs. Martin's scab was an old house converted to commercial use. A couple of prostitutes huddled under a faded awning and looked bored.

Slow night.

A neon sign from the bar next door to Martin's office hummed and gave off a sad pink light. The *P* in O_EN had burned out long ago.

An intercom greeted me at Martin's door. I pressed the white call button and waited.

"Yeah?"

"It's me."

"About time. What's the password?"

"Just let me the fuck in." I sneered up at the security camera. The door lock buzzed. I opened the door and walked in.

After stepping through the mudroom I approached the door that had *Private Investigator-Martin Steele* stenciled on the frosted glass. The door hinges let out a noticeable squeak, probably on purpose, when I opened it.

The room looked like a throwback to the hardboiled detective days of the forties: wood floor, paneled walls, wood desk, wood filing cabinets, and clutter everywhere. Two uncomfortable wooden chairs sat in front of the desk, and a ceiling fan with worn out bearings whirled a lazy, drunken path above the muddle. A crummy floor lamp did nothing to cheer up the dark hole that was Martin's office.

He sat in a high-back padded chair behind his desk, which had been cleared off save for an old rotary dial phone and a deck of cards. "Rough day?"

"Haven't slept in a while either."

He gave me a sly nod. "That could work in my favor."

"Don't count on it." I took off my coat and placed it on the antique oak coat stand.

Martin offered me a seat in one of the wooden chairs.

I'd just gotten seated when he tossed me a flask. I opened it, and the lovely aroma of brandy wafted out. "Don't mind if I do." I took a sip. "Thanks." I felt the fiery swallow make its way down to my stomach. Warmth spread out from there. "Good thing I didn't take my Vicodin." I tossed the flask back.

"Cheers." He took a swallow as well.

"So who starts?" I asked.

"What's the bet?"

"A steak at Hughie's."

Martin's eyebrows shot up. "And dessert?"

"Just deal the cards."

"You must feel pretty confident, O'Shea." He shuffled.

I cut.

He set the deck between us. "Your move."

I drew a ten of clubs.

He drew the queen of diamonds.

I went first.

Martin sat back in his chair and closed his eyes as I told him about my encounters with Thunderstorm and T and what I suspected about Dani being the third accomplice in the armored car robbery. I told him about the photograph of the Reaper and how I found out the Feds had taken control of the STF.

"Impressive work, detective."

"Your turn, Martin. Dazzle me, I'll throw in that dessert."

"Okay, Rick, remember that website you had me check out?"

"Yes, Dex Territory."

"Jeremy wasn't lying. There's an online game solely dedicated to Dexes. Some of us have websites and twitter feeds, sure, but all of us are featured in the game. Players pick from a list of Dexes and their powers. The fantasy superhero league does exist. I was pretty disappointed in my ranking."

"What is your ranking?"

"Better than yours."

"Mine? I'm in the game? I'm not even a Dex."

"And you lose a lot of fights."

"My life isn't a game." I wanted to unplug every computer in the world.

"Welcome to the future."

"Fuck! What about the Chess Dude?"

"There is a player in the game called the Chessman. His superpower is mind control, but he has no ranking because he can't be played."

"We've had mind controlling Dexes before," I

said. "They're locked away on Plum Island. What makes this one different?"

"Controlling someone's mind is hard to do. There has to be a personal connection with the victim, and most importantly, an intimate knowledge of how that person thinks. It's truly a one-on-one experience. However, the Chessman can control dozens of minds at the same time. Maybe hundreds."

"Any proof the Chessman had control of the rioting Dexes?"

"No...but it's a lead."

"Any ISP that traces back to the real Dex?"

"No...but it's a lead."

"If that's all you got, Martin, while impressive, I think you owe me a rib-eye."

"Not so fast, my friend. One other fact I learned while perusing the various websites."

"It better be good."

"The number of Dexes has dramatically increased. I confirmed it. We have hundreds of new people with superpowers."

"That would account for why there were so many rioting Dexes I didn't recognize." My throat sized. "The retrovirus...is it back?"

"Not exactly." Martin leaned forward

conspiratorially. "I found some blogs that talked about a new drug on the black market. Someone has developed a copy of original retrovirus. You take a drink, you get a superpower."

"Holy shit! Dex on demand."

"We know firsthand how quickly the retrovirus spread. It had a very short lifecycle, less than twenty-four hours, and it still spread across the country. This time it's packaged for sale to the highest bidder."

My blood ran cold.

"And it comes in different formulas for different powers. Flight, super speed, super strength, super dexterity, and invisibility, to name a few. You'll never guess who was investigating it, took comprehensive notes and was compiling a list to trace sales back to the seller." He shoved a piece of paper at me.

Paige Greene.

I shuddered. This was the research project she'd told me about. Had it gotten her killed? "Where did you get this?"

"Duke got it off a laptop from Paige's house, sent it to me so I could share it with you."

"How could this have put Paige on the Reaper's radar? He's out to kill the Reyes Cartel's drug dealers. She wasn't a drug dealer."

"And she had no ties to the Reyes Cartel."

"That's two reasons why the Reaper couldn't be her killer." A familiar thought ran through my head. "What if there are two Reapers?"

"A copycat?"

I nodded. "Something the coroner suggested. Why else would the pattern be broken? This fake Reaper wanted the list to protect the seller."

"Or shut her up?"

"She's a nurse, for Christ's sake."

"She was playing with some dangerous information," he said. "In fact, I'm thinking Porterhouse dangerous."

I had to concede. "You earned it."

"Let me get my coat."

"One thing first." I pulled out the slip of paper with the number on it. "I need a burner phone."

"Come on." He got up from the chair.

I followed him to a paneled wall. He *phased* through it. Something clicked from behind the panels and a section of the wall opened.

Martin stood on the other side and led me into a secret backroom. While the office belonged in a Raymond Chandler novel, this room belonged on the USS Enterprise from Star Trek.

Rows of servers linked to a command station with synchronized monitors and an array of keyboards and input devices: audio, video, and some that I couldn't identify.

As Martin rummaged through a cabinet, my attention landed on a wall decorated with newspaper clippings and crime scene photographs of the Reaper killings. Photos of the dead drug dealers were pinned up under a picture of Fernando Reyes. Next to his picture hung a paper with a big question mark on it.

"Here, it's clean." Martin handed me an ancient flip phone. "When you're done with it, wipe off your prints and toss it in the Thames."

"Thanks." I was suddenly more afraid of the phone than the thought of calling Dani's mystery number. I pocketed the burner and pointed to the Reaper display. "You've been doing your homework."

"And this case has taken a disturbing turn." He stepped up to the wall and lifted the paper with the big question mark on it. Beneath it was a photograph...of Dani.

An anvil could have fallen on my head and I wouldn't have felt a thing. "What the hell?"

"Your girlfriend is Fernando Reyes' daughter."

I felt all the color drain from my face. Dani was the daughter of a mob boss? I couldn't believe it. However, if true, her involvement in the robbery just took on some merit. But I still didn't believe it. I would have said something to that effect, but I couldn't breathe.

Martin let go of the question mark paper, again concealing Dani's face. "Heroin, cocaine, and marijuana have always been the Cartel's drugs of choice, but with pressure from DEA and Homeland Security's border crackdowns, they've shifted their focus on designer drugs."

"You mean performance enhancers like anabolic steroids and methamphetamines?"

"There's a huge market for those who want to be better than they can be."

"Including people who want superpowers."

"And as with any product that goes to market you need a distributor."

"So the Reyes Cartel is prime choice for that role."

"And your girlfriend is in the thick of it. I just haven't figured out her involvement, thus the question mark."

I still couldn't wrap my head around that. Dani? The same woman so frightened of horror movies she had to bury her face in pillows was knee-deep in the most dangerous cartel in the country?

Martin stepped back. "I think she's a prime target for the Reaper, the real one. If I was out to hurt the cartel, or Fernando Reyes himself, she's the one I would kill."

My heart damn near stopped. "The Reaper's going after Dani next."

Chapter Fifteen

I didn't wait for Martin. I jumped in the car and started the engine. He leaped toward the car, but didn't bother opening the door, just *phased* through it and settled into the seat. I punched the accelerator, hoping we weren't already too late to save Dani.

As we raced toward her place, I speed-dialed the number to her house. No one picked up. I left a message for her to call me. I tried her cell phone. Again no answer. Maybe caller ID was giving her a reason not to answer.

I turned onto the street to Dani's neighborhood and dug the burner phone from my pocket. "Here." I passed the phone and the folded paper to Martin. "Dial that number."

The phone rang, it rang again, and then it rang again. On the fourth ring, the line connected.

Martin passed the phone back to me.

"Hello?"

A familiar voice answered me. "Rick?"

"Talon?" I glanced at Martin.

His eyebrows knitted in puzzlement.

"You're probably wondering why Dani left my number in your pocket."

"You bet your butt feathers." I pulled up in front of Dani's house. The windows were dark.

Talon was talking to someone in the background. She must have held her hand over the receiver, because I couldn't make out the muffled words. Finally she said, "We'd better meet."

"Where's Dani?"

"I can't tell you over the phone, but we're safe." She spoke with confidence. "Meet me at Fort Griswold...at midnight."

"Done." I snapped the phone shut, hoping they were surrounded by some serious muscle. The car's dashboard clock gave me about four hours.

"I guess we go back to your office and wait," I told Martin.

He stiffened. "Something just moved behind the curtain."

My heart jabbed a rib. "Dani's not in there. Might be the Reaper lying in wait."

"We're going in." Martin *phased* out of the car.

I didn't have my pulse pistol with me, damn it, but I had something else. From the glove compartment I grabbed a can of pepper spray then threw open the door. The interior light came on like a beacon announcing our presence, not that it mattered any now.

When I reached the door, I held the pepper spray in front of me. Martin stood about twenty feet away next to a windowless section of wall. I put my ear to the door and listened. I heard a floorboard creak inside. As quietly as I could I slipped the key Dani had given me into the lock. I held up a finger, then two, and then on three I twisted the door knob and pushed my way inside.

A dark caped figure turned to flee. He was carrying a briefcase.

"Freeze!"

He slammed into Martin's fist, a vicious uppercut, and crumpled to the floor.

"We got the Reaper." I was pulling out my cuffs when he melted into his own shadow, leaving the briefcase behind.

Martin flipped on the lights. There was no one on the floor.

I pivoted right and left, pepper spray aimed

like a gun. "Where'd he go?"

"I hit him hard enough to knock him into next week." Martin rubbed at his knuckles. "Let's look there."

"He's somewhere in these shadows."

I sprayed the shadow beside the couch, careful to keep my face away from the cloud of toxic mist.

Nothing happened.

I sprayed a dark corner.

Nothing.

I took a couple of steps toward the dark hallway when a shrill scream burst from the dark corner. The caped figure staggered about, clawing at the eyeholes of his white skull mask with one hand and swinging his scythe blindly with the other. The pepper spray had done its work.

Martin and I immediately moved in on the struggling figure. He wasn't getting away this time, but before I could blink, the Reaper's scythe nearly got me. I jumped back. The Reaper swung it in blind wild arcs. Blinded or not, he fought with the efficiency of a master martial artist.

The deadly scythe slashed through everything. Solid oak furniture might as well have been plastic, and the walls, cardboard. The Reaper howled in pain or anger or both and whirled in deadly arcs, but as the pepper spray wore off, his swings became more accurate.

The blade slashed into my shoulder. I hit the floor and rolled, leaving a bloody smear on the hardwood floor. I slapped a hand to my shoulder and my fingers came away wet.

"Shit."

Delivering that wound cost the Reaper his footing. Martin clocked him, and off balance as he was, the blow sent him sprawling to the floor. The deadly scythe skittered under the coffee table.

He recovered fast, dove for the couch, and melted into its shadow. I shot pepper spray under the couch, but the dark form jumped into the shadow of an end-table, and then into the darkened hallway, heading toward Dani's bedroom.

We flipped on every light as we made our way toward the bedroom, but his shadow-jumping ability outpaced us. I stopped when I reached the back wall. Martin *phased* through it, still in hot pursuit.

I ran back to the living room to get the briefcase. It was gone. The Reaper had doubled back but didn't have time to get the briefcase and the scythe. When I picked it up, it felt alive and it hummed.

Martin joined me a moment later. He'd come up empty.

"At least we got that," he said through panting breaths.

"I've got to get this to the lab. Fingerprints. DNA."

But holding the scythe felt wrong, all prickly up and down my arms. A chill ran through me then an electric shock, and I dropped the scythe. As it hit the floor, it shattered into countless silver fragments.

I reached down to snatch up the fragments, but the metal slivers melted before my hands got close enough to touch them, leaving me nothing to grab onto. I pulled Martin back as the mercurial metal rolled into the nearest shadows and dissolved into them, leaving no trace.

"Did you know it could do that?" I shrieked at Martin.

He let out a grunt. "Oh yeah, knew it all along, metal shattering, pieces disappearing into the shadows...oldest trick in the book." Then he shouted, "Are you fucking kidding me?"

"Okay then, let's not freak out."

"Right. Both of us crying like little girls would be bad for our images." His panic shifted to concern. "You're bleeding."

"He nicked me."

"Looks a little more serious than a nick."

"Dani keeps a first-aid kit under the sink."

A moment later, Martin returned with it. He spent a few moments cleaning and dressing the wound. I was more pissed about the gash in my trench coat, but I'd learned one thing. The Reaper was a Dex, but what was he looking for?

We searched the house. Dani's documents were piled on her kitchen table. Her mail was torn open and the contents stacked in another pile.

In the bedroom, the contents of drawers and closets lay scattered all over the floor. Boxes were opened and dumped on the bed. All Dani's valuables: jewelry, credit cards, and a small supply of emergency cash hadn't been touched. Then I remembered the briefcase. It wasn't his briefcase. It was the third briefcase. Dani had it all along.

"Damn!"

Whatever was in it had to be mighty important to the killer.

Chapter Sixteen

*F*ort Griswold overlooked the Thames River. During the Revolutionary War it had been overrun by the British. The Americans guarding the fort were killed. The word *massacre* was used in American accounts. The British shied away from the term. But it was still a massacre.

Martin and I were alone at the Groton Monument, a granite obelisk that looked like a miniature version of the Washington Monument. A red aircraft warning light shined from the pinnacle.

A high-pitched girlish scream came from above. Neither Martin nor I moved a muscle as Zack crash-landed into a clump of holly bushes off to our right. His cape floated down on his head like a deflated parachute.

We extracted him from the holly bush. Lucky for him, the thick leather of his costume absorbed the scrapes of the prickly plant.

"Zack, where's Talon and Dani?" I demanded of the rail-thin, scruffy man. He'd been torn up pretty bad at *The Brawl*, but that didn't show now.

"They're coming. I scouted ahead."

"Are they all right?"

"Chill, O'Shea. You're gonna blow a gasket."

Easy for him to say.

He noticed Martin. "Oh, hey, Phantasm!" Zack attempted to slap him on the back, but Martin turned invisible, and Zack's hand passed through thin air.

Martin muttered something about amateurs.

Zack took no notice of the slight. He pulled me aside. "And man, thanks for calling me by my real name. Everyone's been calling me Roadrash since I crashed and burned at *The Brawl*." He grimaced.

"Can't say I ever heard anyone refer to you as Roadrash." I shrugged.

"Cool!" He gave me thumbs up.

From overhead I heard the sound of wings beating in powerful whooshes. Talon circled us once before alighting a few feet away. "You're looking a lot better, Rick." She smiled as she tucked her white wings behind her.

I liked her smile. "You too."

She walked up to me. We embraced in the type of warm hug reserved for old friends. If there were any hard feelings over me shooting her down during The Brawl, they didn't show. Her hair smelled of lavender. After lingering a moment, we separated. I couldn't be certain because of the mask she wore, but she appeared troubled.

Talon was concerned enough to come in her complete costume. She didn't wear it often, usually for special events. It was a dark blue one-piece laced with gold metallic designs that served as armor. A low-cut V ended at her navel, allowing a maximum show of cleavage. She wore thigh-high boots that ended in platform soles and heels.

There were many Dexes who could fly, but the difference in their abilities flabbergasted me. Talon had wings similar to American Eagle, and as far as I knew, they were the only two who had feathers. They could fly higher and faster than the others. I didn't know much about the woman with the dragonfly wings, but I figured her wings were best suited for hovering. Zack could jump really high and soar off like Superman, but without wings he had stabilization problems, so his landings were essentially controlled crash landings minus the control. Talon's wings were by far the coolest.

"Any word about the charges against you?" Martin asked Talon. "Assault on a police officer is serious shit."

"Still pending, but they let me free on my own recognizance. Ironically, the judge doesn't consider me a flight risk."

"Thanks for keeping Dani safe," I said. "We think she's the Reaper's next target. He made an appearance at her house earlier this evening."

"You saw him?"

"We almost got him."

Talon's expression shifted to concern. "Are you two okay?"

"O'Shea will have a new scar to add to his collection." Martin didn't go into details about my shoulder wound.

"I was surprised to find your phone number in my pocket." I held the paper up to Talon.

"It was my idea. Dani had called me. She got a call from croaky voiced guy looking for Danielle Reyes. After what she'd done, she figured it was a hitman. We had to get a message to you."

"Hell, I almost didn't find it."

"I know you and your attachment to that trench coat." She regarded my coat. "You really should think about retiring it."

The coat had seen better days. It had singe marks, a few torn bits, missing buttons, and a new gash in the shoulder, but its weight was familiar, and it hid weapons well.

A sudden impact nearly knocked me off my feet, and I stagger-stepped backward to keep from falling over. Doublewide emerged from a cloud of dust. He cradled a woman in his massive arms. She wore a tight-fitting black costume accented with dark purple swaths. Her brown hair was cut short and she wore a mask that nearly covered her entire face.

She dropped from Doublewide's arms, strode up to me, and kissed me full on the lips. I admit I was a little startled, and my heart did a summersault, but as much as I'd have liked to attribute her actions to my manly prowess, I knew those lips as well as I knew my own. I thought I'd never taste them again. When she finally let go, I pulled back her mask and saw Dani's beaming face. "Hello, Rick."

I scowled. "We have to talk."

Chapter Seventeen

*E*veryone suddenly found the fort's battlements much more interesting, leaving Dani and me alone. We walked a short distance to a bench at the base of the monument and took a seat. We sat silently under dim streetlights. I didn't know where or how to start interrogating my supposed girlfriend.

"Rick, I know you have a lot of questions."

"And the understatement award goes to...Danielle Reyes." My comment had a bitter edge, but Dani gave me a smile anyway.

"Believe me, I didn't want to lie to you, and you don't know how many times I wanted to tell you who I was, where I came from."

I didn't say anything, just let myself stew.

"What we had was real. You saw my real feelings for you. But I love being a teacher, and you love being a cop. How can we have a normal life?"

"Why all the deception, Dani? You're a Dex, and you're the daughter of a crime boss. Did you think if I knew that...that I wouldn't love you anymore?"

"I thought you'd try to rescue me, get me out of my family's affairs." Regret flashed in her eyes and she dropped her head. "It doesn't work like that. There's no getting out."

"We'd have found a way."

"Rick, my father is semi-retired. Geraldo Diaz runs the cartel now. He's like the son my father never had, but he's on a path that'll get my father busted, prosecuted, and imprisoned. The only way to end Geraldo's criminal activity is to dismantle the cartel. The only way to do that is from the inside. I know what I'm doing, and I'm sorry you got caught in the middle."

"Is that what you want to do, destroy your family?"

She nodded. "My father doesn't want anything to do with this new drug that's coming out, but Geraldo wants to branch out. Sabotaging his plans will discredit the organization and cut him off from the supplier."

"Who's the supplier?"

She shook her head. "Whoever shipped that

briefcase."

"What was in it?"

"A formula and samples of the new drug...two vials."

"The drug that gives people superpowers."

"You knew?"

I nodded.

"Not just one superpower, Rick, all the superpowers. Anything you can think of."

"I take it you don't approve."

She shook her head. "Never."

"So what do you do for the cartel, for your family? You're just a...what...a thief for them?"

"I had no choice."

"What made you change your mind and come clean? I mean, you had me fooled into thinking you were somebody else. You're a thief and a liar to boot." I didn't even attempt to pull back the hurt in my statement.

"Don't be like that, Rick, please. This is hard enough."

A pang of guilt slugged my chest, but damn it, I was pissed. "Jesus, Dani, how did you get involved in the heist?"

Her shoulders sagged. "The armored car service was to deliver the briefcase to Diaz. It was a sample of the product up for distribution bids. For some reason, the Dexes went crazy. Hardball and Metal Jim took down the transport. If that formula fell into the wrong hands, the cartel would have gone to war against all of New London to get it back. When my father got word of the heist in progress, he sent me in to steal the briefcase right out from under their noses. I was to bring it to him, but I didn't."

Sounded like a good story, but how could I trust her? How could I test her honesty? I decided the Reaper could help me answer those questions. "Where is the briefcase now?"

"I don't know." Her voice sounded very small. She fiddled with a button on my trench coat. "A courier from UltraGen picked it up at my house."

"Wrong answer, Dani. You hid it in your house. The Reaper tore your place apart looking for it."

"But, I..." Terror ballooned in her eyes. "The Reaper was in my house?"

"And he got away with a briefcase. Why didn't you take it to your father?"

"My father deserves to retire without the shadow of prosecution hanging over his head. I didn't want Geraldo to get his hands on the new drug. I know what I'm doing."

"You're in over your head."

"I need you to stay out of it, Rick. Some very bad people are involved here, and I can't protect you anymore."

That almost made me laugh, and I would have if not for the serious look on her face. Still, I had my pride. "I'm the police, Dani. I'm the one who does the protecting. I'll get you into witness protection. We'll go to the DA, raid the bastards, and put them all on Plum Island."

"No, Rick. It's got to be done my way. My father has to be insulated when the cartel goes down. I need you to trust me."

"Not on your life. Your trust privileges have been revoked."

"I get it. You're pissed."

"I'm scared for you, Dani! The Reaper wants to kill you next."

Her eyes narrowed. "Why? I'm not a drug dealer."

"You're the daughter of the biggest drug dealer in New London."

"Ex-biggest and I want to keep it that way."

"The question is what did your father do to

piss off the Reaper?"

She leaned into me. "I don't know."

I was surprised at how calm Dani was over this bad news. If a psychopathic killer were after me, I'd be a little more freaked out. It forced me to realize I didn't know this woman at all.

I stroked her hair and the back of her neck, until I remembered the fish tattoo. I moved my hand to her shoulder. The show of affection didn't feel right anymore, but I was willing to let the illusion live for a moment longer.

Talon touched Dani on the shoulder. "Time to go."

"Come on, Whisper." Doublewide opened his arms. "Your ride awaits."

I arched an eyebrow. "Whisper?"

She shrugged. "My Dex Territory name."

Dani and I would have to be a total do-over. I turned to Doublewide and got right in the big man's face. "You take care of her, or you'll answer to me."

The man could squash me like a bug, but he gave me a solemn nod. "I will."

"Do I get a goodbye kiss?" Dani swooned and came in to plant one on me.

Our lips touched. I pulled back. The fire was

gone. The love was gone. I couldn't get past the lies. "Maybe next time."

Doublewide set her on his broad shoulders. He took a couple of bounces and jumped off into the night. I had no doubt that he'd reach New London with that single leap.

Talon walked up next to me. "She's safe with us. This is the least I can do for all the trouble I caused you."

"I was only doing my job. You don't owe me anything."

She kissed me on the cheek. "Yes, I do. If you were a better shot, I wouldn't be here right now." She flew off after Doublewide.

I wondered if she could make that argument hold up in court.

Chapter Eighteen

We drove back toward the city. Zack rode in the back seat with his Raggedy Anne cape gathered in his lap like a pauper girl's prom dress. He'd said he'd had enough flying for one night.

"Earth to Zack," I said. "Everything all right back there?"

"Yeah," Zack responded, and out of the corner of my eye, I saw Martin grimace, clearly not impressed by Zack. "I'm just watching the fires down there by the docks."

The docks were five miles away.

Martin said, "You can see that far?"

"Oh, yeah, dude. I can see for miles."

The nonchalant way Zack uttered those pronouncements was one of the reasons he was so well liked in the community.

"Uh-oh, there goes another one."

"Another what?"

"Another building's on fire. Hey! Pink

Panther's down there! She's, like, way hot. You think if I—"

"Zack, focus," I shouted. "What's going on down there?"

"There's some little dude chasing her around, sort of looks like Elvis."

Damn and double damn. Panther had gone after the Arsonist, and now they were battling it out in the middle of a growing inferno. "I told her not to approach him without backup."

Of greater concern was the carnage they were creating. The northern end of New London's shoreline was a cluster of docks where tankers brought in heating oil, diesel fuel, and gasoline to supply all of south-eastern New England. If the Arsonist lit up any one of those, the train station, ferry docks, and City Pier would be incinerated.

"She needs help." Zack opened the window and leaped out. His skinny frame shot straight up. "I'll meet you there." The last word faded into the night.

"I'll make sure everyone's out of those buildings." Martin *phased* through the door and sprinted off at speeds my Charger could never attain. I remembered a time when people used doors to exit cars.

The engine roared. I didn't bother with things like reasonable speed and defensive driving. I came upon an overlook that would give me a good view of the docks. Smoke billowed from my screaming tires as I careened to a stop in the pull-off area just before the edge of an embankment.

A warehouse off to my left was completely engulfed in flames, and a firestorm boiled up a hundred feet from a fuel storage tank. I wondered where Panther was in all this mayhem.

A kid ran from the burning warehouse. I expected to see the Arsonist on his trail, but instead Pink Panther tumbled after the kid in her usual display of gymnastic skills. Her face was set in grim determination as she covered ground faster than I'd ever seen her before. She caught up with the kid, and the two rolled in a tangle of limbs until she pinned him underneath her.

"What the hell is she doing?" I muttered.

All of a sudden Panther flew off the kid and slammed into the side of a warehouse with bone-snapping speed. The impact left a ten-foot deep dent in the aluminum wall. She slumped to the ground and didn't move.

"Fuck!" I gunned the engine, catapulting the Charger down the embankment, over a ditch, through a chain-link fence, and braked to a stop just before I hit the kid.

He was standing in a Superman pose with his right arm extended and palm up to my car. The kid was a Dex. My expert driving and good brakes may not have been what saved him.

I jumped out of the car and nearly fell over as a combination of noxious fumes and superheated air belted me in the face. Keeping low and breathing as little as possible, I sprinted toward Panther, performed a baseball slide, and came up next to her. "Panther, can you hear me?" I felt her wrist for a pulse. It was steady and strong. "Panther. Panther. Monica."

She coughed and took in a breath. "Is the...kid out?" she slurred groggily.

"Yeah, he's fine. How about you? Any broken bones?"

"I'm...okay. Got...the wind knocked...out of me. Get the kid."

I turned to see the kid running back toward the burning warehouse. "Is he nuts?"

"He thinks he's a superhero."

"I'd have to agree with him."

A wave of flame burst from the open door, headed straight for the kid. He stood firm and thrust out his palm. The fire spread in a thirty-foot arc and parted down the middle, falling away like a curtain on both sides of him.

The Arsonist stood center stage. He considered himself a performance artist who loved to make a grand entrance. He had added some features to his costume that upgraded him to Elvis Presley's Hawaiian tour persona. Instead of sequins and rhinestones, the decorations were made of flames that danced from mirco-jet nozzles sewn into his fireproof jacket, and his cape and hood were fireproof too. He wore giant glasses on his burn-scarred face that made his expression look small and pinched.

He carried a large tank strapped to his back with hoses reaching from the tanks to nozzles at his wrists. Pilot flames flickered at the ends of the nozzles. He would squeeze pressure valves in his palms, shooting jets of flame from the nozzles in controlled bursts.

His face twisted in a mad smile filled with maniacal glee. "Going to burn, going to burn, little boys burn."

The kid faced him down. "I'm not going to let you do that, creep!"

"Boys make cheery fires. I know. I know."

That set off fits of giggles.

"Arsonist." I kept my voice steady and calm, like the tone I'd use toward an unfriendly dog. "Leave the boy alone. You've got your fire. It's a beauty, some of your best work."

"It's not enough! Boys have to burn, cheery fires they make." He gritted his teeth and spat, "I would have incinerated that pink bitch if not for him!" He shot a lance of flame toward the kid, who thrust out his hand and stopped the fire short of frying him.

The blast of heat made my forehead bead with sweat. I held up my hands and edged toward the kid. "The boy is leaving."

"I can handle this," the kid shouted.

"Let us take it from here."

"No! He's my criminal!"

"I'll give you a medal for helping us. You need to leave."

The kid held up his hands to the Arsonist. "He's mine."

The Arsonist directed a stream of flame to the asphalt in front of the kid, which turned molten as lava and effectively threw up a wall of black smoke.

All I could do was flip my coat up to cover

my face and use my body to shield Panther. I had never felt heat like that, but I knew what the Arsonist was doing. He'd use the cover of smoke to outflank the kid and fry him. "Kid, you need to back the hell off now!"

The Arsonist giggled and sent out another jet of flame, this time at my car. A tsunami of fire engulfed the Charger. The tires exploded and the smell of burning rubber added its aroma to the already noxious air. The windows blew out and the leather upholstery ignited. The inferno cut off the kid's escape to the left.

"Look out, kid!"

"I got this." A burst of energy shot from the kid's hands and peeled the molten asphalt off the ground. The huge fiery glob slammed into the Arsonist. The lava-hot tar covered him head to toe.

He screamed bloody murder.

His costume may have been fireproof, but he hadn't counted on a phenomenon known as spontaneous combustion. The extreme heat ignited his skin, and then his muscles, and then his bones. He didn't scream for very long. The tank on his back made a clunk sound when he toppled over and struck the ground, his hulk completely encased in fire like a marshmallow on a stick that got too close to the flame.

I was dumbfounded. The kid was good. Damn good.

Panther and I got to our feet and used our hands to shield our faces from the heat. Cape smoldering like a shot-down Zero, Zack spiraled in carrying a couple of fire extinguishers. He tossed one to Panther, and they doused the Arsonist.

The kid gaped with pride at the still form of the Arsonist. "He killed a lot of people."

"And you saved a lot of people," Panther added.

"You tried to stop me."

"I had him under surveillance. He was dangerous. You should've left him alone." She dropped the extinguisher and looked at me. "He started this, not me."

Martin sprinted up to us. "Everyone's safe, Rick. I got all the people out." He smelled of smoke, but otherwise looked unharmed.

Zack ambled up. "Sorry about your car, Rick."

"Shit!"

The four of us stood silently as the kid smiled and everything around us burned.

***

Every fire truck and emergency vehicle from the five closest stations raced to the warehouse district fires. Lights and sirens got steadily closer.

"Martin, Zack. Thanks for having our backs tonight, but unless you want to face official heat, you boys better get out of here. Panther and I will cover."

Zack and I shook hands and he leapt into the air. His course took him toward the Thames River and then south into the city.

Martin sighed. "You're in one hell of a mess, Rick."

"We'll figure it out. I don't need you on anyone's radar right now, Phantasm." I pointed to his attire. "Get going."

"How are you going to justify being here? You're not supposed to be on the case."

"The Arsonist was wanted in connection to the fires at The Brawl." I wiped soot from my face. "I'm just a concerned citizen driving by."

Martin nodded. "Your car sure is fucked up."

"Tell me about it." I looked at the smoldering skeleton that once was my Charger. Made my heart sick.

"O'Shea," Panther shouted. "We have a problem."

The kid was lying flat on his back on the ground, his body jerking uncontrollably. Foamy saliva burbled from his mouth, and his eyes stared out blankly.

"He's seizing." The malady looked like an epileptic seizure. The big one, the grand mal. I turned him on his side so he wouldn't choke on his own saliva. There was nothing else we could do but ride it out with him, keep him safe and comfortable.

Emergency vehicles pulled up, and fire crews jumped out and went to work laying hoses. Two paramedics got out of an ambulance and pulled their equipment from the back. One started toward the Arsonist's smoldering body.

"Don't bother," I barked. "He's dead. We need you here."

The paramedics raced over to us.

"He's in bad shape."

They went to work on him, checked his vitals, and examined him for injuries. "Injection site," one said. They were looking at his arm. By the firelight I could see an angry red patch of skin. Red tendrils spider-webbed up and down his arm, extending from a puncture mark.

"What is it?" I asked.

"This kid's on Vitamin C, and I don't mean orange juice."

The other medic said, "Damn. We're seeing too much of this nasty stuff. It gives users superpowers for a short time. When they come down, they crash hard."

"More cases have been showing up since The Brawl."

"Is he going to be okay?"

"He's dying." They loaded the kid on a stretcher and rushed him to the ambulance.

I stood out of the way as it tore off toward Lawrence Memorial Hospital, lights blazing and sirens blaring. New London was in the middle of an epidemic that was killing our kids.

Chapter Nineteen

Back at home, I took inventory of Detective Rick O'Shea. I looked like hell. I felt like hell. I smelled like hell. Somewhere in heaven my dad was laughing at me.

I took his picture off my desktop and regarded it. He and I shared similar features, but his green eyes showed more wisdom than mine.

"Dad, you warned me about being a cop."

He told me that he did the job so I wouldn't have to. I went to college, and then joined the Army, became a Ranger, a tough guy. Things were good for me back then. I had a future; I had a path to success. I'd survived Afghanistan, but my fortunes changed in Iraq. I lost a platoon. I got wounded. I lost my dad. And I lost my path.

I floundered until I met Duke. He'd said, "I heard your dad was exactly the same way when he returned from Vietnam. Someone kicked his ass, and he became a damn good cop. I hope to be that good someday. You should too."

Duke was a rookie just out of the police academy. From that point on, I wanted nothing else. I realized my dad's wisdom. It wasn't that he didn't want me to be a cop; he wanted it to be my choice. So I pulled myself up by my bootstraps, applied to the academy, and before long they shoved a badge in my hand.

I replaced Dad's photo next to the display of his medals. My eyes fell on the Medal of Valor in the center of the display. That one carried the weight above all others, that one cost him everything. Instead of having him here with me, I had that piece of metal on a ribbon. It made me proud, it made me lonely, and too often it made me cry.

I took a shower and a Vicodin and got a few hours of sleep. I woke up before sunrise and threw on some sweatpants. From a pile I grabbed an old grease-stained shirt and put on a pair of worn boots. Then I strode out back toward the darkened garage.

I could see my breath vapor in the chill air. The smell of the fallen leaves filled my nose, and I breathed in deep. The constellation Orion was visible in the early morning hours as it peeked out over the southern horizon. Orion was The Hunter forever facing the bull, Taurus, and I felt like I could relate.

I pulled up the garage door, flipped on the lights, lit a kerosene heater, and turned my attention to the canvas-covered car, my dad's car.

I pealed back the cover to reveal a 1972 Dodge Challenger. I'd spent the better part of a year restoring it, and now I needed a car. The car needed a little wax and a good vacuuming. I went to work.

Time passed and my attention was so completely fixed on the car's gleaming black finish that Duke's voice startled me.

"You missed breakfast." He stood in the doorway, two foam cups in a tray and a bag in hand. "I waited for you."

Shit. I was supposed to meet him at Y-Knots. "Lost track of time, sorry."

Duke walked around the car, nodding. "I didn't think you were ever going to uncover this hot rod."

"I'm a little extra motivated."

"Yeah, sorry about the Charger, Rick." He handed me a cup of coffee from Dunkin' Donuts. "Heard you had a rough night."

"If you have a Boston cream-filled in that bag I'll marry you."

He threw the bag to me. "Consider it an engagement present."

I set my coffee down and peered into the bag. A pair of Boston creams stared up at me. I grabbed one and munched. Donuts and coffee, the next best thing to heaven. Ask any cop.

"Now you got something for me?"

I stopped chewing. "Oh, right, the Reaper photos. They're in the house. Let me get them."

Chucking the Boston cream in my mouth, I headed inside, quickly changed clothes: jeans, t-shirt, tennis shoes, and battle-scarred trench coat, got my wallet and the envelope with the photos, and bounded back to the garage.

I handed him the envelope and picked up my coffee. "Let's go for a ride."

I got behind the wheel, set my coffee in the cup holder, and turned the key. The engine rumbled to life. I revved it a couple times, the most beautiful sound I'd ever heard.

Duke slid into the passenger seat. He juggled his coffee and the empty donut bag, probably brought it to forage for crumbs.

I eased the vintage Challenger out of the

garage.

"Let's make your dad proud," Duke shouted.

"I already have."

Duke and I laughed like schoolboys as I put the Challenger through its paces. The sun glinted off the pearl black paint, and we threw on sunglasses. We drove until the gas gauge needle hit empty.

After refilling the tank, I drove downtown and pulled up behind the haul-away trash bins on State Street. We sat there and watched crews scour the rubble. Bucket loaders dumped debris into the trash bins and waiting dump trucks.

"Rick, when I told you to investigate under the radar, it was supposed to mean *under* the radar." He overstressed the word *under*. "Now we have a bunch of torched warehouses, a dead Dex, namely the Arsonist, a break-in at your girlfriend's place, another kid in a coma...did I miss anything?"

"I had a good steak last night."

"I'm surprised you had time to eat. This was all in a single day, O'Shea."

"Duke, get off my ass. I had nothing to do with any of it. Besides, what do you care? STF is off the case."

"You're making some people I know nervous."

"All I care about is making the Reaper nervous." I filled him in on our fight with the Reaper at Dani's house. "The fucker is a Dex with more powers than you can shake a nightstick at."

"Fuck!"

A dump truck blew by and got dust all over the car's new polish job. "Prick!"

"Why was the Reaper after Dani? Is she connected to this drug somehow? She dealin'...you know how the Reaper likes to kill drug dealers."

"He was looking for something."

"What?"

"I don't know," I lied.

"Is she all right?"

"Talon has got an eye on her right now, keeping her safe."

"It's probably better that we don't know where she is."

"Meanwhile, I have to catch the Reaper, but I don't know how to stop him from melting into the shadows."

He nonchalantly glanced into the empty donut bag, as if he was about to say something unimportant. "It might be a good time to run this past your mad scientist, Doc Quarks."

"I don't think that's such a good idea. The last time I saw Doc, it ended badly."

"He's a lonely old man who plays with dolls."

"A lonely old man who thought it would be interesting if he reduced me to subatomic particles and transmitted me to his lab fifty miles away."

"He has a way with machines, built that pulse gun you use." Duke wadded up the bag. "I think you hurt his feelings when you declined to be his guinea pig anymore."

"I can't believe you're taking his side."

"It's all in the name of science, my friend." Duke laughed.

"So was the atom bomb," I grumped.

"Which reminds me." Duke patted his pocket. "I got a warrant for Geiger's arrest for masterminding the armored car heist. Nobody will go near him, so I want you to make the bust."

"Are you shittin' me?"

"I think somebody needs a nap."

Duke was right on two counts. I did need a nap, but I had to arrest Geiger first. I needed to get him to talk, find out if he was a pawn for the Chessman, or if he was trying to take over the drug business for himself. He'd hired Metal Jim and Hardball to rob the armored car, not for the money, but for the formula and new drug samples. And more than that, he may have hired the Reaper to retrieve the stolen briefcase from Dani's house. If Geiger was in cahoots with the Reaper, I needed him to cough up a name.

The only issue facing me now was how to keep Geiger from killing me in the process.

Chapter Twenty

I spent the rest of the day getting plans A through C in order. Duke would get me some backup to arrest Geiger. For plan D, the apprehension of the Reaper himself, I needed a mad scientist, and as Duke had reminded me, I knew one.

I pulled up to a very nondescript brownstone on a very ordinary street in an unremarkable part of the city. The antenna array on the roof was the only thing that made this particular townhouse stand out.

I rang the doorbell and waited. A small girl opened the door. "Can I help you?" She was dressed in a red checkered schoolgirl uniform.

"I'm here to see Doctor Thaddeus Quarks."

"May I ask who is calling?"

"Detective Richard O'Shea, New London Connecticut Police Superhuman Task Force," I told the girl very precisely, though it was a lie. I'd been officially suspended, but she didn't need to know that.

She cocked her head and bowed to me. "Please follow me, Detective O'Shea. Doctor Quarks is happy to receive you. May I take your coat?"

I stepped inside the foyer. "I'm not wearing a coat." It was sixty degrees and sunny. I'd left my coat in the car.

"May I take your coat?"

"I don't have a coat," I told her politely.

She cocked her head. "May I take your coat?"

I sighed. "Do you see a coat?"

"Please answer me."

"Doc. Hana is having issues again!"

"May I take your coat?" She started reaching for my shirt.

I jumped back. "Whoa! Easy, Hana, that's not a coat. Doc!"

A small man stepped out from a side door. "Hana, no." Hana bowed to me and walked away, down the hall and disappeared behind a set of swinging double doors.

"She's really coming along, doc." I made sure my voice sounded condescending.

"The answer to her question was a simple

no."

"Boy, do I feel stupid."

Doc nodded in agreement. His shock of hair needed to be combed. He wore a van dyke beard and glasses he must have made himself. Various lenses occasionally changed positions. Depending on which combination of lenses fell in place, the color and size of his eyes changed: sometimes comically, sometimes disturbingly.

"Did you need something?"

"I need your help."

"What makes you think I might help you?"

"The Reaper."

His lenses changed, made his eyes look small. "Come in then." He walked back through the side door.

I followed. The doorway opened to a study. Bookcases filled with leather-bound volumes adorned the walls. A writing desk with a small table lamp sat in the middle of the room in front of a lit fireplace. Above the mantel, a portrait of beautiful woman hung. She had large brown eyes that appeared to watch us as we crossed the study to another door.

We stepped into the next room. Where the study had been warm and comfortable, this room was sterile white and all business. Benches were set at regular intervals. Each contained some kind of gismo in various stages of assembly or disassembly, hard to tell which. Elaborate technical drawings and schematics of life-like androids plastered the walls. They were labeled: *H.A.N.A. and S.H.A.N.A.*

I recognized Hana in her schoolgirl outfit even though she had her back to me. As I approached, she turned. Half her face was missing. It rested on the workbench in front of her, the eye plucked out and held in her right hand. As she regarded me with the other eye, servos and gears spun in her head, complicated as any precision clockwork. She smiled at me, a half-faced smile made possible by the movement of exposed cables and levers. Freaked me out, but I couldn't help but stare at her. She bowed to me and went back to work on the eye.

"That is Shana," Doctor Quark explained. "Hana's eventual replacement."

"I see why. Hana seems to be a little glitchy, doc."

"Good word, Rick, glitchy. Do you mind if I use that in my reports?"

"Not at all." I pointed to the android. "What

is Shana doing to her eye?"

"She's fixing it...having a little focusing problem." He laughed. "I programmed her specs into her CPU. She takes care of her own maintenance."

"I see. Machines that fix themselves. What could go wrong with that?"

"Machines can fix anything." He smiled at me as his lenses switched positions, making him look bug-eyed. "So don't dwell on the negative, detective. Now what can I help you with today?

"There's a new drug on the streets."

"What kind of drug?"

"It gives the user superpowers."

His eyebrows shot up, and his face went ashen. "Cobalt, yes, I've heard of it."

"Cobalt? The EMTs called it Vitamin C and the side effects are coma and death."

"A colleague tells me UltraGen is attempting to recreate the retrovirus that created the Eximius vox humanus res."

"My command of Latin is somewhat underdeveloped."

"Dexes, my boy, what you call Dexes."

"It appears they've succeeded. Since The Brawl, the government's financial aid to find a cure for the Dexes has been approved. But you're saying they're going to use Cobalt to create more Dexes. Why?"

Quarks' glasses shuffled again. "More people to cure."

"A perpetual money machine."

"There's no money in a cure...unless you can propagate the disease. The drug industry learned their lessons from polio. Once cured, all funding for research dried up."

"I need to find those samples." I looked around his lab. "Maybe you can mix up an antidote or something."

His expression turned thoughtful. "How does the Reaper fit into all of this?"

"He's killing the Reyes Cartel's drug dealers." I elected not to tell him about Paige Greene, a perfectly innocent victim of the Reaper.

"If the Cartel is the distributor, murdered dealers can't make UltraGen happy."

"It appears the Reaper wants to interfere with UltraGen's plans. Now he's got the formula and the samples. They were stolen during the armored car heist, and he stole them from the thief."

I neglected to tell him Dani was the thief. I did tell him about the fight Martin and I had with the Reaper, how he melted into the shadows, and how his scythe went into self-defense mode and escaped with him.

Dr. Quarks sat on a stool in front of a workbench. He hung his head down and absentmindedly stroked his beard. I could almost hear the gears grinding in his head then realized it was Shana's gears.

"He's a Dex who can shadow walk. You'll need a good offense and a better defense."

It took a mad scientist to tell me that?

He rummaged through a nearby drawer and handed me a gun that looked like it belonged to Buck Rogers. The barrel was made of glass and a gold metal shaft extended the length of the barrel, and both were spiral wrapped with some kind of tubular conductor. The grip and trigger were similar to my pulse pistol. I hefted it in my hand to gauge the weight, or in this case, the lack of weight.

"It's a plasma gun. It will seal the Reaper's atomic structure in a force field bubble and keep him from shadow walking."

"But how do I put the cuffs on him?"

"That's your problem."

Why did everything have to be my problem?

"And here's a little something that could save your life." He handed me a disc-shaped device with a button in the center: a red button, which couldn't be good. "Only use it if your life is in immediate and terrible danger."

"What is it?"

"What you don't know won't hurt you."

Perplexed, I put it in my pocket.

"Now for your defense." From the same drawer, he whipped out a sleek hypo-sprayer, jabbed the nozzle into my neck, and pulled the trigger.

Pop!

It felt like a bee sting. I slapped my neck. Heat rushed to my head. "What the fuck?"

"You might suffer some side effects," Doc Quarks informed me in the same tone he might use to tell me I had a spot of mayonnaise on the corner of my mouth.

"What did you inject me with, you crazy bastard?"

"Nanites."

"Nanites? What the fuck are nanites?"

"Microscopic machines that fix things."

I glanced at Shana, still hard at work fixing her eye. "You've gotta be shittin' me."

"They'll make you feel better, however, if you get a fever in excess of one hundred and five, you start smelling the strong scent of cookies, you get sudden blood-curdling chills, or die unexpectedly, let me know."

His lenses shuffled into an arrangement that made his eyes look meek and innocent.

I thought he'd done that on purpose...so I wouldn't shoot him with his own fucking plasma gun.

"Now you have all you need." He patted me on the back. "Off you go," he said enthusiastically, as if I was simply a kid on my way to school. "Go get that big bad Reaper."

I tried to say something, anything, but words would not form in my mouth. The nanites must've stolen them.

Chapter Twenty-One

In a few short seconds I stood at the door, staring out at the street. Hana handed me a coat. She must've confused me with someone else. I took the coat. I must've confused myself with someone else.

"Die unexpectedly?" I mumbled. Somewhere between five seconds and two minutes standing there in front of the door with my mouth agape, I finally looked at the coat. I didn't come with a coat.

I wondered if I should operate machinery. Exiting the brownstone, I wondered if I would drop dead at any minute.

The doc had injected me with nanites. He'd said they'd make me feel better. True to his word, my injuries hurt a lot less.

Once I got in my dad's car, I tossed the coat in the back seat, pulled up my shirt, and examined the wounds on my abdomen and shoulder. They had stitched closed. Angry scars remained, but I felt reasonably sure the wounds were healed.

"Cool." I now understood Dr. Quarks' defensive strategy. Wounds inflicted by the Reaper's scythe would heal as fast as he could inflict them. Now I had a fighting chance.

At the Y-Knots diner, Ramirez and Jensen waited for me. Duke had spread the word that I needed volunteers for backup. They jumped at the chance for a little action off the books. Something told me Duke had left out the part about us arresting Geiger.

Rachel Ramirez dressed in street clothes. She wore a brown leather coat and blue jeans tight enough to show off some very pleasant curves. She had her gold badge clipped to her leather belt.

Jensen wore a police-issued jacket and black pants. Sunglasses covered his eyes. His badge hung around his neck on a lanyard. A day's worth of stubble made his face look badass.

They both piled into the Challenger, Jensen in the back, and Ramirez rode shotgun. She settled in the seat and rubbed her hand over the dash. "Now this is a car I don't mind being seen in. I approve."

"It was my dad's."

"I think I would have liked your dad."

"He'd have liked you too."

She beamed, put on her sunglasses, and became all business. "Where are we headed?"

I was right. Duke hadn't told them. "You both armed?"

They indicated they were.

"Good. We're going to arrest Geiger."

The air left their lungs in a simultaneous huff.

"You guys are here to keep things official. Get your game faces on."

"Right," Ramirez acknowledged.

"I'll go up first. Ramirez, you follow me. Jensen, you're backup. If things go squirrelly, you two get the hell out." I handed each of them radiation badges Martin had scrounged up for me. I left mine in my pocket. "Put these on. If they turn orange, it's time to leave. If they turn red, it's time to run."

Ramirez took a turn. "Can't we find another way to get him, trick him, trap him, one that's less likely to make us glow in the dark?"

"Geiger was out to steal this new drug, and he may have connections to the Reaper. There's only one way, and that's to get him to come downtown peacefully."

Down the block from Geiger's place, we

geared up: ear-buds, radios, weapons, vests, the works. I threw on the new trench coat Hana had given me. It fit perfectly. It was a friendly tan and had the benefit of not being full of holes. If I could have added a white cowboy hat, I would have. I wanted Geiger to see me as one of the good guys and maybe keep things civil.

I left the Challenger at the bottom of the drive. Ramirez came with me, and Jensen remained with the car, engine running. We walked steadily up the long drive to a very large house on a hill.

The house had no foliage growing around it. Where there should have been grass and bushes growing, gravel had been laid out in decorative patterns. Tall walls surrounded the property. I hoped they were designed to contain a nuclear blast. Yellow and black warning signs were posted in regular intervals up the driveway.

Ramirez checked her radiation badge and gave me a thumbs-up.

I breathed in a slow breath and rang the doorbell.

The door swung open. A pudgy little man greeted us with a sneer. His face looked like it had caught on fire and somebody put it out with an ice pick. "What do you want, Detective O'Shea?" He held out his boil-festered hand.

I knew better than to shake it. Third degree radiation burns. "I need your help with an investigation."

Geiger's brows crinkled as he spoke carefully. "You must be stumped if you're coming to me. Not interested." He started to close the door.

"People are dying from Vitamin C."

That stopped him. "And how many die from heroin, crack, prescriptions, and alcohol. Honestly, what's one more drug?"

"Come downtown and have a little chat with us."

"I'm not in the drug business anymore."

"Then why did you hire Metal Jim and Hardball to rob the armored car? They turned on you, squawked like parrots."

Geiger's forehead started to glow. "You don't really believe those assholes."

"Doesn't matter what I believe but something tells me a judge will. That'll get you a lead-lined hole on Plum Island."

Ramirez held up her radiation badge. "We're orange, O'Shea."

"And I think you know the Reaper. You hired

him to steal the briefcase from Dani. Give me his name, and we'll just walk away. Forget we ever had this conversation."

Geiger pushed through the door and got in my face. "I can't give you a name. And if I had one, I still wouldn't give it to you. Call it professional courtesy. It's time for you to leave."

"We're in the red, O'Shea. Let's do what he says."

"Get back to the car, Ramirez. I want to have a private word with Geiger."

"I'm not going back without you, Rick."

"Now, Ramirez, you and Jensen get the hell out of here. That's an order."

She got all tight-lipped, but she turned and fled. A few seconds later, car doors shut and the Challenger roared off down the street.

I grabbed Geiger by the shirt. "I need the Reaper's name. You're going to give me a name, or I'll take you downtown and beat it out of you."

Geiger's glowing face radiated heat. "Detective, that strong-arm bullshit won't work on me. I could kill everyone in the police station."

"It's Dr. Douglas Brooks, isn't it? Say it. Tell me it's him."

"Leave now, before your bacon gets fried."

Even though he affixed a smile on his ruddy face, I took his threat seriously. "It doesn't have to go down this way. Give me what I want and I'm gone."

A lot of emotions flashed across Geiger's face but mostly defiance. "Fuck you!" He shoved me back ten feet.

"Wrong move." I whipped out the shiny new pistol Quarks had given me. "You're under arrest."

"I'm never going back to that hole in the ground." Geiger held out his arms. His entire body started to glow and pulse and hum. Talk about a bad temper ready to blow. In seconds my life would be in immediate and terrible danger.

I turned and ran, pulled Dr. Quarks mystery device from my pocket and pushed the red button. A popping sound came out.

Geiger went thermonuclear.

A blast furnace of heat slammed me from behind. I had a feeling those nanites would soon be working overtime.

Chapter Twenty-Two

I regained consciousness in a bright white world. *Go into the light.*

A sound came to me, popping, and then a dolphin's chatter mixed with a Jimi Hendrix guitar riff played on a squeaky chalkboard. I blinked, tried to focus on hazy figures above me, but recognition alluded me. I closed my eyes. The chattering became a garbled voice. Then voices. I opened my eyes to a familiar room, Dr. Quarks whitewashed lab, and soon the world returned to something that resembled the one I had left.

Jensen sat in a chair, chatting with Ramirez while they ate pizza. The smell nearly brought on a round of something colorful from my innards.

"Detective!" Jensen exclaimed. "You're awake."

I swung my legs off a workbench and planted my feet on what I hoped to be a solid floor. "How long was I out?"

"Just long enough for us to order pizza."

Quarks pointed a flashlight in my eyes. He snapped a finger in my left ear. I blinked. Same with my right ear.

"Am I going to live?"

"You're all right," he assured me.

"How did I get here? What happened?"

"You teleported back here just in the nick of time, I must say, or you'd be nuclear waste by now."

"That gizmo you gave me—"

"A GPS remote teleporter. I programmed it to return here. You took my advice and used it. Well done."

"Thanks." I couldn't bring myself to be mad. He did have a way with machines, like Duke had said.

"Drink this." Quarks shoved a glass in my hand, filled with a milky colored liquid, like snake venom.

"No thanks." I pushed it away, but the doc got downright forceful.

"Drink it."

"What is it?"

"Fuel for the nanites. Without them you'd have been out cold for a nuclear winter."

I gave in and took a sip, nearly spat out the foul tasting goo but managed a swallow.

"All of it."

I drained the glass as fast as I could. The nanites seemed to like it. I already felt like a million bucks.

"Wow, doc! What's in that stuff?"

"Let's just say you might want to avoid a drug screening for a few weeks."

I recalled the last second of searing heat. "I think Geiger is dead."

Quarks said, "Nah, he'll coalesce."

"How's that possible?" Ramirez asked. "He was blown to smithereens."

"Matter can't be destroyed, only changed in shape or form. Geiger has the superpower to control nuclear fission *and* fusion. He'll be back."

"Talk about resisting arrest."

Quark dropped the flashlight in a drawer. "No need to shed tears for him."

I paced the floor a couple laps to make sure my legs still worked. I stopped in front of Jensen. "How bad was the blast?"

Ramirez spoke first. "Nothing like Hiroshima, but big enough to level Geiger's mansion. The containment walls around his place took care of most of the concussion."

"It still blew out windows for blocks around," Jensen said, chewing pizza. "Minor injuries, no casualties, unless you count Geiger."

"He doesn't count."

"And for what?" Ramirez asked. "We're no better off now than we were before. We don't know if Geiger was working for someone or for himself, and we don't have a name for the Reaper."

I had a name, I just didn't have proof.

Chapter Twenty-Three

The fallout from Geiger going nuclear received national attention, and once again New London became a hotbed of controversy. I might as well have painted a bulls-eye around the city.

More government agencies were represented here than in all of Washington DC. We couldn't jaywalk without being hit by a government vehicle of some sort, lights flashing, speeding down the road on some vital task.

By the time I got home, bone-weary exhaustion nearly crippled me. I couldn't remember the last time I slept. Stripped to my boxers, I gave it a try.

I awoke at one-thirty. Hell, the bars weren't even closed yet. My tongue felt thick and throat scratchy. I got up to get a glass of water. Sleepily, I turned the corner into my kitchen and came face-to-skull with the Reaper and his deadly scythe.

I jumped, frightened out of my skin, and

damn near out of my boxers. Adrenalin coursed through my body, and I started backpedalling, slammed butt-first into the counter. My hands frantically searched behind me for something to use as a weapon: a toaster, fruit bowl, anything.

The Reaper watched me through a skull mask, his head tilted and black eyes staring in amusement.

I'd show him something funny. My scrabbling hands came up with a wire whisk. I brandished it like a knife. It looked puny compared to his wicked scythe. "Get back. I'll kill you. I swear."

He held up a hand in a placating gesture. "Detective, I mean you no harm." His voice came out through a synthesizer in the mask.

"Rest assured I mean to harm you, Reaper," I croaked, my voice suffering the effects of unbridled panic.

His scythe vanished into the ether. "By now you should know that's not possible." His lower jaw moved up and down as the electronic baritone voice came out, but not in sync with each other. "Detective, if I wanted to harm you, believe me, you'd be hurting right now. I came to talk."

I threw the whisk at him, reach in a drawer,

and pulled out my dad's Colt, the revolver I'd almost given Dani, thank God I didn't. I pumped rounds into him until the hammer struck empty cartridges. The bullets passed right through the Reaper and left six nickel-sized holes in my wall.

He just stood there calmly. "Are you done?" His gravelly voice sounded perturbed.

"You're under arrest," I informed the black-clad figure, though I had no clue how I was going to collar him.

His jaw dropped, and the sound that emerged was synthesized laughter. Not sinister laughter, but amused laughter.

I felt heat rise in my face.

"Detective, I'm not going to allow you to arrest me."

I knew that.

I studied the Reaper. While he looked solid, his edges faded off into shadow. The skull was framed with a deep cowl that hid all but the frontal bones. Damn creepy.

"Why are you here?" I tried to position myself so I could take a run at the pulse pistol hanging on the coat rack.

He seemed to know what I intended and laughed. "Looking for this?" The holster and gun appeared in his upraised boney fist.

"Fuck." The Buck Roger's gun was in the car. I'd be dead before I got that far.

"Detective, like I said, I came to talk."

I folded my arms across my bare chest. "Then talk." Adrenaline had me all shaky by now, but I fought to appear calm.

"I know what you're looking for..."

That damn synthesizer. I couldn't recognize the voice, couldn't know if it was Dr. Douglas Brooks or not.

"...and I think I can help."

"Sorry, Grim. I don't need your help." I let bravado jump in to dampen the fear. It gave my mouth something to do while my brain figured out how to save my ass.

"Detective, we have the same goals. Poison is being spread throughout our streets, and it is killing people."

"I don't mean to pick nits, but you're killing people, too."

He shrugged. "Only those who deserved to die, detective. Those who profit from the suffering of others."

"You killed Paige Greene, someone I cared about."

"I did not." Even through the synthesizer his tone sounded appalled at the suggestion.

"She wasn't a drug dealer. She was compiling evidence of drug sales. In some sick way you two were in the same fight, you piece of shit!"

"All the more reason for me not to kill her."

"What about my girlfriend." Well, ex-girlfriend, but he didn't need to know that. I pointed an accusatory finger at him. "Dani has nothing to do with selling drugs."

"We both know that's a lie."

I had to pause to think about that. A few days ago I would have gave given him a resounding no, but lately Dani's entire life had become suspect. Still, I gave her the benefit of the doubt.

"She's Fernando Reyes' daughter. That alone puts her on my hit list. You should know that about me by now."

"I only know one thing. You killed Paige Greene. There's no power on earth that will stop me from killing you."

"You talk pretty tough standing there in your underwear."

"I wasn't expecting company."

His hand disappeared in a deep robe pocket, and he pulled out two vials of blue liquid. He carefully set them on my kitchen counter. "I think this is what you're looking for."

"Were these in the briefcase you stole?"

"Danielle Reyes stole it first."

I didn't even like him speaking her name. "Leave her out of this."

He shrugged. "Seems I've earned a bit of a reputation. No matter, a little fear can be an effective tool. I've done what I've done all for good reason. I won't stop until the Reyes Cartel is wiped from the face of the earth."

"Dani wants the same thing, an end to the cartel so her father can live out his last days in peace. She stole the briefcase to put a rift between her family and the drug business."

He glared at me for what seemed like an eternity then: "Detective, I'm inclined to believe you. I'll leave your girlfriend to you, but fair warning, stay out of my way."

"I appreciate that, Reaper, don't get me wrong, but nothing's changed between us. You're wanted for murder. I'll get you in the end."

"Then we shall both go our merry ways." He melted into the shadows.

Merry ways? "Son of a bitch."

Chapter Twenty-Four

We met in Martin's office. Emergency meeting 101 with Phantasm and Pink Panther. I gave him one of the cobalt blue vials of liquid human disaster. He held it up to the light. "So that's it?"

"It doesn't seem like much." Pink Panther narrowed her eyes. "How did you get your hands on this?"

"Special delivery from the Reaper himself."

"No shit?"

"I dropped off the other vial at Doc Quarks' lab. He's going to work on an antidote."

Pink Panther looked skeptical. "You sure Quarks is up for this?"

"The doc may be a little eccentric, but he knows what he's doing."

"Like the flesh eating, saber-toothed, zombie squirrels?"

"Okay but—"

"Or the self-replicating jelly beans," Phantasm added.

"And when the Thames River froze solid in mid-July." Pink Panther swished her anatomic tail.

"All right. I admit doc goes a little overboard sometimes. But he can handle this."

Phantasm changed the subject. "So how did your encounter with the Reaper go?"

I filled them in on last night. "He wants to put the cartel out of business."

"Why?"

"He said he had his reasons. He also said he didn't kill Paige Greene."

"Then who did? A copycat?"

"That's becoming the popular theory. I need to talk to Dani again."

"What for?" Phantasm asked. "Haven't you had enough of her lies?"

"I need her to ask her father if the name Douglas Brooks means anything to him."

"Who's Brooks?"

"A hunch. If so, I need to know what happened to make Brooks go out and kill the cartel's drug dealers."

"And if he doesn't remember anybody named Brooks, what then?"

"That could be a problem, but still, I think there's some history there. Reyes would never tell us, but he'll tell his daughter. It's worth a try to ask. If nothing else we're stirring the pot."

"I'll get in touch with Talon and arrange the meet." Phantasm stepped through his office wall and into his secret backroom.

"Make it for tomorrow night," I called after him. Then I turned to Panther. "We've got something else to do today."

"About damn time!" She wrapped her arms around me and pulled me into her like I was a ragdoll. I tried to mount a protest but it was a little hard to speak with her tongue dancing around in my mouth.

When I didn't return the kiss, she opened one eye and focused on my open eye, the one with the sternly lowered eyebrow shading it. Her tongue performed a hasty retreat, and she pulled back a couple of inches. "Not what you had in mind, I take it."

"Not exactly."

"Oh, I see." She let me go and sulked to a chair, sat, shoulders slumped and ears flopped over. Her tail drooped to the floor.

I should have been committed to a mental

institution for rejecting her affections. A certain part of my body would agree, having responded with eagerness only to be left high and dry.

Martin *phased* back into the room. "Okay, gang. The meeting's set, the Viper's Pit, tomorrow night..." His eyes darted between the two of us. "What did I miss?"

"Nothing," we both said at once.

"Right," he said skeptically.

"So what *are* we doing today?"

"You heard?"

"Everything. You two are playing with fire."

"I'm trying to keep it cool, but she—"

He stopped me with a raised hand. "It's nobody's fault that Dexes and non-Dexes aren't a good combination."

Dani and I were proof of that. "I agree."

Pink Panther sniffled. "Fine, O'Shea. We're not that kind of partners. I get it."

I felt like a genuine lunk the way I'd gone and hurt her feelings. *Way to go, Rick.* But we had work to do. "We're going to take a tour of UltraGen's Groton facility. The renovations are finished. They're having an open house."

Panther gave me a bland look. "What are we looking for?"

"Proff they're producing Vitamin C."

Phantasm handed the vial of blue liquid back to me. "What are you going to do with this one?"

"Bait."

I filled them in on my plan.

Chapter Twenty-Five

*T*he tour started with a speech worthy of Jonathan Ford himself. A smartly dressed woman spoke crisply. "At UltraGen, we're inspired by a singular vision, and that is your health. Our researchers are dedicated to developing safe medications to treat and prevent the world's most serious health concerns."

I glanced around the glass and steel atrium of UltraGen's Groton plant on the banks of the Thames River. Oddly enough, I felt very small. I hoped I didn't appear as bored as Monica. Thirty other folks gathered around the speaker.

"Our goal continues to be making medicines available to the people who most need them, even giving them away to those who cannot afford health coverage. We believe that from our dedication comes hope, and from that hope comes a brighter, healthier, and more-peaceful world."

We then started our tour of the world's

largest, most advanced pharmaceutical and genetic research facility on the planet. Our tour guide took us through some impressive labs. We saw dozens of workers dressed head-to-toe in white scrubs, hoods, gloves, protective eyewear and dust masks, making the scene dramatic and futuristic.

Our guide showed us where the machines stamped out the pills. One of the technicians caught my attention. Martin had infiltrated the lab as planned. Walking through walls had its advantages.

"Today we're stamping the little blue pills that help men go from softball players to hardball big leaguers." She extended her fist in the air. "With *big* being the optimal word."

The crowd chuckled. I frowned.

After a mind-numbing hour of droning machines and the tour guide's bad jokes, we finished up in a reception area where they served soft drinks, coffee, and offered all kinds of swag sporting UltraGen's logo: cups, pens, hats, and t-shirts for sale. Reams of literature about UltraGen's medicines and programs cluttered the tables, free for the taking. The coffee and soda cost five bucks a pop, the inflated proceeds going toward curing disease. Ford's billions wasn't enough, the asshole.

And as if to end the tour with a grand finale, Jonathan Ford appeared. Staff members started clapping and the tourists joined in. Applause reverberated throughout the massive structure.

Monica and I added our polite claps to the hubbub.

Jonathan shook hands as he made his way to a small podium in front of the room. Men with video cameras clattered in and quickly set up an array of equipment.

Ford looked just like he did on the newscast interview. However, in person I could see that he stood about six feet tall. A strong jaw line and sharp features gave him a predatory look. His perfectly combed hair was a very dark blue-black, in stark contrast to his pale eyes that scanned the scene with hawk-eye precision. I noticed an ear-bud in his right ear and a mini-mike on his suit coat lapel. Hi-tech all the way. He smiled a shark's smile, lots of gleaming teeth.

A hush fell over the crowd.

"My friends, welcome to UltraGen. I hope you have enjoyed the tour." He started his address with a rich deep voice. "As you know, we have expanded this plant and are about to break ground across the river, right in the heart of New London."

Another round of applause.

His voice had a cadence that came from a lot of practice, probably addressing boardrooms. "We are about to bring two thousand more jobs into the city. Yes, we've been awarded the government contract to find the retrovirus cure. Our Dexes will soon become normal, functioning, and law-abiding people in our city."

Murmurs of awe trickled through the crowd.

"There'll never again be another riot like The Brawl."

Monica and I traded skeptical glances.

"As a token of goodwill with the City of New London and in celebration of the ground breaking ceremony, UltraGen will be hosting the Halloween celebration. Everyone is invited."

Applause came with a few cheers added in.

Meanwhile, Ford scrutinized each member of the tour, one-by-one. When his gaze landed on me, his eyebrows arched slightly. His reaction was much more profound when he spied Monica; his face turned pallid.

"That was interesting," Monica whispered.

"Oh yes, it was. And look at this."

A redheaded woman, powerfully built, deftly made her way around the back of the room. Her hair swayed in graceful arcs as she approached us. While I wouldn't call her beautiful, the confidence in her stride gave her a demeanor that was as attractive as it was foreboding.

She stopped in front of us and smiled pleasantly. "Jonathan Ford would like a moment of your time."

"We're busy." I didn't want to seem easily available.

"He'll make it worth your while, detective."

"In that case, thanks."

"If you'll please follow me."

We fell in step behind her.

Red led us down a well-lit corridor. Photo panels on the walls were set up in groups of three. The first picture showed sickly brown-skinned people in a filthy village, foraging through trash. The second picture showed a collage of photos depicting uniformed teams of UltraGen employees interacting with the people in the village, providing medical care and delivering food. The third picture showed the same village completely transformed, cleaned, and remodeled, and its people well dressed, well fed, healthy, and happy.

Another picture we came to showed villagers lying in the mud, dead or dying and infested with black flies. I had to stop to contemplate what I was seeing.

Red stopped behind me. "This is a reminder that our work is never done. There's always one more virus that we have to outsmart."

"And one more village to save," came Jonathan Ford's voice behind me.

I turned and looked into his eyes. Here was a man who truly wanted to save the world.

We shook hands while we regarded each other.

"Mr. Ford, I've heard a lot of good things about you and your company. You're to be congratulated."

"I've heard things about you too, detective O'Shea." Our eyes remained locked. "You're the STF cop who got that NLPD officer killed, what's his name, Jebrowski."

"Bad news travels fast."

"What are you doing here?"

"Taking the tour."

"I don't believe that for one minute." He blinked.

I'd won. I could stare down a crocodile.

He turned to Monica. "Hello, Miss Voight."

The barest trace of red dusted her cheeks at his use of her real name...as if they were friends. "And how do you know me, Mr. Ford?"

"I make it my business to know the movers and shakers in this town. I can't help but wonder what you're doing here with this officer." Disdain dripped from his final word.

"We're looking into your drug-making operations." Monica showed a bumper crop of dimples. "Does Vitamin C ring a bell?"

She was as subtle as a tarantula in a bowl of bananas.

Jonathan turned to Red. "Give us a few minutes."

She glanced at me and then Monica before walking away.

Then Jonathan got wicked. "What in the hell are you talking about?"

Will the real Jonathan Ford please stand up?

I reached into my pocket and produced the vial of blue liquid. "Are you making this?"

He looked like he'd seen a ghost but quickly returned an implacable glare. "You know, detective, UltraGen has one of the most advanced research facilities in the world. It would be my pleasure to have our scientists examine the sample and provide you with a full analysis."

"No thanks." I carefully replaced the vial in my pocket.

He watched my hand the entire way.

"I have my own scientists working on it. Besides, the look on your face told me what I wanted to know. As soon as I get some proof, you're going to be our guest in the Plum Island resort hotel."

"Good luck with that..." He put a finger on his ear-bud. His expression became unreadable. "Seems we have a virus of our own to deal with."

"I once had a virus in my computer. Perhaps I can help."

"I assure you, O'Shea, we have some very advanced virus protection here, and this particular virus is in deep shit. My assistant will show you out."

Our redheaded escort returned and showed us the way to the front door. Once we were outside, she told the guards we weren't welcome back inside.

I felt like I just got eighty-sixed from a dive bar.

Monica took my arm and turned me to face her. "What virus was Ford talking about?"

"Martin's still inside. I think he's the virus."

"What do we do?"

"We stick to the plan. Phantasm is very resourceful. He knows what he's doing. He'll find evidence that Vitamin C is being manufactured in there."

"Not if they're torturing him to death."

"Come on. He can walk through walls."

"Do you think we have a price on our heads yet?"

"Probably before we left the building." I patted the vial in my pocket. "I've got something he wants."

"Jesus, Rick, we're going to end up victims in a drive-by shooting."

"Not if I can help it. We'll lie low until the meeting tomorrow."

"Okay, where?"

"I know a little bed and breakfast on Block Island."

Chapter Twenty-Six

We jumped on a bus and rode it to State Pier. There I purchased tickets for the Block Island Ferry, in cash, and boarded the next boat out. We didn't have to wait long before the pier fell far behind us and the ferry moved swiftly out into Long Island Sound.

I loved the open water. Gulls flew overhead, oblivious to the state of humanity below. They soared, rising and falling on the winds that blew in from the ocean. I welcomed the saltiness of the sea air into my lungs. It smelled clean and fresh and didn't contain the foamy residue of rotting seaweed and dead shellfish that washed up on the beaches.

We passed New London Ledge Lighthouse. The red-and-white Victorian tower sat on a square basin of concrete and jutted up triumphantly at the mouth of the Thames River.

Monica ducked into the galley and bought us

each a cup of coffee. She also brought a very large selection of snacks in a grocery bag. She offered me some chips, but I refused, to her delight.

She'd lost the Monica wig and let her blond hair fall to the wind.

She caught me admiring her and stopped chewing. "What?"

"I like your hair."

Her cheeks blushed a little.

I turned back to stare at the water.

She leaned on the railing next to me and munched her snacks.

I enjoyed the moment, but eventually typical shovel-in-a-broom-closet Rick O'Shea had to open his big mouth. "Here's what I don't get. You put on your pink work clothes and you're this libido driven dynamo, but as the real you, Monica, you blush like a schoolgirl when I compliment your hair. What gives?"

"It's the mask, silly. Not only does it hide my identity, but it allows me to be someone different. The mask empowers me, liberates me."

"But you're the Pink Panther persona so often, how do you keep them separate?"

"I don't, not always, but it's no different when you put on your badge and gun."

I hadn't really thought about it like that. As a cop, I had a job to do, and I had the authority to use a gun and badge to uphold the law. They were my own kind of mask. Empowering. Liberating. Pink Panther and I weren't so different after all.

Thirty five-minutes later, the ferry pulled up to the dock on Block Island. I found the quiet little Bed and Breakfast I had in mind. We were greeted by the innkeeper, a grandmotherly woman.

"You didn't bring any bags?"

"This little trip was strictly on impulse, spur of the moment, if you know what I mean." I winked at her.

Her face lit up. "Oh, that's so romantic." She gave Monica a little elbow nudge. "Lucky lady."

Monica slid her arm in mine. "How lucky am I, *partner*?"

Ouch. That hurt.

The woman presented us with a small bag. "My husband and I keep a few of these little toiletry kits on hand for our *spur of the moment* visitors."

We thanked her and she showed us to our room.

A fire crackled in the fireplace, giving the room a romantic glow. An armoire and a chest of drawers were the only furniture, save for the cozy bed covered with a comforter my grandma might have quilted.

Monica jumped, flipped and twisted, and landed with a soft *kerplump* on the bed, leaving her shoes neatly parked at the footboard. "What do you think, *partner?*"

"This is going to be a problem," I muttered. "How do you want to do this?"

She rolled to her stomach and wagged her bare feet in the air. "Like anything worth doing, slowly and thoroughly," she breathed.

"I mean the sleeping arrangements."

"Who said anything about sleeping, *partner.*"

"All right, enough with the partner snides. I get it."

I joined her on the bed, lying on my back next to her, and looked up at a star-patterned ceiling spackled with firelight. The only sounds were our breathing and the crackle of logs in the fireplace. Monica's flowery scent soothed me, and her nearness stirred emotions and desires I hadn't felt for anyone but Dani for a long time. I felt at peace for once, the city's Dex and drug problems a distant nightmare.

The bed jostled as Monica snuggled up closer.

I felt the warmth of her breath on my neck. Every voice inside my brain screamed *run*. Dexes and non-Dexes were a bad combination. And what about Dani? I truly loved her once, but her lies became a scab on my heart, a wound that bled until all the love drained out. I still cared about her, and I cared about Monica too. And she cared about me. As Pink Panther, she'd saved my life during *The Brawl*.

"Penny for your thoughts, Rick."

I turned to face her and those beautiful blue eyes. "I'm sorry about—"

"Just shut up and kiss me."

Our lips came together like two lost lovers. This time I welcomed her tongue, let it explore. She tasted like strawberries and red-red wine. Waves of pleasure swept through my body. Our arms entwined, our hips came together, and she moaned when I pressed my happy part against hers.

Her tongue and lips retreated and her hot smoky voice whispered in my ear, "Is that for me?"

"It's your birthday present."

"But it's not my birthday."

"Shut up and unwrap it."

She showed me one advantage to being an agile gymnast, one that I hadn't considered. With smooth speed and elegant grace she peeled off my clothes down to my boxers, which by now looked like a tent.

"My turn." I flung her to her back on grandma's comforter and wrestled her jeans off her hips and down to her ankles. She kicked her pants to the floor while I tackled her blouse buttons. My fingers were shaking, and I performed the task with the grace of jackhammer operator.

"Want some help?"

"I got it. I got it." I finally opened her blouse, revealing a pink bra. What else? Mounds of joy stared up at me. My lips kissed a trail up her neck to her chin to her mouth, a distraction while my right hand slipped around back to attack the dreaded bra clasps.

She arched her back and giggled, let me fumble with the material, then finally let me in on a secret. "Victoria Secret," she whispered. "It unhooks in the front."

"Oh." I found the hook and button between the cups. It took both hands, but I got the sucker undone. The bra fell away, and the sight of her rosy and upright nipples made my heart leap out of my chest and sing.

Bare chest to bare chest, we hugged and kissed and explored each other, up and down, round and round, higher and higher. One beautiful Dex, one beat-up cop, two lovers came together, *come hell or high water, the devil may care*.

Once.

Twice.

Three times that I could recall. And when it was over, neither of us had a stitch of cloth on us or a breath in our lungs we could hold on to.

Grandma's comforter would never be the same.

Monica rolled off me and nestled her back into my chest, and I wrapped my arms around her. Spooning, we caught up with our breathing as we basked in the afterglow's bliss.

She had teased me a lot as Pink Panther, but I had no idea that there were actual desires under all the flirting. I was either blind or in denial of my own desires for the superstar. She didn't seem real enough, down-to-earth enough, always over-the-top with everything she did. I knew now it was her mask that had me fooled. Monica turned out to be every bit as desirable as her Dex persona, but very real, very down-to-earth, and very much over-the-top in bed.

Firelight danced on the curves of her body. It was beautiful. She was beautiful.

She purred a pleasing little sigh.

"Are you okay?" I asked her gently.

"All this time I thought you weren't interested in me."

I stroked her hair. "Me too." I had no doubt that my life had just become one huge complication.

"I love you, Rick. I have for a long time."

A really, really huge complication.

Chapter Twenty-Seven

*T*he next day started off with a gray New England sky. Technically, Block Island was part of New York, but with the pea soup fog and cold damp chill in the air, it felt like New England. We'd be back there soon enough, to faceoff with Jonathan Ford and arrest the Reaper.

Monica and I walked down the narrow street, hand in hand like real lovers. We talked very little, just breathed the fresh air and let breakfast settle. Needless to say we were famished.

I didn't regret making love to Monica last night, though my breakup with Dani felt too fresh to begin a new relationship. I knew there was no going back to her. The lies were too big. How could I trust her again? For a millisecond, I worried that Monica was rebound sex. Hell, what better way to rebound than with Pink Panther?

"Rick?" Monica asked. "Are you all right with us?"

I gave her a sideways glance. "Don't tell my you're having regrets."

"No, I'm good."

"Last night will go down as the brightest moment in my life the next time it flashes before my eyes."

She grinned. "I know what it meant to me."

"So you've always wanted to get into my pants?"

Her grin faded and her expression sobered. "Just so you know, I don't sleep around. You're pretty damn special."

"I've got to confess I'm a little intimidated by Pink Panther."

"Since we're confessing..." she pulled me to a stop. "I took a lot of pleasure in watching you squirm. Here was this man who wasn't afraid to go toe-to-toe with any badass in the city, and yet you'd turn to mush whenever I batted my eyelashes at you."

"I was befuddled. You, the city's most famous sex symbol, had eyes for me, how could that be possible?"

"Just remember there is a huge difference between being a sex symbol and being your sex partner, so if you want to continue to be the latter, then stop whining about the former."

"I wasn't whining, just saying...I mean—"

"Befuddled again, partner?" She showed me a dimpled smile and dipped a little curtsey then walked on, leaving me standing there, slack-jawed.

We took the last ferry off the island, back to the real world of murder and mayhem. By now every thug and assassin in New London would be out to cash in on the bounty Jonathan Ford had put our heads. Though the light weight of my Buck Roger's weapon in its shoulder holster felt reassuring, even with having that and Pink Panther at my side, I worried we wouldn't live long enough to make our meeting with Talon.

Chapter Twenty-Eight

Back at State Pier, we remained seated aboard the ferry until everyone else had disembarked. The parking lot had pretty much emptied, save for a few vehicles that would soon become our only protection.

As soon as we walked on solid ground, Frost Warning and Zip launched an attack on us from the trees. I dodged a wickedly sharp icicle then Frost Warning followed up with a shuriken tossed at my head. I ducked the frozen throwing star. It impacted the minivan behind me, leaving a ragged gouge. That gave me a split second to dive over a Volkswagen.

Monica hunkered down beside me. "So what's the plan?"

"Why do I always have to be the one with the plan?"

"Because you're the only one who can pull something out of his ass."

"But you're the superhero on this team."

"Move over." Monica traded places with me, grumbling under her breath about me being dead weight. "Cover me."

I pulled Buck Roger's from my holster and gave her the *go* nod.

She jumped up, tumbled and twisted to the minivan, executed a perfect back flip, and stuck the landing. That would have earned her a ten-score from the Olympic judges, but what it did was get Zip's undivided attention. I aimed Buck and squeezed the trigger.

Quark's weapon ejected a stream of plasma that tracked Zip as he tried to elude it. He shrieked when it hit him. The plasma congealed into sphere of energy around him and bowled him over. Struggle as he might, he wasn't going anywhere, trapped in a force field like a netted badger.

"Ha!" I looked at the Buck Roger's gun in my hand, way cooler than my pulse pistol, and had to smile. Quarks was a genius with mechanical things, for sure. I had no idea how long the plasma shield would hold Zip or how many times I could shoot the gun before it petered out, but I didn't have a second to ponder over it.

Frost howled at seeing Zip's predicament. "You'll pay for that, O'Shea. Take this, asshole." She threw a flurry of deadly ice shards at me. They weren't well-thrown, she was so pissed, but there were a lot of them, a kind of spray and pray volley that went high. If not, I would have left the parking lot in a body bag.

I bolted to another car and took up residence behind a tire. "Hey, Frost. I'm not an asshole. I'm the police."

"You're dead meat, asshole."

I wasn't getting through to her. No respect.

She responded with a sheet of ice that coated everything around me. It forced me to move in another direction, but she whipped an ice blade at me. I jumped, hoping to jump clear, but I needed another split second. The freezing blade stabbed me in the thigh.

"Fuck!"

Pain spiked directly to my brain. As I hit the ground, I grabbed my leg and rolled, dropping Buck Rogers in the process. "Shit." I'd rather have been caught with my pants down than unarmed. I crawled toward the weapon, but Frost Warning buried it under a thick glob of ice. I tried beating on it to break it, but Buck might as well have been locked behind steel doors.

Frost Warning let out a truly joyous laugh. "Nice try, O'Shea." From fifty feet away, she lassoed my hands with an ice rope, yanked my wrists together, and gloved me with ice mittens.

I couldn't even move my fingers.

"Now we can collect a fat check and go someplace warm."

"Warm seems a little out of character for a woman with a frigid personality."

"Never mind my personality, O'Shea. Now get Zip out of that bubble."

"I don't know how that's even possible."

"Never mind. I'll do it myself." She blasted the force field with a stream of ice until the bubble became a frosty ball. Then a crack appeared across the ball's surface and webbed out like forked lightning. Within seconds, the ball caved in, crumbled, and buried Zip under a pile of ice crystals. He wasn't moving.

"Clever," I mumbled. However, I'd just learned the force field lasted only as long as it remained warm. A glance around did not produce Monica. Where the hell was she when I needed her? I tried to get up, but I couldn't feel my leg. And where were those goddamned nanites when I needed them?

With nothing else I could do, I rolled on my back. By now, Frost Warning stood over me, hands on her hips, and an icy smile on her blue lips. "Any last words you want to say? And don't bore me with 'please don't kill me' blah, blah, blah."

As a matter of fact, Frost, I do have a last word."

"Make it quick. I have an anger management class at the Y."

"Duck!"

"Eh?"

Pink Panther landed a roundhouse kick that would have been the envy of Bruce Lee. Frost's jaw snapped. She went down in a heap, and Pink Panther kicked her in the ribs for good measure. Obviously Monica's absence was due to her changing clothes in a phone booth somewhere. Good thing she didn't have to futz with her makeup. I'd have been a dead man.

"Are you okay?" We both asked each other at the same time.

"I'm good." I smashed the ice mittens on the pavement, freeing my hands.

"But your leg. We have to get you to the

hospital."

"Unnecessary." I struggled to my feet, surprised my leg was warming up. "We've got to get to the meeting."

I took a couple tentative steps. No pain.

She looked at my leg and cocked her head. "It's healing?"

"Thanks to those friggin' hearty little robotic bastards."

"What are you talking about?"

I bounced up and down on my toes. "Doc Quarks injected me with Nanites."

"Nanites?"

"Microscopic machines that fix things."

She rolled her eyeballs. "Whatever you say, Rick."

"We'll stop at Martin's office first. I want him with us when we meet Talon and Dani."

"We're not sticking around for the police?" She indicated the unconscious body of Frost Warning and Zip the snow cone.

I shook my head. "Leave them. I don't want to be stuck in an orange jumpsuit breaking big rocks into little rocks."

"That's right. You're suspended."

"Remember when I told you about that

authority you didn't have? Well, I don't have it either. So we've got to stay under the radar."

"Lucky for those two jerks."

"They'll get their shit in a ringer someday." I stepped to my weapon. It lay under a thick layer of ice. "A little help here."

Pink Panther flipped in the air and landed on the blob with both feet. The ice shattered, freeing Buck Rogers.

I felt whole again.

Chapter Twenty-Nine

We entered Martin's office. The door wasn't locked, so I knew it would set off an alarm in the backroom. That didn't sound like a bad thing. He'd come flying through the wall, probably with gun drawn. I'd have told him we were coming if he would've answered my phone calls.

But Martin didn't appear.

"Martin," I shouted. The office remained as we'd left it. I couldn't get into the backroom so I pounded on the wall. "Martin, you in there?"

"Perhaps he stepped out," Panther suggested.

"He's not here. He's not answering his phone. What if he's still at UltraGen...in some kind of trouble?"

"You told me he could handle himself."

Right. I had told her that. If he was still there it was because he wanted to be there. No room, no cell, no box could hold him. He could turn invisible. I'd have to wait for Martin to contact me.

"Looks like we have to meet Talon and Dani alone."

"What are you going to tell Dani about us?" Panther's tone suggested my answers were limited, so I came back with a question.

"What should I tell her about us?"

"You don't know?"

That backfired, so: "How about *us* is none of her business?"

"You don't want her to know we slept together. You're ashamed—"

"I am not. Where's this jealousy coming from? Let's worry about the meeting for now. We can sort out our personal lives later."

"I'm not jealous." She hugged. "Where are we going?"

"The Viper's Pit."

"Oh, yeah, now I remember Martin mentioning that place. I was in a weak emotional state then."

"Rub it in. I said I was sorry."

"But the Viper's Pit?" Her jaw tightened and disgust flashed behind her eyes. "How awful."

"Hey, I didn't pick the place."

"A Dex strip joint? Come on, Rick. What kind of joke is that?"

"Now you know why I wanted Martin to go with us, for backup."

"Backup for a bunch of naked floosies?"

"Trust me sweetheart, you have nothing to worry about."

"Who said I was worried?"

I cocked my head and smiled. "You're more beautiful than any of them."

She rolled her eyes.

"Okay, it's a haven for badasses. You don't have to go in. You can wait outside and watch the door in case another assassin is lurking about."

She shook her head. "No, I'm in with you all the way, Rick." She kissed my cheek.

We left Martin's office en route to the raunchiest bar in town.

***

We pulled up to the curb in front of a brightly lit building. Its marquee pulsed in neon, a fanged snake curling around a buxom blonde. A crowd had gathered at the entrance.

Panther handed me a mask, black with a nose bill.

"Where did you get this?"

"Really, Rick. I'm a Dex."

~265~

"I don't want to wear a stinkin' mask."

"When in Rome..." She batted her eyes and donned her pink mask.

I sighed with resignation and put it on. I had to admit I felt a little power behind the anonymity.

A valet opened my door. "Awesome car, mister."

I got out of the Challenger, "Not a scratch, you hear?" and tossed him the keys.

Then I surprised myself. I actually swaggered over to the passenger side, opened the door, and held out my hand for Pink Panther.

She slinked out with all the elegance of a superstar.

The crowd went wild with cheers and applause. Kinda made the hair on the back of my neck stand up.

A second later, we actually stood on an actual red carpet. The crowd of tourists and paparazzi waiting behind velvet ropes manned their cameras in preparation for a real treat.

Disorienting flashes blazed from every direction.

I tried to rush inside, but Panther held me back and whispered in my ear, "Relax, Rick. Enjoy the spotlight. See how I live."

I had to give her one thing...this life could be intoxicating.

A flurry of questions chirped from the crowd, but she remained silent and posed for the cameras with me on her arm.

I wasn't sure what to do, so I tried to look worthy, back straight, shoulders squared, phony smile. It quickly became obvious that no one cared about me. That suited me just fine.

Panther, on the other hand, put as much energy into the spectacle as I'd seen her put into the most grinding fight. She knew how to work the crowd, released my arm to sign an autograph, and gave everyone just enough attention to make them feel like they'd received something special.

Additional club security emerged and formed a soft barrier between Pink Panther and the crowd. She grabbed me by the shirt and pulled me along so the bouncers wouldn't confuse me with the masses. A guy gave me a *what-is-she-doing-with-you* look. I smiled at him and continued with Pink Panther into the club.

The Viper's Pit was *the* prominent, non-historical tourist attraction of New London. It was modeled after the red light district in Amsterdam, Club 54, and Boston's Combat Zone. Heavy Metal music beat the air and strobes pulsed above a tri-level dance floor. Frozen rum drinks were dispensed by the glacier and delivered by waitresses who could have subbed for models in Victoria's Evil Secret catalogs. Their skimpy outfits showed enough skin to be a health code violation.

We worked our way through the frenzy until we reached a mirrored back door guarded by two very large goons. They were tough and superhumanly strong and just the sort management would want to employ as bouncers.

A line of young men who could have been off-duty Navy personnel stood at the door and waited for their turn to enter. Their eyes got big when Pink Panther drew near. The men mobbed her with requests to have their pictures taken with her: Maxim Magazine's *Super-Hottie of the Year*. To give them a story to take back to their buddies on the ship, she consented to the pictures and few hugs and cheek kisses.

The sideshow gave me a chance to break away, and I spoke to one of the bouncers, showed him my badge. He allowed me through the great mirrored door.

This was the heart of the Viper's Pit. Men and women gathered around a variety of stages, watching nearly naked women pole dance to pulsing lights and thumping music. Topless waitresses strutted among the tables, delivering colorful drinks. Neon and black lights made the atmosphere stick to me like syrup.

The women gyrating on the stages were inhumanly gorgeous. One woman burst into flames. The crowd around her roared. Another woman wore a body suit, and she made pieces of it disappear in alluring ways. Another half dozen stages held other amazing Dex dancers, male and female, who attracted crowds and big tips.

My eyes fell on the woman I'd been looking for. They called her Black Rose. She wore a black and red evening gown with stylized roses woven into the fabric. She carried a harlequin mask on a thin rod that she casually held to her face. She chatted with a man who made her laugh. My heartbeat thudded in protest as I approached the table where they sat.

Rose's gaze shifted from her companion and fell on me. "May I help you, sir?"

Mute, I removed my mask.

Recognition crossed her face. "If you'll excuse me," she said to her comedian friend. "I have some business to attend." She rose and extended her hand to me.

I brushed my lips on her knuckles. "You look lovely tonight, Rose."

She eyed me up and down. "Still a cop, O'Shea?"

"To serve and protect, ma'am."

She plopped her palm on my chest and ran her fingers all the way down to my belt. "I hear you're single now."

"Something like that." I snatched her hand before it reached someplace I didn't feel like sharing. "Where are they?"

"Your party is upstairs in the suite."

"Thank you for helping us."

"We all lost something during *The Brawl*. I consider this my part in balancing the scales."

"What did you lose, Rose?"

"Business." She eyed me levelly. "Sales are down eighteen percent."

She started to say something else, but her face turned implacable as two pink-clad arms wrapped around me from behind. Pink Panther's chin settled on my shoulder. "Hello, Rose. What are you doing with my man?"

"You can have him, Panther," she replied with forced civility. "I was done with him a long time ago."

"Ladies, please."

"They're waiting for you upstairs." Rose turned and took a couple of steps then glanced back over her shoulder. "And O'Shea, please let me know if you desire some worthy entertainment." She glowered at Panther, "On the house, of course," and glided away.

"Fucking whore!" Panther snarled.

"Easy, tiger. Her title is actually *madam*." I led the way to a private elevator.

On the way up to the suite, Panther purred in my ear. "You've got me for entertainment now."

"Rose didn't mean anything by that."

"Yes she did."

Women.

And I was about to face another one. Dani. A knot tightened in the pit of my stomach.

The door slid open. We walked down a short hallway lined with elegantly framed mirrors. Muffled voices came from behind the security door to the suite. I pressed the button. A pleasant synthesized voiced asked, *"May I have your name, please."*

"O'Shea."

"Voice print confirmed."

The lock released with a click.

"Why all the security?" Panther asked. "It's just a whore house."

"True," I said. "But a secure whore house. No listening or video devices will work here. No cell phone reception. There's a red phone with a secure line, the only connection to the outside world. Who knows how many clandestine, underhanded plots and shady deals have been made in this suite?"

"What happens in Vegas..."

"Same principle." I opened the door.

Talon rushed toward us. "Thank God!" Visibly relieved, she wrapped her arms around me. "We heard you were attacked by Frost Warning and Zip."

"Did you hear how we kicked their asses?" Panther growled.

"Good to see you." Talon hugged her and they talked quietly.

"Yo, my brother," came Thunderstorm's deep voice. He sat in one of the overstuffed chairs, puffing on a cigar.

I nodded his direction.

Zack stood talking to Dani. Her eyes lit up when she saw me, and in a blur, she left him speaking to thin air. Her arms were wrapped around me before I could blink. "You made it." She pressed her body against me. "We heard that every thug on the street was looking for you and Pink Panther."

I peeled her arms off me and made light of the danger. "Now who would spread a rumor like that?"

"That would be me." Duke had a knack for coming in at the wrong time. "I need to speak to you privately." He grabbed me by the arm and dragged me to the corner. "Have you lost your fucking mind?"

"What did I do now?"

"Infiltrating UltraGen without backup, what were you thinking?"

I pushed back. "We went on a goddamn tour. Ford confronted us. I gave him a little surprise. He didn't like the fact that I have one of his samples." I slipped the vile out of my pocket and showed Duke.

"All right, put it away. If having a death wish was part of your plan then your wish has come true."

"Panther and I can take care of ourselves."

"What about Dani?"

"I came to ask her a favor."

"That girl over there loves you," he whispered, pointing to Dani. "You have no idea how much."

"How do you know?"

"I talked with her for an hour while we were waiting for your sorry ass."

"Don't believe a word she says. Dani and I broke up. She's a big girl and makes her own choices, and those choices don't involve honesty and trust."

"That's no reason to ignore her feelings. She's really sorry. You two still have a chance."

I glanced at Pink Panther. "Dani had her chance."

"Then what do you want to see her for, to string her along? She hopes this meeting is to patch things up between you two."

I hadn't seen that coming. Dani and I together again? Her timing was impeccably poor. I'd already moved on. "It's strictly business and I'd like to get to it."

Duke gave me his best dead-eye stare. "You'd better know what the fuck you're doing."

I'd been on the receiving end of that look before, and it never failed to shake me, until now.

"Hey, it's *bull-in-a-china-shop* O'Shea you're talking to." I turned to Dani.

A blind man could have seen the hopefulness in her eyes. "Did you want to talk to me about something, Rick?"

I had to stay focused. We sat together on a plush divan. "I need you to talk to your father."

"What about?"

"I'm looking for a motive in the murders of his drug dealers."

"That would be Geraldo's department now."

"Ask your father if the name Dr. Douglas Brooks means anything to him."

"You suspect he's the Reaper?"

"I know the Reaper has a score to settle with the Reyes family. Brooks I'm not sure about. If there's a connection between them, I want to know what it is and why it turned deadly."

"I don't know if I can see my father for a while. I'm lying low under Talon's protection."

I glanced at Talon. She was talking on the Red Phone, and she didn't look happy.

"Her protection's not necessary any longer, Dani. The Reaper has promised me he'd leave you alone."

"Are you guys buddies or something now?"

I huffed. "Let's just say we have an uneasy truce. I believe he won't harm you. Will you ask your father about Brooks?"

She sighed. "I was hoping you wanted to talk to me about something else."

"No, that's it."

"Then I want to talk to you about something else."

"Like what?"

"Us."

Talon stepped up. She looked worried. "I hate to interrupt, but we have a problem."

I patted Dani's knee. "Some other time." I'd just dodged a bullet. *Thank you, Talon.* I stood. "What is it?"

"Martin never made it out of UltraGen."

"How's that possible?" I swallowed. "He can walk through walls."

"My source just told me he's being held in a radioactive plasma sphere."

"UltraGen has one of those?"

"Duh, evidently. He's untouchable."

"We'll see about that." I gathered everyone around and got them up to speed on our tour of UltraGen.

"Panther and I served as a distraction so

Martin could do some snooping. We just got word he's being held there against his will. We need to infiltrate, find him, get him out, and locate where they're manufacturing these little beauties." I showed them the blue vile.

"It's a big complex," Thunderstorm boomed. "High security, guards everywhere. You're talking Mission Impossible here."

"Impossible or not, we're going in after Martin."

Duke spoke up. "You don't have the authority to conduct a raid on UltraGen."

"He's right." I looked around my group. "Anyone want out, now's the time to opt out, no hard feelings."

No one budged.

"Just so you know..." Duke swept a finger around the room. "You get caught, you go directly to jail. Don't say I didn't warn you."

"Questions?"

Duke raised his hand. "Can I go with you?"

"I thought you'd never ask. Anyone else?"

None.

"All right. Let's roll."

Chapter Thirty

.At night, UltraGen looked more like a high-security prison than a research and development pharmaceutical company. Nightlights lit the perimeter walls, spotlights swept the compound, and windows glowed where employees burned the midnight oil. Hunkered down in the bushes along the north wall, I couldn't help but hear the tune to Mission Impossible playing in my head.

Duke stooped next to me. "Rick, this is a dumb plan."

"Now you tell me."

Duke had supplied us with Walkie-Talkies from the SWAT team's equipment room at STF. I spoke into mine. "Zack. Go."

Zack glided in, landed on the wall, and tossed down a rope that he'd tied to a nearby tree limb. Then he leaped to the sky and joined Talon on aerial recon.

Duke caught the rope. "Do you have any idea

how many things can go wrong?"

"Come on, Duke. I expect everything to go wrong, so shut up and let's get it done."

"It's your funeral."

Talon's voice came over my ear-bud. "All clear, O'Shea. No heavies."

Pink Panther chimed in. "Thunderstorm and I are in position."

"Roger that." I looked at Dani, not an arm's length away. She wore the same black and purple costume that I'd seen her in at the monument. Tonight she wore a black skull cap, the tattoo on the back of her neck clearly visible, and she'd strapped a katana across her back. Several other handheld weapons were attached to her belt. I hoped she wouldn't need any of them.

"After you." Duke handed her the rope.

She made eye contact with me. "When this is over, we're going to talk about us," she said in chilly voice.

With any luck I wouldn't make it out alive.

She scurried up the rope so fast it would have awed any marine. I followed her up without any of the speed or finesse she had displayed. My ear-bud brought bad news from Talon.

"O'Shea, Dani, two heavies coming toward

you."

I froze. There was no place to hide on top of this wall and Duke was halfway up the rope.

Dani dropped to the ground inside the compound, landing in complete silence.

The two security guards pacing by below didn't notice her. She moved so fast that I even lost track of her.

The guards stopped abruptly. One pointed at the tree branch that was jerking up and down as Duke climbed the rope. They drew their guns. I was about to order an abort when Dani slipped up behind them. In the time it took me to blink, she had them hogtied and gagged with their own clothes. She left them in the bushes, wearing only their underwear and boots.

Duke made the summit, huffing for breath. "Remind me to thank her for that."

"She never undressed me that fast." I pulled the rope up and dropped it on the compound side of the wall. "You first this time."

He slid down the rope and I followed. We joined Dani and moved along a wall until we found cover behind a piece of faux art. A spotlight beam swooped by.

Dani pointed out the security cameras. She

didn't miss a thing. "Stick close to me and we'll avoid being seen."

"Did all that ninja stuff come with your superpower?"

"No, that's my training. And I'm not a ninja, I'm a kindergarten teacher."

They didn't make kindergarten teachers like her when I was a little kid. I radioed Talon. "How's our diversion coming?"

"Ten minutes."

"Panther, did you copy that?"

"We're ready for splashdown."

Now I had to get my team into position. We edged up to a door that read: SECURITY. Through the window I counted three guards on duty. They were playing cards. I held up three fingers to Dani.

In a blur she was at the door. I drew my pulse pistol and started dropping fingers for the countdown. On two, she grabbed the doorknob. On one, she opened the door.

I stepped into the doorway and fired a couple pulses into the room. They hit one guard. He spazzed on the floor in an electrically induced fit.

Dani sprang into action so fast I had to pull up my gun or risk shooting her. She had the other two down and bound before I could swallow.

Not a ninja my ass.

Dani and I each grabbed ID badges off the guards. I keyed their radio mike. "Guard check." I'd used my hand over the mike to muffle my voice.

"Who is this?" a guard on patrol called back. "Where's Dave?"

"He'll be back in five. State your positions."

Four teams keyed in with their locations, and Dani marked their positions on a map of the compound Duke had brought with him. Then she fiddled with the security system, and we started looking for likely places where we'd find Martin.

Most of the plant was empty except for a few third-shift workers in the waterfront building. The loading docks were piled high with freight awaiting a cargo ship to places unknown.

"He wouldn't be there." I decided. "Too many people to keep quiet. Besides, a radioactive sphere would probably be located underground."

"Right." She found basement feeds and switched security camera views to the monitor. The shots changed from rooms to hallways to more rooms, some dark, most vacant, all eerie. "How are we going to know a radiation room from a sauna?"

I recalled the radiation warning signs in Geiger's driveway. "Look for a black on yellow sign. Black circle, three radiating arms—"

"I know what it looks like." She flipped through more views. "What I can't figure out is how anyone could have contained Martin in a radiation plasma thingy."

I knew, and I had a Buck Rogers gun to prove it.

"Will you guys hurry up?" Duke was guarding the door.

"Solid matter is mostly empty space because atoms are mostly empty space. Phantasm is able to sift his atoms through that empty space. Plasma force field atoms are so densely packed there's less room to slip by."

"Same as lead."

"Yes. If he tried to walk through a lead wall or a plasma force field, his atoms would be blocked or absorbed in such a way the attempt could kill him."

"So he's screwed." She switched screens.

"Fucked all the way down to the atomic level."

A view of a door with a radiation sign

showed on the monitor. "Got it." She pulled up a floor plan. Zoomed in and out. The maze made me dizzy, but she memorized the route. "Let's go."

Duke and I followed her out of security to a stairwell leading down. Already, Thunderstorm had brewed a hurricane force wind coming in from up river.

Talon radioed in. *"Splashdown in ten, nine..."*

Suddenly, two heavies started bounding up the stairs. They were already reaching for their belted weapons and radio mikes. They'd kill us and put all of UltraGen on alert.

Shit!

"...seven...six..."

I drew my pulse pistol too late.

Dani shouted. "I'm on it."

Before her words finished echoing down the stairwell, the guards had been disarmed and were kneeling at the point of her sword. "Lady, we got no beef with you."

"Dani," I shouted.

"Please don't kill us," one of them pleaded.

"...two...one..."

Duke had little patience for groveling. He grabbed my gun arm, fingered my trigger, and shot them both with my pulse pistol set on knock out.

They wouldn't see the giant container barge plow into the lower waterfront docks and building. Thunderstorm's hurricane wind had broken the barge loose from its moorings upstream. The timing was a little off. We should have already been in position to free Martin, but the results were spectacular. I'd never heard a crash so loud, the sound of metal grinding against metal in whiny rasps as the barge ate up concrete and steel. Lightning forked from the night sky, and giant swells washed ashore. The wreck would be blamed on a sudden storm. Meanwhile, the compound and buildings would be evacuated, giving us free range of the place.

I called up to Talon. "Did everyone get out of the waterfront building okay?" We wanted to create a ruckus, not squish some hapless worker just doing his job.

"Everyone is accounted for, O'Shea. Now get Martin and let's get the hell out of here."

I bolted down the stairs after Dani and Duke. We passed workers running up the stairs, either to escape the building or run toward the crash. No one showed any concern for us.

Talon and Zack remained skyward as

lookouts, while Thunderstorm and Panther joined us in the basement.

We moved quickly down the corridor, covering each other as if we had done this our entire lives. Panther took point. Duke took sweep to guard our rear. We encountered six goons on the ground in various states of hurt. Pink Panther had pummeled them good. None were in any condition to cause us further issue.

"Keep moving." Duke's voice came over my ear-bud.

We made our way down deeper into the complex. Nothing impeded our way until we came to a steel reinforced door. An *Authorized Personnel Only* sign large enough to be seen from space adorned the control panel on the wall.

Dani let out a low whistle. "This door has got to be six inches thick with titanium deadbolts in the walls, ceiling, and floor."

Thunderstorm stepped up to the door and started billowing and bulging. Lightning flashed between his puffy ears. Thunder rumbled as the storm inside him built to unleash a fury on the door.

I made a sweeping gesture to him. "Get back."

He deflated and grumbled. "I can do it."

"Allow me." From my suit coat pocket I whipped out the ID badge I'd taken from the guard. With one easy stroke, I swept it across the control panel's card reader. Solenoids clicked, motors whirred, levers clanked, and the impassable steel door angled open.

My pride of achievement was quickly dashed as red laser sighting beams sliced out of the dark hall beyond the open door and landed on our chests. Armed guards were waiting for us. How was that possible?

Before anyone could say, "Oh, shit," pink and black streaks whizzed by me into the darkness. The speed must have caught the owners of the laser sights off guard, as well.

Huffs and thuds echoed down the hall. Then gunshots and ricocheting bullets. Screams of pain. Cursing and spitting.

Thunderstorm and I wasted no time and darted into the fray. We almost got clear of the door before the panic firing started. Thunderstorm took several rounds as he bulled forward.

I took a blow across my lower back, felt like being hammered with a two-by-four. It knocked me off my feet, and I tumbled into a painful heap.

"Fuck," I shouted.

Thunderstorm got to me, gasping. "You okay?"

"It'll feel a lot better when it stops hurting." I struggled into a crouched position and aimed my gun into the dark corridor, but I didn't dare pull the trigger for fear of hitting Dani or Pink Panther. "We've got to find the light switch."

Thunderstorm threw a bolt of lightning into the darkness, which illuminated the hall for a flashing few seconds.

Dani and Pink Panther enacted the most intricate battle ballet I'd ever seen. They moved with grace, and not a single ounce of energy was wasted. Each seemed to know where the other stood, and more than once rolled over the top of one another or used each other as springboards to strike an armed guard.

I wanted to cheer as they beat the tar out of Jonathan Ford's minions, but something jabbed me in the neck from behind. I staggered and hit the floor.

Chapter Thirty-One

I didn't know how long I was out. My head felt heavy and thick. I couldn't see anything and I couldn't move at all. My lower legs were completely numb, and when I tried to wiggle my toes, they didn't respond. Best I could make out, I was in a kneeling position with a metal rod jammed under my armpits. My hands were shackled behind my back. Sometimes it didn't pay to get up in the morning.

A light blazed on. The glare stabbed at my eyes like pitchforks. Footsteps approached. A scraping noise. When my vision cleared I saw a figure sitting across from me in a metal chair.

"Tsk, tsk, detective," purred the voice of Jonathan Ford. "We have a nasty situation here. There is a container barge parked in the middle of my compound. Would you know about that?"

I shrugged. "Where are my friends?"

"Your pitiful band of thieves is in good

hands. "

I doubted it.

"The women have such amazing abilities, but alas, they are currently being dissected by my scientists. Their DNA will prove invaluable for fighting disease."

"I know what you're up to. You say you're going to find a cure for the Dexes, but then you're going to create more Dexes to be cured. You'll supply your own demand for your own drugs. Talk about pitiful. You won't get away with it."

He gave me an approving nod. "Too bad you won't be around to see my vision for the future come to pass, but we can hardly make a better world without a few sacrifices. I wish you luck in your next life, detective."

"Fuck you." I had him where I wanted him.

He casually pulled out a pistol and fired three shots into my chest.

Pain exploded as my aorta burst and blood flooded my lungs. In the mere seconds of consciousness I had left, I watched Ford walk out the door. As an added cruelty, he had music piped in, *Roxanne,* and that would be the tune playing over and over in my head until I finally died.

Chapter Thirty-Two

*T*o my amazement, I suffered through a hundred and seventy-four repetitions of Roxanne. At around repetition forty-eight the first bullet had worked its way out of my chest and clinked to the floor. At one hundred twenty-eight, bullet number two dropped to the ground with clunk, and by one hundred and fifty–eight, the last one had joined the other two. Dr. Quarks' nanites had earned themselves a big bonus for this round.

"Now if only they could undo locks and chains," I muttered.

A dark cloaked figure emerged from the shadows. "There's more to you than meets the eye, Detective O'Shea." A synthesizer disguised the voice.

"Reaper. How did you get in here?"

"Really, you had to ask that question? Not thank God you're here, or get me out of this mess I got myself into? What's the matter with you?"

"Hey, I'm having a bad day."

He scooped the bullets off the floor, looked at them and then back at me. "You're some kind of Dex, too?"

"No, I'm an idiot with a mad scientist for a friend."

"Okay, idiot, I'm going to get you out of those chains. Stay perfectly still." He swiped at the chains with his scythe, which cut through them like they were soggy noodles. I fell forward and landed on the side of my face. He pulled the bar out from behind my back and cut the cuffs off my wrists.

I had never been so grateful for anything in my life. My legs turned to pins and needles as the blood rushed back to my feet. "I can't feel my legs."

He bent over me and checked my vitals. "Detective, the feeling will return much quicker if you stand."

"Is that your professional medical opinion, Dr. Brooks?"

"What did you call me?"

"I know who you are, just can't prove it." He helped me to my feet.

"You're a better detective than I gave you

credit for."

"More than meets the eye, remember?" I tapped my forehead. "After The Brawl you were downright rude and hateful to me. That got me suspicious. I'd never done you any harm, but I realized that wasn't the problem. It's the harm I could have done to you, like bust your murdering ass. That's what you were worried about."

"Do tell."

I rubbed my aching wrists. "Or you thought that since I knew Dani Reyes, I was on the take with the cartel, just a dirty cop in your book. Since you hate the Reyes family, you hated me. Just guessing again, mind you, but the clincher came when you used words Brooks had said to me the night you broke into my kitchen."

"Merry ways." He shook his skull. "Bad habit. I hoped you'd missed that."

"I don't miss much."

"So you got me pegged. What now?"

"What I don't have is your motivation for murder. Why do you hate the Reyes family? Once I have that I'll put you away for life."

The Reaper held out his hands. "I'm a shadow walker, detective. You can't possibly think a cell will hold me."

"That's not my problem."

"Let me save you some trouble. How about if I confess?" His disguise melted off him and Doctor Douglas Brooks stood before me.

I staggered at the revelation, but there I was with no recorder or witnesses who could collaborate the confession unfolding, no gun to arrest him, and no balls to try to take him into custody by force. Been there, done that, and failed. "Okay, I'm listening."

The Reaper sat in the same chair Ford had sat in. "Fernando Reyes murdered my family, my wife, my son, and my dog. I hate that man with every fiber of my body. Every waking moment I spend plotting to put an end to him."

"Revenge, a great motivator." He'd handed me his head on a silver platter.

"My son, God rest his soul, didn't do very well in school. I tried to encourage him to study hard to become a doctor like me, but he got this crazy idea to set up his own little medical marijuana shop. No college degree needed. He could still help sick people."

"Get real, Brooks. We both know medical marijuana is a front for drug dealers to ply their trade with immunity."

"I tried telling him that, but he wouldn't listen. He set up a little place, but the Reyes Cartel didn't like the competition. They came calling that night, Fernando and his goons. While I was on duty at the hospital, they took out my family, tied and gagged and shot them in the back of their heads. Then the killers shot Fred just for fun."

"Fred?"

"My dog."

"Oh."

"It's all true. By day I'm a healer, by night I'm a killer. Fernando Reyes made me who I am today."

"What proof do you have it was the cartel?"

"That's the problem, no forensics or DNA to tie them to the crime. No witnesses. But they had threatened my son. I had phone messages and emails from Fernando Reyes warning my son to close shop or die. Circumstantial evidence, the prosecutor said, so Reyes got away with murder. And now so will I."

"So you got your hands on some Cobalt."

"You can never know what it feels like to be so determined to get revenge...so full of hate that your own life doesn't matter anymore. I didn't want to level the playing field. I wanted to dominate the battlefield."

"I don't like seeing bodies in the morgue, and you supplied me with a lot of them. The fact that they were cartel drug dealers doesn't mitigate the fact that you committed murder. For that I'm going to throw every book at you I can get my hands on."

"Detective, is that the thanks I get for bailing you out of this mess you're in?"

"I didn't say it would be today."

"Until then, we both have something to prove." He again cloaked himself in the Reaper's garb. From a pocket he removed my pulse pistol and Buck Rogers. "You will need these."

"Where did you get them..?" As soon as the words left my lips I realized how stupid the question sounded.

"Come on. Let's go get your friends."

That synthesizer was just too damn cool.

The Reaper pulled me into his shadow world. I've felt a lot of strange things in my time, but this ranks in the top two of *most weird*, right after walking through walls with Phantasm.

We jumped around a lot, like running through a series of doors, each one opening in a different place. It could be sunny through one door, raining past the next, and darkness filled with water after that. Textures and sounds held no emotional meaning. Light and dark were just gateways into other realms. I felt insubstantial yet completely solid, like being trapped in a kaleidoscope, but all my senses experienced an ever-changing mixture of tastes, textures, colors, smells, and sounds that eluded me.

The first stop we made looked like a factory behind glass: technicians, vats of powder, machines, assembly lines, packaging.

The Reaper growled out, "This is where they manufacture the drug Cobalt, aka Vitamin C on the streets."

Next, we shadow-walked to the dock, badly damaged by the barge that had already been towed back into the river. "This is where the drugs are loaded into speedboats."

"Runners for the Reyes Cartel?"

"No. They missed the opportunity when their samples were stolen from the armored car. Local drug gangs are doing Ford's dirty work for now. But imagine the war that's going to break out when Reyes reclaims what he had lost."

Thanks to the Reaper, I'd found what American Eagle needed to issue a warrant for a legal raid on UltraGen. "You have me convinced. Let's go find my friends."

The shadow walking started again. When we stopped, I was looking through a glassy membrane into a room that held Pink Panther, Dani, and Thunderstorm.

They were restrained in similar-type bindings as I'd had been held, but their chains were much thicker. To see them in such dire straits, completely subdued like lab rats, made my blood boil. I imagined the nanites trying desperately to put out the fires that raged through me.

A couple of technicians busied themselves at a counter of machines and bubbling flasks. A third held a tray that contained vials of blood and what looked like microscope slides, probably tissue samples from my Dex friends.

"Sons of bitches." I brandished my pulse pistol and took a run at the glassy shadow's edge, fully intent on smashing my way into that room. A hand pulled me back.

"Not so fast." The Reaper shifted our position in the shadow and showed me two others in the room. The redheaded escort we'd seen during the tour and an incredibly emaciated man moved about as if overseeing the lab techs. The skeletal man stood over six-foot high with a gaunt face, sunken eyes, and skin so tight over his bones that he looked like a living Jolly Roger, minus the jolly.

The Reaper stiffened. "We n-need to leave r-right now." Even the synthesizer couldn't mask the terror in his voice.

"Not without my friends we don't."

"Do you have any idea who that skinny fucker is?"

It made the hair on my neck rise to see the Reaper afraid of someone who could benefit from a cheeseburger. "Who is he?"

"Plague."

A sudden chill went up my spine. "I thought Plague was an urban legend."

"He's been out of the country."

I blinked. Plague, out of the country? UltraGen working charity in the third world, the photo panels I'd seen during the tour. Disease, death, then salvation via Jonathan Ford, the great healer. He and Plague were in on it together. I compared that theory to my current theory, Cobalt and the cure. A pattern began to emerge. A conspiracy to profit from human misery spanned the globe.

My guts twisted.

The Reaper's scythe vanished. "While you're thinking about it, I'm leaving. But remember, Plague can kill you with a single touch."

My blood actually ran cold. I could feel the shiver rush through to my bones. "Thanks, Brooks, but remember, if I survive this, I'm coming after you."

"Fair enough, but as a warning, I suggest you and your friends get out of here as fast as possible." The synthesizer relayed a sinister tone to that statement.

I suddenly realized I'd forgotten to ask the Reaper one thing: why was he here? Had he somehow learned of my fate and came to rescue me? Why would he? We had no affinity for each other. He must've been here perpetrating his own plan of revenge. "What have you done, Brooks?"

"In thirty minutes this place will be on its way to hell."

"What does that mean?"

"Tick tock, twenty-nine minutes thirty-four seconds." He faded away.

"Shit!" I checked my watch. He'd set the place to blow at 10pm sharp.

I waited for everyone to turn their backs to me, and when I saw my opportunity I exploded out of the shadow.

My entrance startled the technician carrying the tray of blood samples and slides, which promptly crashed to the floor. "Holy crap!"

Another bolted from the room screaming. Everyone else was paralyzed with surprise and fear, which gave me a couple of seconds to make my move on Red and Plague with Buck Rogers leading the charge.

I blasted them with plasma streams. The familiar bubbles entrapped them. Red started punching the force field with her fists. As long as the room temperature stayed warm, she could punch that bubble until her fist turned to hamburger. Plague just stood there and glared at me through the translucent wall of his bubble, as if I was food.

I used the threat of shooting again to push the lab techs against a wall. "Don't anybody move." I always wanted to say that.

Time check: Twenty-four minutes 'til ten.

Panther was the closest to me and I unbound her first and pulled off her blindfold. Her eyes looked dazed and unfocused, and when she saw me, she blinked.

I pointed at the others. "Free them."

She blinked again, and then my instructions must have clicked. She moved, rather wobbly, to Thunderstorm while I guarded her back. Then she freed Dani. Their faces, too, were dazed and disbelieving.

"No, don't, Plague, don't!" Red shouted.

I spun around. The air inside Plague's bubble had turned cloudy. A foul-looking mist swirled around him, like he was trapped in some ungodly snow globe. The gaseous fog started to thicken and push outward against the bubble.

"We gotta go, now!" I pointed at the swelling globe.

Thunderstorm grabbed me like I was a little puppy, tucked me under his arm, and rode a thunderbolt to the open door. Panther made it out with an elegant tumble. Dani was already waiting in the hallway.

"Don't leave us!" Red looked frantic.

Thunderstorm slammed the door.

My watch read: *9:40*. Twenty minutes...

The technicians scrambled for the door, but in their frenzy, they couldn't get it open. It must've locked automatically. They pounded on the bulletproof window, their terrified faces pressed to the glass, clawed fingers raking the impenetrable barrier.

Thunderstorm looked back. "I can save them!"

"No! You can't! It's death to go in there."

That same mist from Plague's bubble now fogged the window glass. The force field had failed and turned the lab into a gas chamber. Technicians morphed into struggling silhouettes. They screamed inhuman howls as their flesh blistered and melted. Blood exploded from one guy's mouth and laid a crimson streak down the glass.

Thunderstorm turned his eyes away. "It's too late to save them."

Panther took my arm. "We have to save Martin now."

I glanced at my watch and cringed. *Fifteen minutes.* "We'll be lucky to save our own asses."

Chapter Thirty-Three

Dani lead the way to another door. This one displayed the radiation warning sign. "Martin's in here."

Thunderstorm bulled up to the door.

"Wait." I fished the radiation badge out of my pocket. It remained white. "Now."

He knocked down the door. We burst in the room ready for a fight, but unlike the other lab, this one had only a single tech monitoring a large glowing sphere.

I took care of him with my pulse pistol, sent him to T-Rex la-la land.

The sphere pulsed and shimmered blue and yellow, like an oil stain on water. I expected my radiation badge to turn red, but it didn't. The danger was a ruse, probably to scare guys like me away.

Small openings appeared in the sphere's surface at irregular intervals. Each opened to the size of a baseball, lasted for a second or two, and then closed up, only to appear somewhere else at random. I assumed this was an elaborate ventilation system for the Dex trapped inside.

Martin sat cross-legged on a half-moon seat that floated in the plasma sphere. He appeared relaxed as a Yoga instructor or drugged up to the gills.

"Martin, are you okay?"

"If I move, I die, so don't rock the boat." His voice sounded muffled through the plasma force field.

"We were in the neighborhood." Panther buffed a polished claw. "Thought you might like a ride."

"Get me out of this contraption."

In ten minutes we were all going to die.

Thunderstorm walked right up to the sphere, balled a club-hammer fist, and reared back to deliver a powerful blow on the sphere.

"Careful, Thunderstorm," Martin said. "You don't want to touch it." He held up a hand with a painful looking burn. "I found out the hard way."

Thunderstorm backed off and threw a mighty burst of lightning at the sphere. Sparks flew as it bounced off and seared the paint off the far wall.

His grumble sounded like rolling thunder.

Dani, try this." I scooted a chair to her. "You have a knack for computers."

She sat at the terminal, typed, thought, pursed her lips, then: "Password protected."

About now I wished I hadn't knocked out the only technician in the room.

"What's the plan, O'Shea?" Panther delivered that famous line with her famous smile.

"Not again."

"Unplug the fucking thing," Martin shouted.

I traced cables the diameter of my arm, extending from the base of the sphere and snaking off into the next room. I followed them to a refrigerator-sized transformer-looking monstrosity plastered with yellow and black radiation signs and humming like a bad toaster. My hair started tingling. The closer I got to a panel of blinking lights and levers, the more intense the tingling became.

My radiation badge turned bright red.

I could imagine those nanites shoveling sand on the nuclear fires igniting inside my blood cells. On the panel, one lever stood out. It sported a T-handle. I grabbed it and pulled it down.

The humming ceased, the blinking lights

stopped blinking, and a loud crash and cursing came from the lab. I ran back to find Martin on his ass, the half-moon chair shattered beneath him.

My watch read: *9:55.* We had five minutes, then boom.

"You can thank me later," I told him. "Let's go." I threw open the lab door and a volley of automatic gunfire greeted me. That sent me sprawling to the floor.

Thunderstorm stepped into the barrage and blasted the guards with a lightning blitz of Biblical proportions. Screams and the smell of burnt flesh wafted in through the bullet-riddled doorway.

9:56. Thank God that fight didn't last long.

We bolted for the stairs. Son of a bitch there were a lot of stairs. By the time we got to the top, we were all winded. At least we'd finally reached the ground floor.

A pizza sounded really good right now. And a beer.

I led the way through the double doors that opened to the main lobby. Any hope of a pizza and beer anytime soon flew out the proverbial window.

Jonathan Ford stood in the center of the lobby, all polished and proper. "Good evening,

Detective O'Shea. We really have to stop meeting while you're still alive." He was flanked by two individuals.

Ruff 'N Tuff stood on his right. I could only guess the Coast Guard finally fished him out of the ocean, and on Ford's left stood another Dex I had seen before. At *The Brawl.* She had short blond hair, dressed in green spandex all the way down her shapely legs to a wicked-looking pair of spiked heels, and like before, she fluttered her dragon fly wings at me and giggled.

"Tink," Panther whispered to me. "Don't let her squeaky little voice fool you. Her sting is worse than her bite."

Ruff 'N Tuff struck his right fist into the palm of his left hand.

Jonathan Ford stood between his henchman and henchwoman. "Leaving us so soon?"

I glanced at my watch as if I was waiting for a bus. "Gotta go, Jonathan. Pizza and beer awaits. The word is out on you anyway. In no time this place is going to be crawling with cops and firemen."

"Get 'em," Jonathan commanded.

Ruff 'N Tuff moved forward, fists balled. Tink buzzed into the air, circled around, and dived at me, spiked heels first.

A gigantic explosion rocked the complex. Flying debris took out Tink, shot her down like Raid downed flying insects. A chunk of falling concrete crushed Ruff 'N Tuff flat as a pancake. Dust filled the air so thick I couldn't see Jonathan Ford bite the bricks.

We huddled around Phantasm. He walked us out under the protection of his *phasing* superpowers. The building collapsed in a fireball, but we were only atoms in the midst of a fiery maelstrom. I imagined this was what it would be like to walk through hell and witness fire and brimstone erupt beyond the safety of an unbreakable sheet of glass.

Chapter Thirty-Four

I guessed we had won the day. We got Martin out, the drug lab was reduced to rubble, we all had our fingers and toes, and I had a new respect for the Reaper. I would hate to have been on his shit list.

None of us felt like celebrating with pizza and beer so we went our separate ways.

I called Duke. He informed me that Talon had dragged him out of the basement and flown him to safety. Zack took ground fire and was forced to bug out. Duke had tried to rally the STF to mount a rescue mission, but NLPD had no jurisdiction, since the facility was across the river in Groton.

"You did the best you could," I told him.

I supposed he could have done much worse. He could have been the one to let a killer loose, slept with his superhero partner, and Dani could have been in the car with him, telling him that she still loved him. I hung up the cell phone.

"Rick, I still love you." Dani's large brown eyes pleaded with me to say the words back.

"Dani, look." My heart was stuck in my throat, making my words fight to get out. "A lot's happened since we broke up. Believe me, I can't pretend that everything is all right so we can start over, but..." I let the punch line trail off: *But I slept with Pink Panther.* Maybe she could forgive me that transgression, but the truth was I liked it and couldn't wait to do it again.

"Damn it Rick! Do you think I wanted to lie to you?"

I wasn't looking at her, but I could feel the heat of her stare. "I think you had a choice, and when it came time to make it, your choice was to deceive me. Even when you fessed up you lied again...about the briefcase."

"I-I didn't want you to know I had it, Rick."

"You couldn't tell the truth if your life depended on it."

"You don't understand." She lowered her head. "I lied to protect you from my family. Don't tell me you never lied for a good reason."

Right. There I sat preaching about the truth, but I couldn't find the nerve to tell her the truth about Pink Panther and me. I had to man up before she found out the truth from someone else. "Dani, there's something I've got to tell you."

"Rick, I have to tell you something, too."

Normally, most folks would nurse an awkward silence at a time like this, and then one would want the other to go first, but the other would insist the other went first. Dani and I developed a short hand for these situations.

We closed our eyes and counted to three together.

"One."

"Two."

"Three."

"I slept with Pink Panther."

"I'm pregnant."

Awkward.

Chapter Thirty-Five

I sat in the car with Dani for a long while. The silence had become a physical entity with bad breath and sharp teeth gnawing at my brain, my heart, and my guilty conscience. I'd fallen out of love with the mother of my child. He or she would be one hell of a super kid born of a super mom, but his or her problem would be a real downer; their father was a genuine dunce. Not knowing where to begin, I broke the silence by saying something stupid. "How could you be pregnant?"

"How could *you* sleep with Pink Panther?"

"We were investigating a case. It just happened." I left out the part about how I was happy that it happened.

"That's pretty lame, Rick."

"And lying to me isn't?"

"I had no choice."

"Well, I do have a choice, Dani. I'm really sorry things didn't work out for us."

"I thought you loved me?" Tears flooded her eyes.

I saw the hurt run down her cheeks, turned my head, and spoke to the window. "I did love you, Dani."

"Did? What about now?" Her voice was very small.

I closed my eyes and took in a breath. "I can't go back to a relationship built on lies."

She grabbed my hand from the steering wheel and pressed my palm against her abdomen. "This child wasn't built on a lie."

If my heart was a speeding train it would have left the tracks on that curve. I wanted to gather her in my arms, kiss her teary cheeks, and tell her I was sorry I said I didn't love her, that I was in the middle of a PTSD episode, I wasn't thinking straight, that I did love her more than anything in the world, and I'd rather die than let her go.

But I didn't. Instead, I started the engine and drove her home.

***

I approached Dani's door with my coat unbuttoned and the holstered pulse pistol within quick reach. Dani could take care of herself, but the least I could do was see that she'd be safe entering her house.

Her reaction to the mess the Reaper made tossing her place broke my heart. This was the first time she'd returned home since she'd left under Talon's protection. Some of the damage was caused when Martin and I battled the killer, but I didn't say anything. That fight seemed like a lifetime ago.

"You sure he's not coming back?" Dani started to straighten a few things. "If he does, I'll kill him myself."

I let her rant and picked up some papers. It gave my hands something to do. She wouldn't stand a chance against the Reaper, nor would I. A day would come when we'd faceoff, probably to the death, but not today, not tomorrow, and probably not the next day, but someday.

"The Reaper won't bother you, but I can't say the same for the rest of your family...or the cartel."

She sat on the floor Indian style and sorted through strewn books. "I'll ask my dad if he knows why—"

"I already know why Brooks has a vendetta against your family."

"Why?"

"It's best you don't know."

"Rick, don't treat me like a child."

I tossed a broken lampshade on the couch. "Wouldn't dream of it."

"What about Ford? He knows who we are—"

"You were there. You saw the building come down on him and his flunkies."

"I saw dust, Rick." She threw a paperback at the wall. "I didn't see him die. He's not dead until I see him dead."

She had a point. Corpus delicti. Without a body, there was no proof.

"I can't stay here."

Someone knocked on the door.

The air in my lungs turned to ice.

"See?" Dani stood and grabbed for weapons on her belt, which had long been taken from her at UltraGen. "They're here already."

I pulled my pulse pistol. "Who?"

"Every lowlife assassin in Ford's arsenal."

That was something I had experience with, personally.

The doorbell rang.

Dani ducked into the hallway. "Hide back here. We'll ignore them. Maybe they'll go away."

"Yeah, and maybe daylight savings time will be abolished." I tossed her my pulse pistol. "Run out the back door and don't stop running unless you have to shoot somebody."

Now the assassin was pounding on the door. Why would a killer make so much noise..?

"Come with me," Dani rasped.

"Just go." I drew Buck Rogers. "It's my turn to protect you and our baby."

She ran. I heard the back door slam. She was out.

More pounding.

I stalked to the front door, Buck Rogers ready, willing, and able. "We don't want any. Go away." In case I was lucky enough it was just a salesman.

"O'Shea, we know you're in there. Open up."

I cracked the door an inch. Two NLPD officers stood on the porch. Dirty cops doing Ford's dirty work? "What do you want?"

"You have to come with us."

They surely weren't intent on taking me to a birthday party. Probably a drive into the woods to a shallow grave.

"Got a warrant?"

"Come on, do we need a warrant? Stop fucking with us. Let's go downtown."

"Wait a minute. I have to get dressed." I closed and locked the door then bolted for the back door, flung it open, and came nose-to-barrel with a very large and intimidating weapon.

"O'Shea, don't move."

A bomb blast couldn't have made me move.

I shifted my wide-eyed gaze from the barrel to the yellow scaly hand holding the pistol. My eyes traced a feathered arm up to a well-rounded shoulder...and more feathers, blackish brown, and then white on the neck and head. The Dex stood six-five, and displayed an enormous wing span. A police lieutenant's shield was affixed to his red belt. He wore a white and blue uniform and a half face mask complete with canted eye holes and a yellow beak. His lips were narrow and tight. There stood American Eagle in all his glorious flesh and feathers.

He relieved me of Buck Rogers. "You're coming with me."

I was fucked.

Chapter Thirty-Six

*T*he last time I walked through the police station doors I was treated to a hero's welcome. This time there weren't any pats on the back or "atta-boys" from my colleges. Instead, I read disdain in their cold, hard stares. My piers held nothing but disgust and contempt for me, as well as newcomers assigned under Eagle's command, officers who didn't even know me. American Eagle paraded me through the squad room, handcuffed and shackled, past reporters and cameramen, for all to scoff.

A microphone was shoved in my face. "O'Shea, why did you go rogue?"

"Is it true you dynamited UltraGen?"

"Are you a Dex lover?"

Somebody just shoot me and get it over with.

Downstairs in the STF department, most of my fellow squad members chose to remain noncommittal. A brave few nodded in solidarity. I nodded back and kept shuffling along.

My captors led me down familiar halls and past my office. I eyed my desk, still cluttered with the same perpetual stack of paperwork. My Pink Panther coffee cup was barely visible, but spotting it forced me to wonder if I'd ever see her again.

Jensen sat in his chair. We made eye contact and he pumped his brows as if the joke was on me. Ramirez, on the other hand, leaned on Jensen's desk and gritted her teeth like she wanted to beat American Eagle into a featherbed. She mouthed the words, "Good luck."

American Eagle stashed me in an interrogation room. Mirrored wall, metal chair...I expected to see the dreaded medieval rack and thumb screws.

"Sit down."

"Why am I under arrest?"

"Shut up."

Two NLPD officers removed my cuffs and shackles. I sat in the metal chair positioned under a cone of light.

An officer I didn't recognize brought me coffee in a Styrofoam cup. "I wish it was something stronger."

"Me too."

A commotion in the hall drew my attention to the doorway. "Where is he? I demand to see him." The familiar whoosh of flapping wings followed. "I'm his lawyer."

The NLPD officers barred Talon's entrance. She screeched over their outstretched arms, "Don't say a word, O'Shea. We'll sue the bastards."

At least someone had my back. Dani must've called her, but I had to bite my lower lip to keep from asking her where Pink Panther was at: probably in a phone booth somewhere, putting on her makeup.

"It's all right, Talon." I held up my cup. "Let them have their say, and then we'll sue the bastards."

She folded her wings. "I'll be right outside, O'Shea."

American Eagle stood by the door. Captain Grundle swept in and closed it. "You look like hell, O'Shea."

"I've been hearing that a lot lately."

"What happened out there?"

I sipped coffee. "Is this interrogation being recorded?"

"You're damn right it is."

"Turn it off, video, audio, no pens, no paper,

nothing."

"I'm not sure I can do that." He looked at American Eagle, who shook his beak back and forth, a definitive no.

"Captain, your other choice is for me to lawyer up. Then you get nothing. At least this way, you'll know the truth."

Grundle turned to the one-way mirror. "Turn that shit off and leave us." He waited a few moments then stuck his nose in my face. "Goddamn it, O'Shea. What the fuck were you thinking? Undercover means undercover, not take cover. You've been a one-man wrecking crew out there."

"You gave me a job to do."

"Did you have to use a nuclear blast?"

"Geiger lost his temper."

"And UltraGen? You blew it to smithereens."

"I..." My first instinct was to deny responsibility and finger the Reaper, but he was in enough trouble. As far as I was concerned, the end justified the means. "I don't know how that happened."

The captain paced to the door and back to my face. "My guess is you and Duke and a bunch of your Dex friends put together a vigilante strike force, trespassed on UltraGen's property, and blew the place up."

"Not exactly."

He leaned over me. "Then tell me, O'Shea, exactly."

"Jonathan Ford wanted everyone to think he was looking for a cure for the Dexes, but in reality he created a drug based on the original retrovirus. Vitamin C. Cobalt. His plan was to infect the population and cure the Dexes, making money on both ends."

"That's a pretty serious charge. You got any proof?"

I blinked. Whatever proof there was, the Reaper had destroyed it. "No. But I do have a sample of the drug." I removed the vial from my inside coat pocket.

He reached to grab it, but I locked it in my fist. "The other one is being analyzed. Dr. Quarks hopes to find an antidote."

"That guy scares me."

I re-pocketed the vial. "The scary guy is Plague."

The captain turned white. "What's he got to do with this?"

"Jonathan Ford created the image of UltraGen

as a charitable company, invaluable to the third world, but he conspired with Plague to make villagers sick. UltraGen swooped in and cured them. Ford got world-wide support, investors were happy, stocks sored and tons of money went into Ford's pocket."

"How did you get this information?"

"Confidential sources." Again I'd covered for the Reaper.

"Are you saying you saw Plague and Ford together?"

"No, but I saw Plague in a basement lab that belonged to Ford. I'm sure they both died in the explosion."

"Recovery teams are still pulling bodies from the rubble. No sign of either, yet."

"When the men reach the basement, they better wear hazmat suits."

The captain ran his hand down his face. "What a fuckin' mess."

"Captain, I did my job. The drug lab is out of business. No more new Dexes to terrorize the city. That's what you wanted. That's what the mayor wanted. It's done."

"Oh yeah, then tell me this, smart guy." He bent to my face again. "What's this I hear about the Chessman?"

"He's the mastermind behind The Brawl."

"Duke briefed me on that theory. Tell me something I don't know, like who is he?"

He had me stumped on that one. I shrugged.

The captain stepped up to American Eagle. "We've got to pull him out from undercover. Give him his gun back. Give him a medal. Get him back on the street to find the Chessman."

My eyebrows shot up.

"I agree." American Eagle fluttered up to me and produced Buck Rogers. "O'Shea, I don't know how you do it, fall in a bucket of shit and come out smelling like a rose."

He wouldn't have said that if he knew the bucket my love life was in.

"But let's get one thing straight. This is my squad now, so unless you want to be busted down to meter maid, you better toe the line. No more bodies. No more warehouse fires. No more explosions. Do we have an understanding?"

I wrapped my hand around Buck Rogers, glad to have at least one friend in this world. "I'll try, Lieutenant."

Chapter Thirty-Seven

*J*reedom felt good. Before I got my ass into another jam, I figured it was time to meet Dani's family, after all, I was the father of Fernando Reyes' grandchild. However, a cop among thieves and drug dealers would not make us a family. I knew that, Dani knew that, but we went anyway.

The Reyes' property rested on the edge of Stonington Borough, a thirty-minute trip from New London. It's a quaint place, but the idyllic New England setting could have used Martha Stewart's decorating skills. The niche shops, historic buildings, and home-style restaurants liberally displayed the typical autumn ornaments of Indian corn, bundled husks, carved pumpkins, and hay bales. The air had an earthy smell filled with the sweetness of fallen leaves and the delicious aroma of apple cider.

The estate itself was roughly the size of Texas and contained a main house, winery, and several guest villas with names like the Gate House, the Harvest Barn, and the Tack Room. Winery folks gave tours and hosted many charitable events.

This time of year the trees were barren and the grape vines dormant. Summer-lavish lawns had turned brown, and the gardens had been tilled for winter. Well-trimmed holly bushes boasted the only green that remained. An array of scarecrows had been planted throughout the grounds in preparation for the Halloween haunted hayrides and other fall festivities.

I parked the Challenger at the winery, and Dani led me into the building. A very attractive woman met us at the door. She wore a blue and red tartan blazer and slacks, which appeared to be the standard uniform of the winery. "Miss Reyes, so wonderful to see you."

Dani introduced me to Emily and we shook hands. She took us downstairs. Stacks of barrels added a rich smoky flavor to the wine and gave the cellar air a pleasing aroma that teased the senses.

Several men had arranged themselves around an oak barrel. Each held a wineglass filled with a deep red liquid. I could see that the bunghole had been opened, and an oak ladle rested on the barrel rim. Everyone appeared to be guests of the eldest man of the bunch, whom I took to be Fernando Reyes.

He looked up as we approached, and at seeing his daughter, his face lit up in a broad grin. "Dani." He stood, hugged her, and kissed her on each cheek. "How's my little ragazza?"

"I'm not your little girl anymore, papà."

Fernando stood five-foot-nine and looked comfortably overweight. His thick but well-trimmed mustache was as salt-and-peppered as his hair. I could see where Dani got her dark brown eyes. He cupped the sides of her face. "I'm so happy to see you." Then he cast me a sideways glance. "Who is this now, another putz you bring home?"

"Father, this is Rick O'Shea."

He regarded me for a long moment and then accepted my offered handshake. His bony grip was like the Reaper's hand at my throat. The killer of a wife and son, by Dr. Brooks' account, shook my hand so long I feared I'd get it back dead. As I sized up the man who once led the cartel, I realized he was sizing me up just as hard.

"You are that detective I hear about on the news."

I wanted to say, and you're the murderer I heard about, but instead I elected to live another day. "I hear stories about you too, sir."

"What kind of stories do you hear, Officer O'Shea?"

"I'd rather not answer that and keep this meeting pleasant," I nodded to Dani, "for her sake."

"Stories," he grumped. "I prefer to take measure of a man when I look him in the eye and shake his hand."

"I agree."

He finally let go of my hand. "You brought my Danielle to me and for this I am grateful. That you are a cop is regrettable."

"We all have our crosses to bear."

"Let's walk to the house. We can have lunch."

Dani responded before I had a chance to refuse. "We'd like that."

"Excellent." He beamed. "If you will follow me."

Dani looped her arm in his, and they made small talk on the trek across the grounds.

I looked around. The outer buildings were hallmarks of a world-class resort. While the main house had the façade of an old-world estate, it was nothing less than a fortress of high walls, barred windows, and embrasures. Cameras tracked our movement, and I was sure motion detectors were hidden among the harvest decorations. A staff of armed security posed as gardeners and attendants. They blended with the scenery as flawlessly as the hedges and sugar-maples.

Fernando led us up to the veranda, and we stepped inside Chateau Reyes.

Opulent didn't begin to describe the main house. Gleaming black-and-white marble created an intricate pattern in the floor. Tapestries and paintings I'd expect to see in museums adorned the walls. Rich dark-wood trim framed the room in glorious fashion, all speckled with light from a crystal chandelier.

Dani reached up and gently closed my gaping jaw.

Fernando grumped and led us farther into the palace. He spoke a few words to a tall and sober-looking man standing idly by. "This is Javier. He will show you where to wash up."

Javier gave us a short bow.

"What happened to Simon?" Dani asked her father.

"It is with deep sadness to say Simon is no

longer with us."

I was probably better off not knowing what he meant by that.

Fernando left us with Javier who showed us to a suite where we could freshen up. "Lunch will be served in twenty minutes just down the hall. I believe Miss Dani knows where."

"Thank you, Javier." She dismissed him.

The sink was shiny and round and engraved with Roman images. I washed my hands with lavender soap. "You grew up here?"

"Yes."

"Jezze, my place must've looked like a third world dump to you."

She didn't respond, just dipped her hands in the flow of faucet water.

I flicked water from hands. "So your father runs everything from here?"

"Geraldo does most of the work now."

"So he's the kingpin?"

"He's a threat to my father, but father doesn't see it."

I dried my hands with an Egyptian cotton towel. "So your father knows little about Geraldo and his dealings with Ford?"

Dani snatched the towel from my hands. "He

knows nothing."

"He knew about the armored car shipment."

"Geraldo, he knew and ran to my father for help. My father came to me for help."

"And you helped yourself to the briefcase to help your father go straight. I think you're delusional."

"Damn it, Rick. Don't you ever stop being a cop?"

"Not where you and my baby are concerned."

"Let me worry about me and the baby. Go back to Pink Panther. You two deserve each other."

"If this cartel comes crashing down, I want to be sure you're not under the shit pile."

Or worse, dead at the hands of Geraldo Diaz, as I was sure had been the fate of *no-longer-with-us* Simon.

***

Dani and I seated ourselves at a small table in a cozy nook. The area seemed more informal, like where the family would eat when not entertaining. Four places had been set. I saw the number of place settings and frowned. "Is your mother here?"

"No, she's shopping in New York. She won't be back until tomorrow."

"So who is joining us for lunch?"

My answer came soon enough. Fernando walked in with another man, a little taller and a lot leaner. While Fernando seemed relaxed and at ease in his white silk shirt, the man with him walked with squared shoulders and moved like a jackal. A scraggly beard did a lousy job of hiding his pockmarked face. He wore a business suit that didn't come off a Walmart rack and showed that he knew how to dress the part of a cartel thug. The most striking thing about him was his eyes. They were cold, dead eyes, gray and pinched, the kind of eyes that belonged to a reptile.

We stood as the men approached. The thug strode to Dani, they hugged awkwardly, and he came away smiling. "It's been too long, Danielle."

"Why, Geraldo, what makes you think that?"

Oh there you go, poke the big snake. She had no fear.

She gestured to me. "This is Detective Rick O'Shea from the NLPD."

"STF, really." I'd said it to make sure Geraldo knew I wasn't just an ordinary beat cop.

He bobbed his chin.

I returned the gesture. "Geraldo Diaz I presume."

"Do you know me?"

"By reputation only."

"What do you know? My name is known far and wide."

So was mud, but I kept my mouth shut.

We sat down, stiffly not casually. A pasta dish was served, some garlic bread, and of course, a sommelier brought the wine.

I stopped his pour at half an inch in my glass.

Geraldo pierced me with a dagger stare. "You look uncomfortable, Officer O'Shea. I hope it's not our wine that displeases you." He showed me his teeth. "Or our company."

"Nothing like that, I assure you."

"Then what brings you here, detective? Hopefully not your work."

If this trip was work related, I'd have already shot the bastard. "Actually, this visit is personal. Dani and I were hoping to speak with her father privately."

"What's this privately about?"

"Privately means it's none of your business."

Dani put her hand on my arm. "We'll tell him

another time, Rick."

"Tell me what?" Fernando set down his fork. "You may speak freely in front of Geraldo. We have no secrets."

Sure they did. "Like she said, maybe next time."

"Speak your mind," Fernando insisted, and when he insisted on something, his voice took on the menacing quality of a rabid dog.

"It's okay, Rick." She patted my arm and withdrew her hand. "Papà..." Dani smiled at him. "I'm pregnant."

Geraldo coughed up his pasta.

I held my breath, expecting all hell to break loose.

But Fernando's face lit up like an Easter sunrise. "Well, I'll be damned. I am going to be a grandfather." Then the happy sun sank in his eyes, and he shot me an accusatory glare. "And you are the father of this child?"

I nodded and let go of my breath.

His lower lip quivered as he glanced back and forth between Dani and me. "So when is the wedding?"

Our faces became uniformly grim.

"What? There is a problem?"

I decided to deliver the punch line. "We're not a couple anymore."

"We have a lot of problems to overcome," Dani added.

"Problems?" Fernando slammed his fist on the table, making the dishes jump. "Solve these problems. And quickly."

"Papà, please. Be calm."

I didn't like his tone but the picture was clear. He was used to getting what he wanted. And quicky.

"Mi scusi." Geraldo excused himself, probably wishing he had not imposed on our privacy. He took his plate and wineglass with him.

"See?" Fernando fumed. "You have upset my guest." He picked up his fork and stabbed his pasta. "A nice lunch is all I ask, and you bring me problems. Why do you do this to me, Dani? Tell me good news. Tell me bad news. And you let this cop put his hands on you? You know how I hate cops."

"That's why I never told you about Rick."

"Don't feel bad, sir," I put in. "She didn't tell me about you either."

That earned me a burning glare. She retaliated with, "He has another girlfriend already."

Reyes stood and pointed a stiff finger at me. "You reject my Dani, the mother of your child, for another woman? I should kill you where you sit."

I stood to meet his challenge. "No matter what happens, I'll always be there for them. You have my word. But we cannot be together because we don't trust each other."

He regarded me for another long minute, then: "Trust is everything. I believe you," and he returned to his seat. "Please, sit, finish your lunch. Maybe tomorrow you will have come to your senses and marry my daughter as any honorable man would do." He chucked a forkful of pasta, leaving a smear of marinara on his lips. "You can trust her later."

I sat down but didn't feel like eating another bite. "Fernando, sir, I have a favor to ask of you."

"What's this favor?" He sipped wine.

"At the risk of making your daughter angry, I want her to stay here for a while, under your protection. I believe she is still in danger."

"Rick," she shouted. "You told me—"

"I know what I told you, but until Jonathan Ford's body is positively identified, I don't want you out there."

"I can take care of myself."

"See?" Fernando set down his wineglass. "It is settled. She doesn't need or want protection."

"I'm talking about the safety of your grandchild, not what Dani needs or wants."

"You're asking me to keep her here against her will?"

"That's right. Until I know it's safe for her to go back home."

He nodded. "Very well, for my grandchild, I will agree."

"Papà."

"I have decided. Now eat your lunch, both of you."

Dani stuck her tongue out at me.

Like father like daughter, they were both used to getting their own way.

My kid's safety had trumped them both. *Voila.*

Chapter Thirty-Eight

*T*he next day I was happy to be back in my office and far from Fernando Reyes and his cartel-financed lifestyle. He was proof that crime paid, in spades. The thought of one day calling him father-in-law turned my stomach. Dani and I were farther apart than ever.

The latest coroner's report lay on my desk, a list of casualties pulled from the bombed out UltraGen complex and positively identified. Jonathan Ford's name was not listed, nor the Dexes: Tink, Ruff 'N Tuff, or Plague. The death toll was at eighty-nine. There'd been no survivors found. When the Reaper reaped, he took all their souls.

A gut feeling hit me. No body of Jonathan Ford meant no safety. I wanted to be sure Dani was all right. I called her phone. It rang and rang and went to voice mail. I left a message. "Call me."

I slammed down the phone.

That got Duke's attention. "What's up?"

"I can't get hold of Dani."

"So?"

The worst part was the not knowing where she was, if she was all right. For all I knew she could have been drinking tea or taking a bubble bath. But I had to be sure. "Get your gear."

"Where we going?"

I threw on my trench coat. "The Reyes Estate."

"Right behind you, partner." He strapped on his vest.

We bolted toward the parking garage and ran smack into America Eagle. "Just the two guys I'm looking for."

"Can it wait?"

"Pink Panther, Ramirez, and Jensen have a situation at the mall."

"Shopping?"

"Another Dex riot."

"Fuck, Eagle, we don't have time for this."

"Deploy, and that's an order."

I was about to pluck his feathers when Duke grabbed my arm. "Easy, hotshot. We'll keep trying to reach her on the phone. Meanwhile—"

"I know. Keep the Dexes under control."

We took Duke's official car, a Ford Police Interceptor, cramped but classy and fast. Chatter on the radio was frantic. "Officer down," came through.

"What the hell's going on?"

Duke hit the siren. "I bet the Chessman is at it again."

"Makes no sense. What for?"

"Cover another heist is my guess."

"At the mall, what's to steal, gumball machines and ladies lingerie?"

The Interceptor careened to a stop next to the SWAT van. Armed riot officers in full gear were already deployed and forming a line to mount an assault through the front doors. The mall was decked out for Halloween shoppers: ghosts and goblins, black cats and bats, jack-o-lanterns and flying witches everywhere.

Duke started barking orders, as usual. "I want squads at all exits."

American Eagle landed in a flurry of wind and feathers.

Then the unthinkable: Ramirez staggered from the mall entrance. She cradled her bloody left arm. Her uniform hung in bloody shreds. She made it ten feet before she collapsed.

"Officer down!" a shout went out, but I was already running to her. I scooped her up and ran back to the line.

My adrenalin pumped so fast that she felt as light as a child. A gurney stood by and I hefted her onto it.

"Jensen's...hurt pretty bad," She managed. "Not like these...scratches. You need to get to...him."

"And Pink Panther, is she all right?"

"Haven't seen..." her eyes rolled back in their sockets.

"Ramirez, you don't have permission to die."

Paramedics rushed her to the ambulance, and it left in a fury of lights and sirens.

"I'm going in," I told Duke and pulled my pulse pistol.

"Get back here, O'Shea," American Eagle shouted from somewhere behind me, but I entered the mall anyway. Duke fell in step alongside me. We could cover each other better that way.

Groups of shoppers cowered everywhere, as if they were too afraid to make a break for the exits. We motioned them to go. Some did. Some didn't have the nerve to move.

We cleared the north wing and stalked

deeper inside. The sound of rioting got louder up ahead. A little farther down a loud crash echoed the length of the mall followed by a choking cloud of dust. The roof had caved in.

I hadn't seen any sign of Panther or Jensen.

A gigantic hammer head crashed through the wall. Duke and I dove for cover behind a cookie shop counter. "What the fuck was that?"

I peeked around the corner in time to see a giant muscleman dressed in brown spandex and Viking leather. He wore a horned helmet, a long beard, and a nasty snarl. I ducked back down with Duke. "It's Thor."

"That's a new one."

"Gotta give the new Dexes credit for non-originality."

"How we gonna stop him?"

I took another peek and saw, to my horror, where he was headed. Legs askew, Jensen lay sprawled out in front of a Chinese restaurant. Worse, Pink Panther hunkered down over him, as if she could protect him from the approaching hulk.

"Shit!"

Buck Rogers to the rescue. I hit Thor with a plasma beam, which quickly encased him in a translucent bubble. He went crazy, swinging that hammer, but the force field held.

"Go," I shouted to Duke.

He took off toward Jensen, but slowed as he circumvented the undulating bubble, almost tiptoed past it, his eyes wide and glued to it as if it might pop at any second.

By the time he got to Jensen, Pink Panther had already slung him over her shoulder.

"Cover her on the way out."

We saluted each other with our gun barrels. He went north. I went south toward the food court.

It opened up to a cavernous room with a glass and wood-beamed ceiling. Tables and chairs were tossed about, not a single one properly standing, and food substances dripped from every surface. There had to be a dozen or more teenage Dexes perpetrating the world's largest food fight. They wore gang colors: green and orange spandex with matching bandanas.

Over the fray I heard a buzzing sound. From out of the glass ceiling's glare dropped a hovering figure, her dragonfly wings a blur. She was dressed in green lingerie and wore dangerously spiked high heels. The last time I saw her, she was shot down by flying debris, just before a building fell on her.

"Tink!"

"Good evening, Officer O'Shea," she said in a saccharine-sweet voice. "I've been expecting you." She laughed a shrill laugh.

I set my pulse pistol to T-Rex and took aim. She was buzzing around like a damn fly, damn hard to get a bead on her, and then everything went black.

Chapter Thirty-Nine

*R*ule *number one of police work: don't do stupid shit.*

When I awoke from my impromptu concussion, a beautiful woman in sexy green lingerie had me pinned down and straddled. Normally, I would approve of such things, but she greeted me by biting my lip so hard it bled.

All I could do was grit my teeth and hope she wouldn't get past them and bite off my tongue. My head hurt, and the floor let me know my skull had grown a lump the size of Stone Mountain, Georgia. She held me down with surprising super-strength and rubbed her bottom on my manly body part. The little guy was scared shitless and kept his head down.

I managed to yank my lips from her teeth and paid the price with more pain. The nanites actually tickled the sensitive skin of my lip as they went to work erasing Tink's teeth marks. A sideways glance located Buck Rogers lying dead on the floor next to me. If I could only get my hands on it, but she had my arms pinned to my body with her hot little thighs. One question kept clawing at the neurons in my brain. Why was I still alive?

"Hello again, O'Shea." She giggled. "I found what I want in my stocking for Christmas." With a lizard-like tongue, she licked my bloody lip. "I hope you don't break easily."

"I saw you go down like a kamikaze...I thought you were dead."

"You're going to wish I was dead."

"I already do...how'd you get out of that building alive?"

"Same as the others."

"Others? Who else?"

"You're the detective. You figure it out."

Then I knew the recovery teams were not going to find Jonathan Ford's body in the rubble. "Fuck!"

"All right." She nibbled at the tip of my nose and then kissed it tenderly.

"You are one crazy little bitch, Evil Tink."

"That's between me and my psychotherapist." She giggled that stupid giggle again. "Oh, and he says I'm certifiable." She head-butted me. Blood splattered and pain blinded me.

"You broke my nose, goddamn you."

"Aw, so you *do* break easily. What a shame."

I pushed my hips up with all my strength and tried to buck her off, but she had me locked down tight. My nose throbbed. "Do you always play this rough?"

"You ain't seen nothin' yet, Rickie."

"Why don't we get to know each other better? I'm not Rickie, I'm Rick, as in Detective Rick O'Shea of the STF, and you are under arrest for assault on a police officer."

"Shut the fuck up!"

"So I guess marrying me is out of the question."

She lunged forward and grabbed my throat. The weight shift freed up my left arm enough that I was able to pull it free and give her a swift left hook to the jaw. Normally that would have rung anyone's bell, but she didn't flinch.

"Rickie, Rickie, Rickie, why did you have to do something so stupid?" She pinned both my hands to the floor, jumped up off me, and came back down, knee to my crotch.

And there was the penalty for doing stupid

shit. I thought my eyeballs would pop out of their sockets, screaming bloody murder. Her knee stole my breath and probably my next three kids. And to add insult to injury, she sat on me and rode me hard; each thrust of her crotch against mine delivered a new level of agony. If I were those nanites, I wouldn't go anywhere near the place she was tearing up.

Her body shuddered, and she thrust her head back and cried out in orgasmic bliss, well, if a cat could have an orgasm with its tail caught in the door. I could do nothing but endure her pseudo-erotic antics. Talk about a turn off.

When she settled down, she gazed at me with dreamy eyes. "I can see why Pink Panther likes you. You just don't give up, do you?"

"It's a character flaw. Who the hell hit me?"

"Ruff 'N Tuff, of course."

I'd seen him get splattered to four points of the compass. And he wasn't dead? What the fuck? "Where is the little prick?"

"When you get angry I get so fucking hot." She pressed her lips to mine and then licked blood off my face. "I just might marry you after all."

"Actually, I have enough women problems right now."

She buzzed her dragonfly wings. "I hear your dance card is about to open up."

"Dance card?"

"Dani dance card."

"Dani?"

"Poor pregnant Dani."

I saw red. "If even one hair on her head gets ruffled, there won't be a spot on this planet where you can hide from me. I'll find you. I'll kill you. And I'll cut you up in so many tiny pieces there won't be enough left to dust off a mantel."

"Let me make you a counteroffer, O'Shea. Jonathan Ford wants his briefcase back, the one with the two vials and the formula for Cobalt."

So the bastard got out with his life but not his livelihood. "He doesn't have any left, does he?"

"When you blew up his lab, he lost everything."

I was about to tell her it wasn't my doing, that the Reaper had done it, but decided not to waste my breath.

"If you don't return what's rightfully his, consider your life fucked, O'Shea."

"My life is already fucked."

"And Dani's, and your baby's, and...hold still, you'll want to see this..." She let my hands go and showed me her cell phone, a picture...no a video...of Dani, gagged and tied to a chair, and next to her the incomparable Fernando Reyes in the same situation.

Kidnapped from the Reyes estate, the guarded fortress? "How the hell did that happen?"

"My boss, Jonathan Ford, has a very dear friend in the cartel."

"Geraldo Diaz, that backstabbing son of a bitch."

"Wait for it." She indicated the video, which panned the room and landed on none other than Plague himself, in all his puss-and-boil glory.

Those fuckers were like bad dreams, they kept coming back. I wanted to scream.

Tink giggled. "You have exactly one hour to deliver the briefcase. Dani goes free and you can go on with your fucked life, O'Shea."

"Where do I deliver it?"

She patted my cheek. "Good boy. Bring it to State Street, behind the haul-away trash bins. Someone will be there."

"Ford?"

"I don't have to tell you to be alone and unarmed."

"Is Ford going to be there?"

"Once the contents have been verified, you will be given an address where you can pick-up your honey-pie and baby-pooh. No tricks, you hear?"

"And Fernando, him too."

"I think Geraldo has other plans for him."

Simon's fate came to mind. "Both of them or no deal."

Her dragonfly wings buzzed like a squadron of Zero's over Pearl Harbor. "O'Shea, you're not into the whole team spirit, are you?"

"Fuck you, Tink."

"No thanks. I've had enough...for now."

"I get both of them or Ford gets nothing."

"Be a shame for mother and baby to die because you're a stubborn son of a bitch."

How familiar did that sound? According to Dani, Geraldo was running the cartel. Not Fernando. So it was Geraldo who killed Brooks' wife and son. The Reaper had it wrong. Fernando might have done a lot of bad things, but murdering Brooks' family wasn't one of them. Only now would Fernando learn the true nature of Geraldo's treachery.

Tink hovered above me. "By the way, your

hour started three minutes ago, O'Shea." Then she flitted away like the end of a Disney movie.

Somehow I had to rescue them both and put Geraldo Diaz in his place, preferably six feet under.

Chapter Forty

I emerged from the mall into a huge crowd of people. A line of uniformed officers helped funnel them out of the area. SWAT had rolled the plasma ball out to the parking lot. Thor sat on his hammer, sucking his thumb and bawling like a baby. He claimed he had no idea how he got to the mall, had no memory of what he'd done. Familiar story. The Chessman was definitely behind this riot.

American Eagle came bounding toward me, feathers flying and shouting at me, "Stop, O'Shea. I want a full report."

"Get out of my way."

He wouldn't move so I shot him with my plasma gun. "Sue me." I ran toward Duke's Interceptor.

He ran up behind me. "Rick, have you gone crazy?"

"I have forty-nine minutes to deliver a

package or Dani and my baby are going to die."

"Baby?"

"It's a long story."

"What happened to your nose?"

"Another long story." I jumped in the Interceptor.

"Where are you going with my car?"

"Dr. Quarks." I started the engine.

"What about Thor and American Eagle? We can't leave them like this."

"Hit 'em with a CO_2 fire extinguisher. It'll freeze the bubbles and they'll crumble." I threw the shifter in reverse.

"I don't like you running off like this, O'Shea."

"You don't have to. Just stay out of my way."

I tore out of the parking lot and flipped on the lights and siren, but even with those, traffic was problematic. The roads were jammed with vehicles, people fleeing the mall as others rushed in to take a look. Getting to Jefferson Avenue required a few dents in Duke's bumper. He could sue me too.

I'd chewed up twenty-two minutes getting to Dr. Quarks. I spent half that time on the phone explaining to him what I needed. The sky was already getting dark by the time I careened up to his front curb.

Hana let me in without any hassle about my coat. Shana probably fixed the problem with her programming. My nose felt better, my lip was healed, and the bump on the back of my head had shrunk to the size of a grapefruit.

Quarks met me in the study, set a briefcase on the desk.

"Doc, you did it."

"Exact replica. I printed it on my 3-D printer from a photo I got online."

I dug the blue vial out of my pocket.

He opened the briefcase and set my vial alongside his. "Sorry I didn't have time to make an antidote."

"I'll get it back to you as soon as I can."

He grumped. "No rush. It's colored water. I put the real stuff in a flask."

"And the formula?" I pointed to the envelope.

"A mathematical equation I wrote in college. Only a chemist can read it."

I got a cold chill. "Look, doc, if Ford finds out this is phony baloney before I get Dani back, he'll kill her."

"Then be sure you get her back first." Quark presented me with a familiar disc, the one with the red button in the center. "Take this. If you get in trouble and your life is in immediate and terrible danger—"

"I know, push the button." I wasn't looking forward to that ride again.

"I've set the GPS to take you back to the police station. Good luck, my friend."

Luck? What the fuck was that?

Chapter Forty-One

I had eleven minutes to make five miles. Dani's life meant everything to me, as did the little life growing inside her. It wasn't love that drove me, but the instinct to survive, to procreate, to leave someone on this earth more important than myself. Nothing would stop me from making this delivery. Jonathan Ford had to have known that, and no doubt he counted on my fatherly instincts, as well.

I weaved in and out of traffic, and when I got to State Street, I turned off the sirens and lights and navigated toward the area where the haul-away trash bins were stored. Construction had traffic at a standstill. I parked the car, grabbed the briefcase, and ran the rest of the way to the rendezvous point.

Crews had worked nonstop on State Street since The Brawl. Most of the large rubble had been cleared, and I had nothing impeding my way to the meeting spot. When I got there, no one was around. I checked the time. I was two minutes late.

"Goddamn it," I shouted. "I got hung up in traffic. Like that's never happened to you." I turned a circle, heard my voice echo. No response.

Up until that moment, I hadn't given much thought to what being a father really meant. Only now, at this very moment, when Dani and my baby were being murdered, did fatherhood actually dawn on me. What could have been was suddenly and irrevocably gone. That smiling face in the crib, looking up and mommy and daddy, the smell of baby powder, the thrill of first steps, first days at school, first loves, first proms. All gone.

I felt like slamming the briefcase to the dirt. Oh now I knew exactly how Dr. Brooks felt and why he poisoned himself with the drug to become the Reaper and sought revenge for his family, just as I would do from here on out, until Jonathan Ford and all his cronies were dust in the wind. I didn't know if I was blinded by rage or heartbreak, but whatever it was that drove me to open that briefcase and remove the blue vial, the real one, I would never know, because as I began to unscrew the lid, a synthesized voice stopped me.

"I wouldn't do that, detective."

I turned slowly to see the Reaper standing there, the deadly scythe held across his robed body. My next breath damn near choked me. That didn't make sense. The Reaper was Dr. Brooks, not Jonathan Ford.

"Surprised to see me?" The jaw moved out of sync with the words.

"Shocked."

If he looked like the Reaper and sounded like the Reaper, he had to be the Reaper.

"Don't worry. I'm not here to kill you."

"That's a relief." The Reaper was working for Ford. Hell, that made even less sense. He just blew up UltraGen.

"You have something that belongs to me."

"Oh." I returned the vial to its place in the briefcase and closed the lid. "Take it and we'll both be on our merry way." Kind of an inside joke. I handed him the briefcase.

"You must be very angry."

"I just want Dani back, my baby safe, so we can be on our merry way."

"And when you thought my boss had killed

her because you were late, tell me, were you thinking what I think you were thinking?"

"I was pissed enough to turn myself into a Dex so I'd have some kind of superpower to fight back with."

"That's enough to convince me the contents are real."

"Of course they're real. As long as she's safe, I'll be on my merry way."

"She's fine."

"Merry way, get it?"

"Her father will not be so fortunate."

He didn't get it. "Fernando didn't kill your family. Geraldo Diaz did it. Let the old man go home."

"You don't know what you're talking about. Diaz is my boss's inside man at the cartel."

I felt like I was talking to a complete stranger. My gut told me I was face-to-face with the copycat Reaper. Paige Greene's killer. But I couldn't do a damn thing about it until I knew Dani was safe. "Where is she?"

"The warehouse district. Number thirty-eight." He turned to leave.

I couldn't just let him walk away. "Wait."

"Our business is finished. Go get your

girlfriend."

"The briefcase." Thinking on my feet, I ran up to him. "It's got a dead-man switch in the lid."

"What are you trying to pull, O'Shea? You had the lid open when I saw you."

"But you didn't see this." I showed him the teleport disc. "It overrides the switch."

"And what happens if I open the briefcase without it? Will it blow me up? How trite."

"No. It'll trigger a mechanism that contaminates the samples and renders them inert. Unusable. Lost forever." I hoped he didn't know the difference between brilliance and bullshit. "My boss didn't want you to get usable samples, but here, take it. Press the button before you open the briefcase. Your samples will be all right."

"Why are you telling me this?"

"Reaper, I've got a lot of scores to settle with you, but right now, because you haven't harmed Dani and my unborn baby, I owe you the truth and a thank you." Saying those words almost made me puke.

He took the disc. "You're all right, O'Shea. I don't give a damn what everybody else says about you."

"We'll be seeing each other real soon."

"To better days."

He disappeared into the darkness, but not like I'd seen him melt into the shadows before.

"Merry ways," I called after him. This clown was definitely a fake, maybe the Chessman, maybe Plague, or Jonathan Ford himself. Whoever opened that briefcase would be in for a big surprise.

***

Warehouse number thirty-eight was two buildings down from the burned out husk the Arsonist had torched. I drove past the hole in the asphalt the kid had made with a push of his hand. Whatever happened to him, I didn't know, but he probably died while he was still in that coma.

I stopped at thirty-eight and turned off the engine. The place could have been a cemetery, it was that quiet.

When I slid open the warehouse door, it made a hell of a squealing noise. No way could I sneak in. I drew Buck Rogers and carefully stepped inside. In the middle of an open floor space stood Ruff 'N Tuff, fists on his hips and mean on his face.

"What are you doing here, runt?" I walked

up to the dwarf.

"You like the knot I left on the back of your head, O'Shea?"

"I liked it less when I woke up." I trained my weapon on him, but we both knew that it didn't mean much. "How did you survive that explosion? I saw a chunk of concrete take you out."

"Trade secret, but if it wasn't for my boss's plasma shield, the outcome would have been much different."

So Ford had something like Buck Rogers to shield himself and his cronies. I could believe that. Quarks didn't have the corner market on techno-toys, and Ford had the ability to create force fields, though Martin's plasma bubble was on a much larger scale.

"All right. Let's get this over with. Where are they?"

"I'll take you to the Reyes bitch and her dad."

Bitch would have gotten him killed on any other day. Well, I liked to think that anyway. I followed him through a maze of racks filled with crates and pallets. We stopped at a door. "They're inside here."

"Go get them, bring 'em out."

"Go fuck yourself."

"Hey, I made a deal with your boss."

"Ford don't own me. I ain't going in there." I actually saw terror in his bug-eyes.

"Why? What's in there?"

He pushed open the door and stepped back. "See for yourself."

As promised, Dani and her father were exactly where I saw them on Tink's phone video. Plague stood behind them in quiet contempt.

I trained Buck Rogers on Plague. "First the girl, runt. Untie her."

"Don't look at me," Ruff 'N Tuff said.

"Plague's not going to move. Ain't that right, Plague? He knows what this gun will do to him."

The runt stumped over and untied Dani.

I called to her from the doorway. "Dani, come on."

She rushed out of the room and stood behind me. "Thank God you're here."

"Now her father, runt."

Ruff 'N Tuff started toward him, but when Plague laid a boil-infested hand on Fernando's shoulder, Ruff 'N Tuff froze in his tracks.

Dani's father went completely pale.

"Don't," I shouted at Plague.

He showed me his blackened teeth, some gruesome attempt at a smile. "Mr. Ford doesn't need him anymore."

Dani started toward her father. "Papà."

I held her back. "It's too late."

"No!" she cried.

"I gather Geraldo Diaz is the true criminal mind in the Reyes cartel."

"Sorry, just business," Plague hissed.

Fernando slumped over. If not for the ropes, he'd have crashed to the concrete floor. His last breath gurgled from his suddenly diseased lungs.

"Father!"

I had just witnessed the true angel of death at work. "Back up, Dani, and you too, runt. Let's go."

"But my dad—"

"We'll recover his body later."

"Fuck, O'Shea!" Ruff 'N Tuff's mouth hung open. "You just gonna let Plague get away?"

A plasma bubble wouldn't hold him for very long and I wasn't getting anywhere near that fucker.

"It's done."

I had to get back to the station.

Chapter Forty-Two

I met Duke in the hall. He held two cups of coffee. "You that tired?"

He handed me a cup. "Rick, you don't look like a fresh spring day either."

"Did you get everything locked down at the mall?"

"Those poor kids, they had no clue how they ended up in gang colors and the food fight from hell."

I sipped the coffee, damn near burned my lip. I guess it was still sensitive since Tink's affectionate kiss. "The Chessman was at it again."

"Looks like it. Is there any way we can shut down that Dex Territory website?"

"Not unless we can prove the Chessman is using it illegally. Otherwise it's just a harmless fantasy superhero league game."

"Yeah." He looked into his coffee as if it were a crystal ball. "We're living in Dex Territory anyway. Everywhere you look, Dexes and more Dexes."

"Including our new boss."

"Man, you really ruffled his feathers with that last stunt you pulled."

"Fuck him if he can't take a joke."

"I'm not as young as I used to be and all this excitement is kicking my ass. Its days like this that make me think it's time to quit, find a nice job selling ladies' shoes."

"Then how would any real police work get done around here? Besides, we're down a couple officers...with Jensen ambulatory with two broken legs and Ramirez's broken arm."

"Maybe next year."

"At the end of the day we have a shit load of unsolved crimes, not enough arrests, a bunch of casualties, and millions of dollars' worth of property damage. Where else can you have this much fun?"

We both laughed.

A popping sound stopped us. I knew that sound. It came from the squad room.

"What was that?" Duke jumped to full alert.

"Come on, early Christmas present." I ran as fast as I could down the short hall, weapon drawn, as did everyone else.

"Freeze!" I heard someone command.

"Put the weapon down now!"

A chorus of similar commands echoed through the room.

By the time I got there, a sea of uniformed and plain clothes officers swarmed an area toward the back of the room.

I saw a flash of steel then something metallic clanged on the floor. Someone kicked the weapon out of the fray, and it slid toward me. My heart pounded when I saw the wicked-looking scythe skid to a halt. But I knew this scythe was a hoax. The real one had some kind of defense mechanism. It would have broken into slivers and been long gone by now. The copycat had fallen into my lap.

"Don't touch him!" I shouted.

I rushed in and pushed officers out of the way. "He's my prisoner. Everyone back! Now!"

They all backed up and gave me room. I knelt before the fallen Reaper. "I told you we would meet again soon. Well guess what. I was right."

"I'm not the Reaper," the synthesized voice said calmly.

"Skull mask, black robe, nasty weapon. Let's

have a look." I pushed back his hood and pulled the mask off over the top of his head.

When he looked up, it wasn't the face of Dr. Douglas Brooks that stared at me, but the confused face of Jonathan Ford. He still held Doctor Quarks teleportation remote. "What happened?" Then he saw it in his hand and dropped it like a hot potato. His eyes got big and mean and mad. "You tricked me, you son of a bitch."

Good as any confession. "I finally got your ass."

I called for a neck restraint, the kind dog catchers used when dealing with vicious strays to keep them at a distance.

"Jonathan Ford, you are under arrest for the murder of Paige Greene, seven cartel drug dealers, crimes against humanity and for being an asshole."

"You've got the wrong guy. I'm a pillar of the community."

"You have the right to remain silent. I suggest you use that right, Mr. Ford, because anything you say can and will be used against you in court of law."

"You can't possibly think those charges will

stick."

"You have the right to an attorney. If you can't afford one, one will be appointed by the court for you. But we know you can afford an army of attorneys, now don't we."

"I'll have your badge for this, O'Shea."

"Body search him," I instructed my men.

"Right here, sir?"

"I want to make sure he's got no aces up his sleeves or tricks up his ass." Like a personal plasma shield generator. "Send his clothes and the scythe to forensics. I'm betting we'll find DNA from Paige Greene and the other Reaper victims."

All that really mattered to me was solving Paige's murder. I knew who was responsible for the others, but for now Dr. Brooks deserved his retribution. I'd do everything within my power to put all the heat on Ford.

Four officers had him stripped and bent over a desk for a cavity search. Robinson snapped on latex gloves.

"I'll kill you for this, O'Shea."

Robinson stepped back. "He's got nothin' on him or in him, sir."

"Get him out of here."

Dog collar and stick in place, the officers

wrestled his naked ass out of the squad room. I could hear him screaming all the way down the hall toward the jail cells. "You can't possibly think you've won, O'Shea."

I rolled my eyes at that.

Duke and I high-fived each other then burst out in laughter.

At the end of the day, this was the most fun ever.

Chapter Forty-Three

*T*he morning of Fernando's funeral turned out gray and cold. I put on my dress uniform. When I stepped outside, the chill hit me right down to the bone. I had on my trench coat over my suit coat over my bulletproof vest, but all that wasn't enough to keep me warm.

I finally met Mrs. Reyes. I wished it were under better circumstances. Dani took after her mom. They had the same fierce dark eyes and rich olive skin. Other than a few gray hairs touching Mrs. Reyes long lustrous locks and a few laugh lines touching her cheeks, the two women could've been mistaken for sisters. They both wore the same stoic expressions.

The ceremony was Catholic and took place at St Paul's Cathedral where the Reyes family attended mass. The priest spoke of Fernando's generosity and involvement in local charities and that his philanthropy was an inspiration to the

City of New London. No mention of him being a mob boss and drug lord.

In the first pew with Mrs. Reyes sat Geraldo Diaz, who looked genuinely upset at his mentor's passing. He wore a tailored black Armani suit. He'd removed the beard and took on a more polished appearance, but I could still see the gangster under the polish. He held Mrs. Reyes like she was a member of his family in need of comfort. Dani sat opposite her mother and wouldn't look at Geraldo. That battle was yet to be fought.

In the back pew sat Pink Panther, Zack, and Talon. Phantasm was around here somewhere, invisible, probably so no one could see him cry. They had no love for Fernando Reyes, but they were there to pay their respects and lend Dani their support, more because I told them to rather than genuine give-a-shit.

Fernando's body had been cremated due to the nature of his death. Inside the closed casket lay the urn, ready for a traditional burial, surrounded by expensive silk and mirrors.

Outside, as the north wind rustled leaves along the stony path to the cemetery, I lingered with Dani. "I'm so sorry about your father."

We hugged.

"Rick," she whispered in my ear. "I can't see you anymore."

My heart thumped in my chest and my throat tightened. "You sure? I think I'm going to make a good dad." I nearly choked on the words.

"I have family business to attend."

The meaning was clear. She was going after control of the cartel. What she planned to do with it wasn't clear. What I didn't like was her going up against Geraldo Diaz, especially on her own, but such were the genes of the Reyes family. They always got their way.

"I'd like to be there when our baby is born."

"I know you want to be in our baby's life, but how can I allow our child to worry sick every night you don't come home, and worry that every morning might be the last morning we see you."

"I'm a cop. That's what I do. Doesn't mean I can't be a father too. It happens all the time."

"Will you quit the force?"

"No."

"Then we both know there's no future for us." She put a finger to her lips and moved it to my cheek. "I need you to be the cop you are now when the cartel comes crashing down. Besides, my world rots people from the inside, and you're too good a man to be a part of that."

"You didn't answer my question. Can I be there when the baby is born?"

"I'm going back to Miami to run things from there. If it's possible, then yes. My guess is you'll be tied up with some case or another and not be able to make it to the hospital anyway."

Her words cut me like a knife. Could I really be that callous to put duty before family? The reason my heart hurt was because she was right. I'd never gotten married. I could never commit half of me to a job and half of me to a wife. It was all or nothing for Rick O'Shea.

I felt a panging loss, though she stood right in front of me. "Take care of yourself."

"You too."

I turned away and walked off. She walked the other direction.

We each had our own problems to attend to.

Chapter Forty-Four

Halloween was one of New London's biggest holidays, and even with the problems and rampant danger that had torn through our streets earlier, the crowd seemed larger this year than in previous years. Somehow, along the way, the normal ghosts and ghouls had been replaced with superhero costumes. A few die-hard goblins prowled the streets in search of treats, but most folks had come downtown for the parade.

I walked the route and ended up standing at the site of the new UltraGen complex. Plans were going forward in spite of the fact that their CEO, Jonathan Ford, was sitting in a cell awaiting trial for the Reaper crimes. The judge had revoked bail based on the severity of the charges and the flight risk Ford posed. He was welcome in every third world country and had the means to get there and hide out, immune from prosecution.

The New London site was a massive piece of

vacant land across the Thames from Groton and the rubble of his original complex. A small area had been cordoned off with yellow tape, and seats and a podium had been set up for the groundbreaking ceremonies. A few dozen people had gathered around the site. Reporters stalked the grounds asking questions that had nothing to do with the ceremony.

UltraGen's presence said something about its ability to endure. In spite of everything, they were down but not defeated. Crews had set up hundreds of chairs for hordes of people, and it seemed a little sad that all the effort would go to waste. I felt a perverse sense of amusement about it.

I wandered onto the grounds and was quickly approached by security. They asked me for my ticket. I flashed my badge, and they backed off. A new face of UltraGen, Jessica Harnett, took the stage. She had dressed in a very smart business suit. Long dark hair fell below her shoulders. The suit accentuated her curves and made her look sexy and powerful. I recognized her face, those lips, those teeth, and even without the presence of dragonfly wings, I knew Jessica Harnett's Dex persona was in fact, Evil Tink.

She stood poised, proud as a woman of power, oblivious to the fact that her speech would largely go unheard. She effortlessly charmed the small group of attendees. That made her dangerous on a whole other level. She mouthed the words, "You're mine," toward me and followed that up with a suggestive wink. I couldn't stop her from dreaming, but I sure as hell could wake her ass up.

The ground-breaking went off without a hitch, and soon the place would be rife with bulldozers and earthmovers and the promise of new jobs. As the ceremony ended, I attempted to make my way toward Jessica. She managed to stay far enough ahead of me and was soon whisked away in a limo.

I watched the limo depart and disappear around a corner. "Next time," I muttered and walked back to the crowds.

I bought a funnel cake with cherry pie topping from a street vendor and watched the parade. The floats were colorful and fun. Thunderstorm's was certainly the loudest of the displays. A flock of exotic dancers gyrated to pulsing music. He stood on a papier-mâché mountaintop dressed in his leathers like a Norse

Thunder God. Every once in a while, he'd hit a metal drum and create a thunder crack. The crowd cheered with every rumble.

Talon rode a beautiful float. It had a blue and gold theme, and she looked dignified and graceful as she waved to the crowd and spread her white wings for all to see. From the crowd's reaction it seemed they all believed in angels.

Zack cruised by on a motorcycle, his patched and singed blue cape flapping behind him. He waved to the crowd but mostly went ignored. I felt a little bad for him. On the fantasy superhero game, Dex Territory, Zack was considered the most powerful of all the Dexes. His spectrum of powers was enormous, strength, flight, senses, healing, but he ranked dead last in playability. He couldn't win a fight with his shadow. Forever he'd be a down and out demigod. Someone shouted, "Roadrash," and he nearly crashed his motorcycle into a row of Port-a-Potties.

Several TV and movie stars rode floats or in the back of fancy convertible cars. Ghouls and goblins walked by tossing candy to the kids.

I nearly jumped out of my skin when I felt an arm slide though mine and wrap around me.

Monica nabbed a cherry off my funnel cake

and popped it in her mouth. "Having fun, O'Shea?"

"Now that you're here."

We exchanged powdered sugar kisses. "I was wondering why I didn't see a pink float go by."

"I just didn't feel like it this year. Get a little queasy in the mornings."

"Queasy? You all right?"

"And besides, I have to be more careful now."

"Careful? You? Ha. That's like trying to tell the sun not to rise."

She sighed and moved to look me straight on in the eyes. "And, my love, I'm not hungry like I usually am."

"You, not hungry?" I looked at her dumbfounded. "What could possibly cause that?"

"A positive pregnancy test."

"A...positive...what?" I looked at her sparkling eyes and then down at her belly. I did this a few times as my brain processed the data. "...pregnancy test?" I almost dropped my funnel cake. "You...you're..?"

"Yes, me." She smiled. "But don't worry about it, O'Shea. I know you still have to work things out with Dani, and although I think she's all wrong for you, I—"

I shut her up by placing my mouth on hers, and it didn't take her more than a second to realize that I was kissing her madly. She fell into my embrace. I dropped the funnel cake, and from everywhere around us came applause.

Yeah, life is complicated.

About the Author

Mark Aberdeen was born and raised on a family farm along the Southeastern Connecticut shoreline. He cobbled together an education and a varied career, which includes: armament technician in the US Army, submarine builder for the US Navy, cook, restaurant manager, retail sales, highly unpaid actor, and currently works in field of telecommunications despite a lack of talent, skill, or the study of anything useful. He currently lives in North Georgia with his wife and two rescue dogs.

http://www.twbpress.com